A great victory has b
over.
The Boy-King now n
Only the young office
they have their own battles to face and their own demons to fight. And those inner demons are not proving so easy to control as they are lured to the blood-soaked moors of Culloden for the final confrontation.

The dead are rising. A new darkness is fast approaching. Victory is close…but will the hands of Martin and Sean be too bloodied for them to grasp it?

The conclusion of the critically-acclaimed Watchers series!

Praise for the Watchers Trilogy!

"...horrifying Highland vampires from the bloodline of the diabolical Stuarts. This first novel...offers excitement that never slackens." -- Margaret L. Carter, author of the Eppie Award-winning vampire novel DARK CHANGELING

"...superb story. Thoroughly enjoyable from the first word to the last. William Meikle has a wonderfully unique style..." -- The Eternal Night Science Fiction, Fantasy and Horror

"Breathtaking, Scary and Original. A must read. An impressive blend of horror, history and imagination." -- Dave Dreher, Horror News Network

"I was captivated from the very first scene...Very well written." -- Patricia Altner, author of Vampire Readings: An Annotated Bibliography

Gryphonwood Books by William Meikle

The Watchers Trilogy
The Coming of the King
The Battle for the Throne
Culloden!

The Midnight Eye Files
The Amulet
The Sirens
The Skin Game

Berserker
The Invasion
The Valley
Island Life
Concordances of the Red Serpent

CULLODEN

BOOK THREE OF THE WATCHERS TRILOGY

WILLIAM MEIKLE

Gryphonwood

Culloden!
Copyright 2016 by William Meikle
All Rights Reserved

Published by Gryphonwood Press
www.gryphonwoodpress.com

This book is a work of fiction. All characters and situations are products of the author's imagination. Any resemblance to actual persons and events is entirely coincidental.

ISBN-10: 1-940095-48-4
ISBN-13: 978-1-940095-48-6

CHAPTER 1

NOVEMBER 10, 1745 DERBY

"Sit still, lad," Fitz said. "It is many years since I had to do stitch-work, and I would not want to leave you with a bad scar."

They were in Martin's billet, and the innkeeper was working on the younger man's head wound. Martin knew it was a bad wound, and guessed that the work was bloody and nauseating, but Fitz kept up a steady stream of chat, as if he was merely fixing a darn in a shirt. Martin only took in snatches of it.

"The Duke has sent out search parties, but rumor has it that the Boy-King and his army have fled north...five hundred lost at the south-wall...Megan has been sedated, but she'll be all right...Barclay has control of the west wall and has ordered the gate repaired...they say yon Other you sent to the true death was over a thousand years old, from the land of the Magyar, and that he'd killed over two thousand men-and-only-men single-handed...and it's said Rollo was seen fleeing the field...I will not miss him the next time."

Martin sat and stared at his hands. He turned them over, again and again, as if not believing they belonged to him. Am I yet man and only man? he wondered, for maybe the tenth time that morning.

He stopped Fitz in mid-stitch.

"Tell me again," he said. "When I staked the old man...what did you see?"

Fitz finished the stitch he was working on and moved so that he was eye to eye with Martin.

"Leave it be, lad...it does no good to go over it again...it won't bring anything, or anyone, back."

"Tell me!" Martin ordered.

The innkeeper sighed deeply.

"As I've already said...you raised your arms, as if to show me something. You were raving, telling me to keep away from you, that you would only tear me limb from limb. But I could not see what you wanted me to see. I saw only your bare arms. Then you jumped up and...."

"Aye," Martin said in disgust. "I remember the rest."

"You say you were...what's the word...transformed?"

"Aye," Martin said, "into a wolf...and I suspect it to be the self-same beast that I killed on the other side of the wall. 'Tis the woodsman's doing, some magic that I cannot fathom."

"But how can that be?" Fitz said. "I saw nothing but your own flesh."

"I have a suspicion," Martin replied.

He started unrolling the bandage on his left arm.

"Maybe you should leave that alone," Fitz said.

"What...so that Menzies can tend to me later?" Martin replied, and sobbed. "Besides, I have to see it...I need to know."

Fitz gasped as the bandage fell away.

"Not a pretty sight...is it?" Martin said.

His arm was a mass of scar tissue, rough ridges running through new pink skin. But there were no thick hairs, and Martin let out a sigh of relief.

"A sore wound, indeed," Fitz said.

"You should have seen it last week," Martin said. "Menzies thought I would certainly lose the arm."

"Surely not?" the innkeeper said. "The wounds are indeed bad...but not that bad." Fitz held up his stump. "Remember, lad, I have some experience in these matters myself."

Martin nodded.

"Maybe not now...but they were grim. Very grim. I was delirious for a long time. But it seems the magic is potent. I have healed much more than old Menzies ever anticipated."

"Then let us hope the magic is still working," Fitz said, returning to his examination of Martin's head wound. "Your skull is intact but your scalp is badly torn, and you've lost the top part of your ear."

"Mayhap I'll grow a new one," Martin said, and laughed grimly again. He fell silent once more as Fitz went back to his stitching.

His mind was full of images from the night before...Gord at the gate...the dark army marching slowly towards them...the huge bear-like Other biting into Menzies' neck.

Tears rolled down his cheeks, but his eyes were cold as flints.

"It is done," Fitz said a while later, "But it is not pretty. I fear you will have a scar...and I've had to take off a lot of your hair to get at the wound."

"I do not have to look at it," Martin said, "But the men do...Tell me. Will they still follow me after last night?"

Fitz looked embarrassed.

"Some will...but too many will not," he said. "They say that no man-and-only-man could have survived for so long in that throng of Others."

"A Berserker is not to be trusted...is that it?" Martin said.

"They say you are more than that...they think you are in league with Auld Nick himself. But you're no Berserker, lad," Fitz said. "You were simply over-wrought after the old man's death and..."

"No," Martin said. "We both know it is more. I don't yet know quite what it is...but it is still growing, still taking form, of that I'm sure. The woodsmen called it a gift, but I am not so sure."

"I am," Fitz replied. "It is no bad thing...from what Menzies told us, the woodsmen have no bad in them."

Martin shook his head.

"I am not so certain. It may not seem bad to them, but it is so different to our Christian way of doing things that it might not be compatible. Whichever way it goes, if the men will not follow me, I cannot command. I must go to the

Duke."

He stood, and a wave of dizziness and nausea ran through him. His knees threatened to buckle, and it was only force of will that kept him upright.

"It can wait. You need to rest, lad," Fitz said, and made to push Martin back into the seat. Martin pushed him away.

"No. It must be done now...if it is to be done at all it is best done sooner," he said. He managed to steady himself and stepped out of the tent.

The men in the courtyard went quiet, and all eyes looked at him. Several of them poked their fingers at him...the sign against the evil eye. When Martin walked through the yard the men parted in front of him, as if they didn't want to get too close.

The Duke was already in conference with his other officers in the billet under the north wall.

"Ah, the young hero," the Duke said as Martin was shown into the tent. "I was told you were mortally wounded."

Martin moved his hair aside and showed the man his new scar.

"It was a close thing," he said, "But I am still here."

"And glad I am of it," the Duke said. "For I have a task for you, if you will take it. Come...let us hold counsel together."

Over the next half-hour Martin heard just how close the city had come to falling. Nearly a thousand of the Duke's army had been killed, and two hundred more were missing. The south wall had been breached, and only the sudden retreat of the dark army had saved the city from being infested and overrun.

"And why did they fall back?" Martin asked. "For surely they had us beat."

The Duke stared directly at Martin.

"They say in the ranks that you were the cause of that," he said, "There is talk of a twelve-foot Other with demon's eyes which killed a hundred before you slew it."

Martin started to protest, but the Duke stopped him.

"I know...it was fat and bloated and slow, and your training was too good for it. I have heard your excuses before...do not be so quick to decry your achievements."

Two of the other officers were mumbling in the corner, but the Duke paid them no attention.

"Whatever you did, it was your act in holding the West Gate that stopped the certain destruction of the town. But many Others managed to enter, especially by the South Gate. We have teams out staking the dead," the Duke said. "But we cannot be sure we have got them all. We have to abandon the city."

The other officers complained loudly until Martin spoke up.

"The Duke has it right," he said. "If any Others remain in the city, they will cause havoc after nightfall. We cannot take the chance."

"And what would you know...Berserker?" one of the officers said, then stepped back quickly as Martin advanced on him, eyes blazing.

"I killed more than I can count last night," he said. "I have no compunction about adding another to the list."

"That's enough," the Duke said. "I will not have us fighting amongst ourselves."

"But sir..." one of the officers said.

The Duke cut him off with a wave of his hand.

"I will not be swayed. We burn the city and head south to Sheffield...within the hour. Make it happen," he said. The other three officers saluted and left. Martin too was about to leave when the Duke called him back.

"Did old Barclay survive the night?" he asked.

"Aye, sir. He's too stringy for an Other to fancy."

"Then as of now he is in charge of your men," the Duke said. It wasn't a question. "I have another task for you. I need a scouting party."

"To the north?" Martin asked, and the Duke nodded.

"Aye. Rumors tell that the Boy-King has taken flight and is heading back north of the wall. I need to know if that rumor is true."

"How many men can I take?"

"Take fifty," the Duke said. "And stay out, if you can. If he has retreated, we need to know where he goes."

"And where will I send word to?" Martin said.

"Sheffield, at first, then we will be following on your heels. The Protector has decided that enough is enough. He is resolute...he will harry the Others until there are none left in all these islands."

"Then I volunteer," Martin said. "I will leave before noon."

"You had better," the Duke said with a grim smile. "For the city will burn within the hour."

When he got back to his billet Martin called his officers together.

"I need volunteers," he said. "But not you, Barclay...the Duke has given you command of the militia."

The old soldier looked shocked, but said nothing as Martin outlined the Duke's orders. He saw the shock on the men's faces when he told them about the burning and abandonment of the city.

"I'm with you," Fitz said when Martin finished. "We started this journey together, and together we'll finish it. Who knows...we may even pass near to Far Sawrey."

"And I too am with you," said the smith. "Especially if there's a chance to sample Fitz's beer...he has talked of little else since we met."

"I will be glad to have you," Martin said.

Barr looked at his feet and shuffled from side to side.

"Barr?" Martin said.

"My men will not follow you, sir," he said finally. "But I will."

"That's not necessary," Martin said, "For I can only take fifty. If Toby has that many, it will suffice."

The big smith smiled.

"The hard bit will be keeping the numbers down," he said. "With your permission, sir, I'll get onto it now."

Martin nodded, and the man left.

"Fitz. I need provisions for fifty. Horses, winter gear, food enough for a long stint. Weapons, bulb, silver... everything we've got. And I need it now." Fitz smiled.

"We'll be ready in an hour."

"Make it forty minutes," Martin said. Fitz's smile disappeared.

"The burning starts so soon?"

Martin nodded.

"Then I will go," Fitz said. "For there is a duty I must perform."

"And if you'll forgive me, sir," Barclay said, "Barr and I must also make preparations. If you speak the truth, the Duke has plans for all of us."

Martin nodded again. The officers departed, and he was left alone for the first time since that morning.

He sat on the chair, put his head in his hands, and wept...for himself, for Gord, and most of all, for the loss of the only link he had back to Milecastle, the old doctor, Menzies.

But when he left the tent five minutes later he was back in control and his eyes betrayed nothing but steely resolve.

The yard was a hive of activity—camp was being broken. Even as Martin left his tent three of Barclay's men moved in to dismantle it.

Most of the other tents had already been taken down and packed; the braziers and buckets had been taken from the wall, the cannon were secured for travel and the food pots were being loaded on the back of carts.

All the bodies from the night before had been cleared, and the remains of the Others had been scraped away from the yard. If it hadn't been for the stench of death and powder in the air, it would be hard to tell there had even been a fight.

Lieutenant Barclay saw Martin, and broke off from supervising the loading of carts to talk to him.

"The Duke has ordered immediate evacuation," the old

soldier said. "We are to march for Sheffield within the hour. Barr is getting the men organized. Toby has picked his men for your unit, and has handed the rest over to me. It seems we go our separate ways."

"Aye," Martin said, "Let us hope we meet again in better circumstances."

The old soldier lit his clay pipe.

"It may be a while," he said. "This has the feeling of a long, arduous campaign."

"But we will prevail," Martin said. "I don't know what sent the Boy-King running, but we must be thankful. We have had our first victory."

"At what cost?" a voice said. Martin turned to see Fitz helping Megan across the yard. She had a livid purple bruise covering her neck below her jaw, and she was limping, but there was a deep fire in her eyes. "I'm pleased to see you are well, Megan," Martin said.

"Maybe you won't be so pleased…" Fitz said. "She insists she is coming with us."

Martin started to shake his head, and Megan stepped forward, almost stumbling, and grabbed him by the shirt to keep from falling.

"You are not well, lady," Martin said. "You should be in bed."

"Only if you will come with me," she said, and rubbed herself against him before laughing. "See. I am well enough."

Old Barclay laughed with her.

"I will miss you, milady," he said. "You make an old soldier remember his youth."

"Come over here and I'll bring the memories closer yet," she said, but Barclay merely grinned.

"I have a long walk ahead of me. I need to save my energy. At my age you are more likely to kill me."

"Oh, I know how to be gentle. Just ask my old man here."

"'Tis true," Fitz said. "Gentle as a lamb one minute…ferocious as a she-cat with threatened cubs the next."

Megan turned and stared into Martin's eyes.

"I will not go to Sheffield and hide like some weak, infirm woman," she said. "And Fitz and I have not been parted for the last fifteen years. I'm coming with you, wherever you go."

Fitz had a rueful grin on his face.

"I would not naysay her," he said. "She's apt to give you some new scars."

For the first time that day Martin managed a laugh.

"Well then, Fitz. You had better find more food...it seems our cook comes with us."

Megan kissed him on the lips.

"Thank you," she said. "But there is one more favor to ask of you."

Martin looked over her head at Fitz, but the innkeeper pointedly looked the other way.

"Ask then," Martin said.

"The Duke has ordered all bodies to be taken to a pyre in the center of town," she said. "We saved one for you to carry."

She led Martin to a cart in the corner of the yard and lifted the tarpaulin.

The body of old Menzies lay there. He wore a uniform of an officer of the Watch. His wounds had been cleaned and stitched and he had been washed...he looked like he was merely sleeping. Only the butt end of a stake protruding from his chest betrayed that fact.

"Fitz cleaned him up," Megan said. "He wouldn't let anybody else touch him."

Martin had a hitch in his throat, and was almost unable to speak. He had to swallow, twice, before he managed a hoarse whisper.

"I thank you…as his friend, and as his Thane," he said. "I know he would want to look his best to meet his maker."

"He was a good man, a loyal friend, and the only man I knew who could drink more ale than me," Fitz said, and forced a smile through his tears. "I know he would want you to take him on this last journey."

Martin had sudden tears in his eyes again as he nodded, and lifted the body from the cart. It was as light as a feather pillow in his arms.

The size of the pyre in the city square amazed Martin. Bodies were piled nearly twenty feet high. They lay tangled among wood, straw, paper and cloth...anything that would burn. They covered an area nearly forty yards on a side and at least half of the bodies wore the red tunics of the Protector's army. They had all been staked.

Men of the cloth said prayers over the bodies, and more dead were arriving every second; loaded high in carts or carried by weeping family or friends.

A crowd of the townspeople had gathered to watch the pyre being lit. They were a surly looking bunch; plump, well dressed and obviously well fed. They reminded Martin of the fat Proctor back in Carlisle.

The Duke was already in the square, standing by the edge of the pyre, as were his three senior officers. He saw Martin arrive. It was obvious that he had been addressing the crowd and he raised his voice as Martin walked towards him.

"Here is a man that has faced the army of Others three times now...three times, and still he walks, straight-backed and proud, an English man-and-only-man. Ask this man if he would bow to the Boy-King or give his city to the Others. Ask him what it would be like if we gave ourselves over to the dark."

There was dissension in the crowd, and some of the people booed the Duke.

"He is a soldier, like you are," someone shouted. "He gets the shilling, like you do...he does not have to make a living. How are we to live if we leave?"

Some shouted in agreement before the Duke strode to stand in front of them.

"And how will you live if you stay? You will be turned Others ere the next night is out," the Duke said. "Or, as is more likely, drained to the limit for your sweet blood…I'll wager you all have more than your fair share."

"We don't know that," someone else said. "The Boy-King has gone…we have beaten him. The Maid is already back over the wall."

"Mayhap," the Duke said, "But there could be Others anywhere in the empty houses…it won't be known 'till darkness falls…and then it will be too late."

"We have searched our houses," a voice shouted, but the Duke shouted him down.

"But you haven't searched them all…and you do not have time."

Martin could see that the Duke was getting angry. Some of his men were nervously shifting their muskets from arm to arm, and looked ready to shoot at any time.

A voice called out from the crowd.

"Mayhap we would be better with a King…at least the King never asked us to abandon our homes."

Martin walked forward, still carrying Menzies' body.

"This old man…" he said, holding the body in front of him, "…fought Others all his life. He saw them for what they are…abominations in the eyes of the Lord. He died for the people of this city, when he could easily have walked away from the fight. He burns, so that he stays man-and- onlyman. This city must burn to ensure no one comes back."

He placed the body on the pyre and stepped back.

"I burn his body, but his spirit lives on…in me, in his friends, and in this city."

The Duke handed him a lit torch.

"It is your honor," he said. "This city owes you for the lives of those who remain." The Duke raised his voice once more.

"While you were cowering, afraid in your houses, this man…who isn't even from this city…held your West Gate against the Others. He slew a lieutenant of the Boy-King, and he has volunteered to scout the north for the Protector."

He shot a withering look of disgust at the townspeople.

"This is what I call an Englishman…and he is worth a thousand of you."

The townspeople still looked sullen as Martin lowered the blazing torch to a large piece of straw. The fire lit quickly, flames crackling through the wood and sending sparks into the sky.

"Burn the city," the Duke called, and his men ran forward to light torches and apply them to the surrounding buildings.

"You have two choices," he told the townspeople. "Either stay here and die, or come with the army to Sheffield. I leave it up to you."

He marched off, and Martin followed him.

"I have my scouting party ready and waiting. I depart as soon as I get back to them," he said, and the Duke nodded.

"Good. You are better off away from this rabble. Cattle…" he said, and spat in the dust at his feet. "They will follow us. That is what cattle do."

"And what if they do not follow?" Martin asked.

"Then my men have orders to shoot them and burn them…we cannot give the Boy-King any more easy recruits."

He saw the look on Martin's face.

"Oh yes…I would shoot them. Make no mistake, lad, this is a war we must win. The plague the Others carry is too virulent to be placated. The Old Protector burned half of London and killed twenty thousand to eradicate it…we cannot do any less."

He shook his head sadly.

"Find The Maid for me," he said. "Find him, and pen him in. I will have him before this winter is out."

By the time Martin led his party out of the West Gate ten minutes later, the city was already well ablaze. Thick smoke rose from the center of the town, soon joined by other plumes as houses began to blaze. There was a thin stream of people going south with the army, but equally, there were large groups leaving by the West Gate…and heading west once they were beyond the walls.

"Ho, there!" Martin shouted at one of them. "Where are you going?"

"Nottingham," a woman shouted back. "The Others have already been there, and the Duke hasn't burned it. Mayhap there is a living to be made if the town still stands."

The woman's face looked pinched and worn with care. She had a babe in her arms, and two more tugging on her skirts.

"You would be better off with the army," Martin said. "The Duke has offered all people his protection."

She spat on the ground in front of her.

"The Butcher? We'd be better off with the Boy-King." She was out of reach of a shout before he could reply.

Martin got his men mounted and led them out of the gate. The smith had got over a hundred volunteers, and had weeded out all the married men or men with other family to look after. What was left was fifty lean fighting men, all hungry for more action.

"They won't let you down, sir," Toby said. "They are stout Englishmen, and they want nothing more than to be rid of this blight on our land."

"As do we all," Martin said. "And we will do it, even if we die in the trying."

Martin stood up in his stirrups and addressed the men. "The Protector has asked us for a favor," he said. "He wants us to find a maid for him...someone to keep him warm on the long winter nights. He has heard the women of the north are fair. Shall we go and find one for him?"

The men laughed.

"Lead them out, Toby," Martin said.

The big man saluted and led the band through the gate. Martin had one last look at the yard, remembering the battle, fixing in his mind the spot where old Menzies had fallen, then followed them out.

Fitz had provisioned them for travel...and for battle. Each man, Martin included, wore a long brown leather coat that hung to his ankles. Beneath that, they each had leather vests and breeches. In bedrolls slung behind their saddles they had canteens of bulb-water, traveling cloaks and blankets for bedding.

Each man also had two pistols, a musket, a sword, a dagger, and a bandoleer of stakes with a small hammer slung beside them. Some of the men also had crossbows slung across their backs, and small quivers of silver-tipped bolts. And many of the men wore large wooden crosses on their chests. One even carried a Bible in his left hand at all times.

Megan drove a long, high cart that was laden with water butts, from which wafted the sour taste of the bulb. The bruise on her jaw had gotten darker; a livid welt of purple that looked like someone had tried to throttle her. Her eyes were red-rimmed...she had been crying again. Fitz had told him earlier that he didn't think she would ever get over being attacked by Gord, but she was strong, and she was determined.

Behind her were three more carts.

The first carried whatever other weapons Fitz could purloin; muskets, silver shot, even a small cannon and a stock of iron balls. Riding it was an old man Martin hadn't seen before, a man who wore a faded uniform of the Watch.

"An Officer of the Watch?" Martin said. "Where did you serve?"

The old man spat out a wad of tobacco.

"Wexham," he said, "The name's Barr. Thomas Barr."

It was too much of a coincidence.

"Your son was the Sergeant Barr who has gone south with Barclay?"

"Aye," the old man said, "I didn't fancy the walk, and I might get to see home again if I come with you."

He spat out another wad of tobacco.

"Come on, you dozy buggers!" he shouted at the horses, then bit another lump off his wad.

"It's good to have you with us," Martin said. "An Officer of the Watch is always welcome."

"Aye," the old man said. "Even though we might no longer have a use."

He went back to chewing tobacco and cursing the horses as Martin fell back to survey the rest of the train.

The second cart carried tents, bedroll and cauldrons for their overnight camps. It was driven by one of the smith's men, a tall, taciturn man who saluted Martin but said nothing.

The third was full of food, for men and horses, and was driven by Hillman's twin boys.

Martin raised his eyebrows when he saw them.

"She would not leave without them," Fitz said, seeing Martin's look. "Besides…we are all family now."

Martin nodded.

"If it comes to battle, keep them out of it," he said. "Enough of my family has died already."

Martin rode up to the front of the line where the smith was leading his men out.

"I'm glad you are here, sir," the big man said. "For I was wondering where we would go first."

"As was I," Martin said. "I feel it in my water that the Boy-King is long gone. Something has happened to dent his confidence…he is headed for the wall, as fast as he dares."

"You have the sight?" the smith asked, but Martin shook his head. "No…'tis just a hunch. But the Duke needs proof. We will head for Ashbourne," Martin said. "…the place where Rollo was taken. We know they used it yesterday…let us see if they are stupid enough to use it again."

They found the first evidence of the dark army's passing in a field some eight miles north. It had once held a herd of some fifty cattle, but now there were only the dried-out husks of drained carcasses and a horde of bustling flies.

"Will they turn?" Edward Hillman said, "I saw the horses of the Others last night…will the cattle too be turned?"

"Aye," Martin said grimly. "They too will turn…although it is hard to imagine it."

"Should we stake them?" the smith asked.

Martin shook his head.

"We have not the time to stop and stake everything the Boy-King leaves behind...if we did we would still be south of the wall come winter."

Fitz rose up beside him and spoke quietly so that the rest of the men couldn't hear.

"I disagree, sir. We must take the time to stake these here...I have faced a stampede of turned beasts before. It was with Menzies in the colonies, and they were oxen rather than cattle, but we barely got out alive. I would not be caught such a way again."

"But look at them," the smith said. "They are full drained."

"That will only make them all the more dangerous," Fitz replied, "for they will rage with the thirst. We must stake them...either that, or use the bulb."

"Stakes will take too long...and the bulb would be too costly," Martin said. "We are caught between two stools." He sighed deeply. "Use the bulb. Issue men with buckets...one man, one beast. Let us get this done quickly."

Soon the stench of boiling flesh was rising in the air.

"Well, young Hillman...they will not be back now," Martin said, but Edward did not reply...he was lost in thought. They rode for the rest of the afternoon in relative silence. At one point one of the men started to sing, but the air was heavy and oppressive and seemed to suck all joy out of the song. That, and the heavy pall of smoke on the horizon from the burning city, dampened all their spirits.

It was nearly four o' clock in the afternoon before they came to Ashbourne.

The town looked unchanged since their visit the day before. The only differences noticeable were the open door of the church at the north end...and the disappearance of the pile of bodies on the green. The Boy-King had yet more new recruits.

Martin called the band around him.

"Some of us were here yesterday," he said. "And we lost

men to the Boy-King's mind-slaves. I want no mistakes today. We will stay together, and search a single house at a time...and only the larger ones. Keep muskets loaded at all times."

"We will need to be quick," Fitz said, "It is just shy of an hour till nightfall."

"Then we had best get to it," Martin said, and led them down the hill towards the town green.

"Fitz. Get a bellows hooked up," he said as they reached the bottom of the hill. "If we are to be here for more than an hour, I do not want any Others to take us by surprise."

The smith watched Fitz set up the bellows and slapped his forehead in exasperation.

"I knew I'd remember sometime," he said, and turned to address Martin.

"Begging your pardon, sir, but it was during the fighting last night. I realized that the bellows could be improved...we smiths use bigger bellows in our forges...two-man bellows. If a way could be found to hook them up to the butts, we would be able to more than double the distance and power of the spray."

"And will there be a smithy in this town?" Martin asked.

"No doubt, sir," the smith replied. "There's one in every town...and if I had remembered this morning, we could have had three or four from Derby."

"Then take ten men and find us the forge. But be very careful...I will not lose another like Rollo."

The smith saluted, and left at a run.

"Well, Fitz," Martin said. "Where shall we search first?"

"The church," the innkeeper said. "If it pleases you, I should like to see the place where Gord was taken."

Martin led the party up the long street. Fitz stopped at the inn, but Martin shook his head.

"It is a charnel house," he said. "And there is no ale."

"No ale? In an inn? That is a disgrace."

Before Martin could stop him, the innkeeper darted in to the premises, but came out again just as quickly. He rubbed at his mouth as if removing a bad taste.

"A fine premises," he said, "but it could do with a clean. Let us see if the church has been kept in better order."

"It happened in there?" Megan asked as they approached the church, "That is where they took Gord?"

Martin nodded. He ordered that the carts be placed in a protective cordon round the church door, and left one of the smith's men in charge of the bellows. It was only then that he felt safe leading the men into the shadows.

The church was cold and dark inside, but otherwise it was empty. Only the fact that some of the pews had been overturned showed that anything out of the ordinary had happened.

"Tell me," Fitz said. "How was it done?"

"In truth, I'm not sure," Martin said. "I sent him to search the church. I believe they were ambushed by mind-slaves, and he was carried off...that was the last I saw of him."

Megan sat on one of the pews and put her head in her hands. Fitz stood beside her with a hand on her shoulder. His eyes were cold and bright. Martin would not have liked to make an enemy of this man.

There was a shout from outside, and Martin's stomach seemed to drop. Not again, he thought. But this time, it was only a yell marking the return of the smith. Martin and Fitz went back out into the sunshine, leaving Megan in the church.

Three of the smith's men pushed a huge contraption ahead of them. It was a large pair of oak and leather bellows, nearly four feet long, mounted on thick oak legs and heavy wooden wheels.

"Well, they are certainly big," said Martin, "but will they work?"

Megan appeared at his side. Once more her eyes were red-rimmed and moist, but they had their fire back.

"I'm sure they will work," she said. "I helped Sawney make two of the hoses last night...I can make one for these, out of tent canvas if needs be. Give me two hours."

Martin looked at the sky.

It was already getting dim.

"We shall stay here for the night," he said. "A church is as good a place as any. Toby...set a watch. Fitz...if Megan is making the hose for the bellows, can you feed us?"

The bald man smiled. "Will ale and cold pies suffice?"

It was full dark before Megan announced that the hose was finished and connected to the bellows.

"We only have a butt of spring water," she said. "We cannot afford to lose any more of the bulb."

They unloaded the cannon and its shot from the weapons cart, and mounted the bellows in its place.

"I need two strong men," Megan said. The smith and Fitz stepped forward and jumped on the cart. Martin noticed that Megan had attached a leather strap to one arm of the bellows, so that Fitz, with his stump, would be able to use them.

The two men stood on either side of the bellows and pumped, just two short pushes. A spout of water arced nearly thirty feet high into the air and landed with a splash more than fifty yards away in the dark. In just five pumps over the next ten seconds they emptied the butt of water, and soaked an area of road nearly thirty yards square.

"It will make a formidable weapon," Martin said, "but it is somewhat impractical. I can see that we'll need huge amounts of water."

"But it will be useful for an element of surprise," said the smith.

"Or if the Others are tightly packed," Fitz said, and Martin agreed with them both.

"Keep it attached to a full butt of garlic water," Martin said. "And keep two men near it at all times during the night-time hours."

"Excuse me?" a small voice said. One of the Hillman twins was pulling at Fitz's vest. "I have been thinking about ways to save our stock of the bulb. I have an idea...what if we put silver in the water?"

"It would be too heavy, Harold. It would merely sink to the bottom of the butt," Fitz said. "It is Edward, sir...and it would not be too heavy if we ground it up to a fine powder, and kept the water well-stirred."

"Come away and leave the men be, Edward. It cannot be done...it…" Megan said, but the smith interrupted her. The big man was getting excited.

"Yes, it can. The boy is right. If we melt the silver, then cool it fast, it will be brittle and easily crumbled. If we mix it with the water, we might not need the bulb."

"But what use would it have?" Fitz said. "Would the water not negate the effect of the silver on the Others and put out the flames?"

"We will not know if we do not try," the smith said.

"Can we do it here...tonight?" Martin asked, and Toby nodded.

"If we have the silver."

"I have sacks full," Fitz said. "The people of Derby were very generous...even if they don't know it yet."

"Then all I need is a fire," the smith said, "and a helper. What do you say, Master Edward. Can you work a small pair of bellows?"

The boy's face lit up and he followed the smith like a happy puppy.

The men were all billeted inside the church, with watches set up of five men at a time. Inside the church the large candles were lit and shadows danced and played across the walls. The pews had been righted, and some of the men sat, heads bowed, praying. Others were at the back of the church accepting flagons of ale from Fitz.

One of the men had a small squeezebox, and was quietly playing hymns. Suddenly a high voice started to sing. Martin turned towards the sound.

Harold Hillman stood in front of the altar, tears running down his cheeks. One at a time, the men joined in, until the old church rang with their singing.

The Lord is my Shepherd,
I shall not want,

When the psalm was finished everyone sat in silence, lost in his or her own thoughts. Harold Hillman sat beside Megan and she gathered him to her bosom where he sobbed uncontrollably.

After a time the man with the squeezebox began to play soft sea-shanties, and slowly conversations started up again around the room.

"There was a man," Old Barr said to Martin. "Back in Derby. He told us to repent, for the Day of Judgment was at hand. He said that only a thousand times twelve-score would be raised in rapture to see the millennium of the Lord's reign. He seemed very sure of the fact.

"He was even gathering a following. He was selling pamphlets for a groat...parchments that promised entry to the chosen band. He already had a small bag full of coins."

"What happened to him?" Martin asked.

"The Butcher shot him for spreading dissension and gave his money to the poorhouses."

The old man spat a wad of tobacco on the floor of the church and turned away. Martin wondered if he was quite right in the head.

Martin walked slowly to the back of the church.

"Ale, sir?" Fitz said, and Martin gratefully took a flagon from the innkeeper.

"What do you think, Fitz? Has the Boy-King really retreated? Or is old man Barr right? Are the dark days upon us? Have we been called to judgment?"

The innkeeper shook his head. "I haven't heard any heavenly choirs. And I cannot believe the Boy-King has retreated...unless something has happened we do not know about. He is merely biding his time. We must stay vigilant, for an attack could come anytime."

But the attack didn't come that night.

At some point in the night Martin was able to sleep, but his dreams were red and bloody.

He runs through deep forest, his brothers and sisters by his side. They are swift and silent, their paws barely touching the ground as they speed after a frightened doe. He sends his gray brothers and sisters off to the side, covering the prey's retreat, and leaps forward after the deer, feeling its back leg crush under his teeth, bringing it down easily and hungrily burying his snout in the soft parts.

The pack cowers beneath a bush as a dark army of shadows streams past in the night. He sniffs the air and finds it full of death and corruption as, for the first time in his life, he cowers, tail between his legs, shoulders hunched in submission until the dark shadows have passed.

He sits back on his haunches as a tall figure with a wounded arm stands above him. He springs, just as a sword comes down in a flash of silver....

Martin woke, covered in a cold sweat.

He slept no more that night. He sat with the men of the Watch, staring out over the town, seeing nothing, saying nothing. By the time the sun rose and Fitz brought him a cup of strong black coffee he felt more like himself, but he was quiet and taciturn during the breaking of the camp. It wasn't until late afternoon that he raised a smile in response to a bawdy song started by the smith.

For the next two days Martin and his men crisscrossed the countryside north of Derby. They found no sign of the Boy-King.

By noon on the fourth day, Martin was becoming convinced that the dark army had fled. He sent a messenger south to the Duke.

"Tell him the country is empty, and that we go to look further north," he said as the smith's man mounted their fastest horse. "We will make for Milecastle...he can get a message to us there."

"And tell him about the smith's bellows and the silver!" Edward Hillman shouted from the small crowd that had gathered to watch the man leave.

Megan cuffed him around the ears, and he blushed redly.

"Yes," Martin said, "tell the Duke about the use of smithy bellows, and tell him about young Edward's idea. Mayhap the Duke has some engineers who can use the information."

That night back in the church the smith and young Hillman had managed to create a fine silver powder that they had mixed with the bulb in a water butt. Both were infuriated by the fact that they had yet to have a chance to test it.

The band of men watched the messenger ride south until he was out of view.

"Milecastle?" Fitz said. "Does this mean we will pass my inn?"

Martin smiled.

"I believe there is some Winter Porter waiting to be drunk," he said. "I have a mind to retrace our steps to Thornton-in-Lonsdale, and thence to Far Sawrey, and on to Carlisle and Milecastle."

Fitz danced a little jig.

"Megan!" he shouted. "Get your clean bloomers on...we're going home."

Later that afternoon the band rode up the long driveway to the manor at Thornton.

They were in a somber mood, for they had passed through three villages since noon, all of which had been recently overrun by the Others. There had been old people and children to stake, and the work had been grim.

Both Hillman boys had tears in their eyes, as did Megan. But among the men Martin noticed only a steely resolve...a resolve born of a rising anger.

The manor looked exactly as it had on their previous visit, and as they pulled up outside the front door, Martin felt a sense of déjà vu. He almost expected Rollo and the dogs to come round the corner of the building at any moment.

He led the men round to the rear of the house and looked out over the sprawling lawn that stretched away to a large pond ringed by tall trees nearly a hundred yards away. The lawn had been recently disturbed...partially dug up and turned over. Martin knew it had been disturbed a week ago...Rollo had told him...but this digging was much more recent. The disturbed earth was still brown and damp.

"That must be a very large, velvet-coated gentleman," Fitz said.

"No gentlemen, these," Martin said. "although they share a fear of the light. Toby, Edward, I believe we have found a test for your bellows."

"Sir?" Edward said, but the smith saw Martin's intention immediately and moved to man the bellows.

"Fitz. Give Toby a hand," Martin said. "Everybody else, load your weapons...silver shot. It may yet be daylight, but 'tis best to be prepared."

Fitz and Toby climbed onto the cart to man the bellows, and Megan leaped up to the driver's seat and pushed Barr to on side. "Move over, old man," she said. Martin expected the man to complain, but he merely spat a lump of tobacco to the ground, raised an eyebrow, and shuffled across the seat. Megan maneuvered the cart into a position where the bellows could be put to best use, and Fitz gave Martin a thumbs- up...they were ready.

Martin lined the men up in two ranks facing the lawn, then nodded to the smith.

"Let us see if we have a new weapon. Start the bellows."

Toby and Fitz began to pump and the spray arched out over the lawn. It landed on the grass...and nothing happened.

Edward Hillman groaned and turned away in disappointment…just as the soaked ground exploded in blue flame.

Great screams came from beneath the soil and the ground heaved. Martin thought it was like watching a child playing under a bed-cover...the whole lawn rose and fell in great ripples and undulations.

"Soak it!" he shouted. "Soak it all!"

Spurting gouts of the water surged over the lawn, and everywhere it landed blue flame erupted. In parts of the lawn where the water had yet to reach, dirt-stained Others dug themselves out from the ground, only to burn in the rays of the sun. Some pulled themselves completely out of the ground, only to explode violently as the water from the bellows found them.

An arm burst out of the soil at Martin's feet...too close for the water to have reached it. The hand reached for him, and Martin was still lowering his musket to shoot when Edward Hillman threw a handful of silver powder on the limb. It exploded with a blue flash, and the flames started to spread to the immediate area of lawn.

"Fitz," Martin called. "Down here. Soak the closer ground."

Seconds later the ground at their feet scorched and burned as it was soaked. The ranks of musket-men had to step back as the heat began to grow.

Down in the distance among the trees, pale forms began to appear.

"Mind-slaves!" Martin shouted. "Rear rank, load with normal shot. Prepare to fire."

A score of the mind-slaves came on at a run, but they were mown down by two volleys from the muskets, and kept down forever by a third.

"Another barrel!" the smith shouted, and Edward and Harold Hillman manhandled the hose into another butt. Out beyond the range of the bellows, Others were dragging themselves out of the earth and trying to escape into the trees, starting to burn as they ran.

"After them!" Martin shouted. "None shall escape!"

Megan gave the horses a touch of the whip and rode the cart over the lawn, the bellows pumping over her head all the time. Martin's men charged behind it, muskets firing, silver shot bringing fresh flames in the backs of the fleeing Others.

Small flames burned all around them, but no more Others rose from the soil, and the only screams came from the fleeing shadows.

They caught the last Other just as it was trying to dive into the pond. Fitz soaked it, and Martin fired a shot into its forehead, having to stand back as the head exploded, showering them all with dry, gray matter and burning pieces of scalp.

"Well," Megan said to Edward, "It seems your idea worked."

Martin stood by the pond, washing the remains of the Other from his leather coat. When he was done he turned and surveyed the carnage.

The whole length of the lawn was a sodden, blackened mass of greasy slime. It still burned in places, and thick gray smoke drifted heavily in the air. The bulk of the men patrolled the area, giving the final death to any Others still showing signs of movement.

Some of the party were filling buckets from the pond and using them to replenish the depleted water butts. Edward and Harold Hillman added silver powder to the mix, and ensured it was well stirred in.

Martin made his way back to the carts, being careful what he stepped in, trying to breathe through his mouth to minimize the stench.

"How many?" he asked the smith.

"Nigh on three hundred as far as I can tell," the man said, an incredulous look on his face. "Fifteen score Others sent to the true death with only two butts of silver, bulb and water. And we didn't lose a single man. Would that we had thought of it sooner...Derby might not have been abandoned."

"Aye. And many a good man might still be here," Martin said. "But old Menzies would have been proud that his idea has led to such a great weapon."

"I will make sure they refill all the butts," the smith said. "Yon new weapon uses the water at a great rate."

"Aye," Martin replied. "And have a team of men search the house for silver. I don't think the Lord of the Manor will return looking for it."

Old Barr was swapping places with Megan...taking charge of the weapons cart once more. He dismounted again quickly as one of the horses began to choke. It had been chewing some grass near to one of the sodden zones, and Martin guessed it had swallowed some bulb, maybe even some silver.

Martin moved to hold the horse's head as the old man took out his canteen and poured water into the horse's right ear. The horse's head jerked, and it sneezed loudly, covering Martin in spittle, phlegm and partially chewed grass.

The old man grinned.

"That's two more lessons you have learned today, lad," he said as he climbed back up on the cart. "If you want to make a horse vomit, pour water in its right ear."

"And what's the other lesson?" Martin said ruefully.

It was Megan who replied.

"Don't stand in front of the beast when you do it," she said, and they all laughed.

Martin found Fitz drawing a flagon of ale from a barrel on one of the carts. Martin took it from him and drained it in one draught.

"What say you, old man?" Martin said. "I would like to be in Far Sawrey this night. Should we travel under the stars like free men?"

Fitz drew another flagon and clinked his mug against Martin's.

"Aye. I do believe the Boy-King himself would fear this new weapon."

I hope so, Martin thought, and I mean to find out one day soon.

The smith came out of the house with ten men behind him. All were carrying sacks, which the smith assured Martin were full of silver.

"He was a bit of a miser, the lord of this house," the big

man said. "Teapots, candlesticks, trays and spoons...almost enough to make me want to take up thievery."

Martin allowed the men a flagon of ale and some dry biscuits each, then got them mustered and mounted once more before leading them out on the road.

The lawn was still smoking as they pulled out.

The beast did not come. Martin thought. The band was tightly packed around the carts, and although it was still light, the sun was beginning to go down behind the moor ahead of them. The sky was painted in deep red and purple, a riot of color. But Martin didn't notice. He was lost in thought.

It did not come. And there was no tingling, no doubling in my mind. But why?

Not for the first time, he realized that the beast only came in moments of severe danger...in the heat of a battle going the wrong way, or fighting a strong Other. This time the new weapon had ensured that he had never been in any personal danger. Although he believed he had found the reason, it was a theory that he did not want to test anytime soon.

The men were in high spirits after the battle. They had killed fifteen score Others without losing a man...they had a right to be happy. The man with the squeezebox...Jim Black, a shipwright from Whitby, began to play again. Harold Hillman kept time on his small drum.

Jim started to play "John Barleycorn" and Harold started to sing. His voice rang, clear as a bell, in the evening air.

> There was a Thane came from the north
> A Thane both great and high
> And he hath sworn a solemn oath
> That Thornton's Lord should die
> That Thornton's Lord should die
> Now the Thornton Lord was cold and vain

And a man of iron will
But the Thane of the North was stronger yet
And he bent him to his will
He bent him to his will
Then he took a stake both long and sharp
And he staked the Other's heart
And then he treated him worse that that
He burned it in a vat
He burned it in a vat
Then the silver flood burnt the Other's hearts
And took them to the cold But the Thane of the north took better yet
He took the Dark Lord's gold
He took the Dark Lord's gold
So let us toast the Thane of the North
A man both great and high
For he has sworn a solemn oath
That the Maiden King will die
The Maiden King will die.

The men cheered loudly and Harold blushed.

"I call it The Lay of the Thane," he said. "It is still rough, but I will work on it."

"Do that. You can sing it in the hall of Milecastle when we get there…I'm sure my people will want to know their sire is a hero," Martin said dryly.

The boy blushed even deeper.

A man both great and high? Martin scarcely knew whether he was yet a man at all.

They rode deep into the night. The moon lit their way, and there was no sign of any Others. As they got closer to Far Sawrey, Fitz became more agitated, eager to ride on ahead. He was always at the front of the column, always pushing on, eager to see his old inn once more. Martin fell back so that he was alongside Megan's cart. She was alone and he could see, further back, that the Hillman lads were asleep in the rear of the cart.

"Your old man is in a hurry," he said.

"So it would seem," Megan replied with a smile. "Sometimes I think he cares more for good ale then he does for me."

An old soldier riding on the other side of the cart called out, "I care more for bad ale than I do for my old lady."

That brought another bout of name-calling and catcalls before things began to settle down once more.

"So how did an old seafarer like him come to bring himself to a land-locked inn?" Martin asked.

"It is an old story, and a long one," she replied.

Martin looked around. There was nothing to see but bleak moor and the rutted path.

"It would seem that we have plenty of time, milady."

"Time," she said with a sigh, "Aye. That is something that is always with us. But never think you have enough of it…for it has a habit of draining away when you are not watching."

"It starts nigh on thirty year ago, back when my man was thin, had a full head of hair, and two good arms, back even before I met him. I was a Miller's daughter, helping my father scratch a living in a forsaken swamp in a forgotten corner of New England. "We had arrived on the New Hope in 1716, full of joy at the promise of a new life. It didn't take us long to learn the truth of it…the New World was much the same as the old, just warmer in summer, and colder in winter…not the best place for a Miller.

"Oh, we heard rumors of fine open grasslands to the west, where farmers were crying out for my father's skills, but we were unable to afford passage in any of the trade caravans, and my father was too proud to ask any man's aid.

"So we stayed in the hovel he built for us, and watched the swamp eat both the building and the builder till the damp destroyed both of them. He lived barely six months after getting off the boat, and my mother followed him a month later. I was left, all alone with not a single living relative, in a country far from anything I could call home. I was just passed my fourteenth birthday."

Sparkling tears formed at the corner of Megan's eyes.

"If the tale is too sore to tell..." Martin began, but Megan brushed him aside.

"I have started it now," she said, and managed a smile. "Haven't you learned yet...a man should never interrupt a woman once she gets started.

"For the first two days I did little more than sit in a dark corner and weep, but father had not raised a weakling. I buried mother in a plot of almost dry land, and I walked away with little idea of where I was headed. I carried an axe in one hand...the one Father used for splitting wood, and a sack over my shoulders containing what few clothes I had.

"I had a mind to go to Boston, a dream in my head of being taken in by a rich Lady, but I didn't even know whether to travel north or south. And after a mile or so I was so coated in mud that I knew I would never be received in polite society.

"The nearest town to us, Dover, was little more than a hamlet. The people were friendly enough to me...they fed me, for one night, and they allowed me a wash, but it was obvious that they had no wish for me to stay. When I moved on I was carrying an extra loaf and some cheese, but that was all they gave me.

"And so I walked for many a long mile. Father's axe came in handy for chopping firewood but, despite my fears, I wasn't bothered by bear or wolf. And I knew there were natives in the country around me for I found signs of encampment, but I never saw one of them. Not then, away.

"I was headed for Boston...so I wasn't surprised when I came to the sea. But it wasn't a metropolitan city that I found...in fact it was little more than a ramshackle collection of huts and shacks piled around a natural harbor. They called it New Haven, and you would have been hard pushed to find a bigger collection of rogues and villains anywhere in Christendom. And that's where I met my old man...although at the time I'd have been happier killing him then marrying him."

Megan stopped. Her tears had stopped, and there was a wistful smile on her face.

"But I am getting ahead of myself. You asked for my story, and I should try to tell it properly. But wait…all this is thirsty work. Will you join me in a flagon?"

She reached behind her and turned back with an earthenware jar in her hand.

"Fitz has his porter, but I have something stronger."

She passed it to Martin, who took a long swig, then coughed and spluttered as his throat burned and his stomach felt like fire had been lit there.

"In God's name, what do you have there?"

Megan smiled.

"'Tis my own recipe. Good wine and French brandy, combined with herbs and spices from the Carib. It keeps me warm on cold nights. I learned of it in New Haven. I learned many things there."

She started talking again, and if Martin thought she might be taking too many swallows from the jar, he was too polite to mention it.

"There is not much use for a fourteen-year-old girl in a whaling port…nothing gentile and ladylike, anyway. I got a bed in the largest of the inns by doubling as barmaid and kitchen maid. In the mornings I cooked…fish, fish and more fish, and at nights I tended bar and fought off the men as hard as I was able. I slept when I could, and I grew up more in the next year than I had in the last ten.

"As I said, New Haven was a whaling station. And at times it resembled nothing more than a charnel house. But there is money in whaling, and many traders were drawn to the port like moths to a flame. The inns in town were drawing ever-larger crowds, and gambling and prostitution were becoming big business. It was only a matter of time before the excise men started to take notice."

Suddenly there was a look in Megan's eyes that Martin had not seen before. He was no longer sure he wanted to hear the rest of this story, but Megan looked set to tell her tale to the end. He took a long swallow of her concoction the next time she offered, and was grateful for its heat as her story unfolded further.

"They came in September. It had been a good year for whaling, and the bleached bones were piled high all around, only accentuating the tar-black darkness of the excise men's garb as they counted this and tallied that and wrote their figures in ink as black as their souls. And after a hard day's counting, they came to the inn, hell-bent on drinking and wenching.

"I remember it as if it was yesterday. The place was bursting at the seams…one long riot of cursing drunks, one sea of stale beer and vomit. I was kept so busy that I only occasionally had time to notice the black-haired youth that kept staring at me as I delivered pitcher after pitcher of ale to him and the old cove with whom he was sharing a table. "Some old sailor was belting out "Barbara Allen" at the top of his lungs when the place suddenly fell quiet and the excise men came in.

"I knew immediately there was going to be trouble…when you work in a busy inn it is something you learn quickly. They set about ruling the roost like arrogant black cockerels, shoving sailors from their tables, demanding the best of food and drink, and showing no signs of payment. Yet we had to put up with it…for these men had the power to take what they wanted…they had the Protector's authority behind them.

"At first the only sign of trouble was some abusive shouting and pushing, but things really started to get ugly when they began to paw at the serving girls.

"I want you to know, the inn was not a whorehouse. We girls all made our livings on our feet, not on our backs. Oh, some of the women did an extra shift or two in the inn down the road, where they had rows of beds in the barn out the back, but I had never partaken.

"It didn't stop the crows thinking I was fair game, though. They latched onto me from the first…maybe because I was young, maybe because I still had all my teeth. For the first two rounds of drinks it was all good-natured, and I had them well in hand. One of them tried to lift my dress, but I slapped him, hard in the face. The raucous laughter of his companions was enough to stop him. From the corner of my eye I saw the black-haired lad rise from his seat, only for the old man to pull him back down.

"The real trouble came with the next round of drinks. The one I had slapped was still nursing a red welt on his face, and there was a rage deep in his eyes that I didn't like. I gave him a wide berth, but when I leaned over the table I felt two hands grab my bosom from behind."

"A fine pair of pillows for a man to lay his head on," a coarse voice said behind me, and the hands began to roughly massage me, as if I were a lump of dough being prepared for the oven.

"I had a pewter flagon in my hand, and the weight of the beer that remained in it lent impetus to my swing as I brought it round and smacked it, hard, against the side of his head. He fell away from me, and I was left standing in a suddenly quiet room, with a lump of mangled pewter in my hand and a moaning body at my feet.

"The silence only lasted for a second. Just long enough for me to register the black-haired lad getting out of his seat, then the crows grabbed me as their companion got groggily to his feet. There was blood pouring from a tear in his right ear, and his eyes seemed to have trouble focusing on me, but his voice was steady when he spoke."

"'Hold her tight, lads,' he said. 'It seems the wench needs to know who has the power around here.'

"To his credit, Old John, the owner of the inn, tried to stop them.

"'Here! I'll have no trouble. Just be seated, lads. The next beer is on the house.'

"'Aye,' the crow replied, 'And the rest of the night too. But if you would still have your inn on the morrow, it would be best if you left us to it.'

"A look passed between John and myself, and I knew what it meant. If I wanted to still have a job, I had best let the crows have their way. Old John had already turned his back on me, and I do believe I was about to submit, when a cold voice spoke. I knew before I turned that it was the black-haired youth."

"It was Fitz, wasn't it?" Martin suddenly said. Megan smiled at him, and took another long swig from her jar.

"Do you want to hear the story or not?"

Martin smiled back at her and waved for her to continue.

"As I said," Megan continued, "it was the black-haired youth. And, yes, I later found out his name was Fitzsimmons."

"'I would ask you to unhand my lady,' he said. He had a pistol in each hand, and the old cove stood behind him, a crossbow pointing at the bleeding crow's heart.

"'Unhand her?' the crow said. 'Aye, but later. For now, she has a debt to pay…and we men of the excise always collect our debts.'

"The crow lunged towards me, and a crossbow bolt seemed to grow from his chest, just before both the youth's pistols fired and the crow fell away from me again. This time he wasn't going to be getting up…half of his head was blown away."

"'You had better come with us, lass,' the old cove with the crossbow said. 'You won't be safe here.'

"'Come with you?' I cried. 'Never!'

"The black-haired youth sighed and stepped forward. In one swift movement he reversed one of his pistols and, using it as a club, rapped me, hard, on the head. I fell into a swoon, and the last thing I remember is him lifting me over his shoulder. After that everything went black."

Martin couldn't contain himself.

"He abducted you! Him and Menzies. It was Menzies, wasn't it? They killed an excise man and abducted you!"

He didn't know whether to show outrage or admiration.

"Aye," Megan said. "And that was how I met the love of my life. And there's more…I haven't told the half of it yet. But maybe I should leave that for another time…"

"Oh no you don't," Fitz said from beside Martin.

Martin didn't know how long the man had been there, but guessed that he knew which story was being told. "You've started it now. You had better finish…and tell the true story…the Thane has earned the right to hear it."

"The true story it is then," Megan said, "Though it is a long time since it happened, and no one but we three who were there has ever heard the tale."

She passed the flagon around, and all three of them drank deeply before she started again.

"I came around in a dark, damp place, and I believe I would have screamed had a cold hand not been pressed over my mouth.

"'Shush, lass,' a voice said. 'The crows have sharp ears.'

"My eyes slowly adjusted to the darkness, and I realized I knew where we were…we were in the stable block behind the inn, up in the hay loft. I started to struggle, until the voice spoke in my ear again."

"'We can give you to them now…if that is what you really want?'

"I remembered the look in the crow's eyes, and I held my peace. But we were not found anyway…the barn stayed quiet.

"'Luck is with us,' the black-haired youth said as we climbed from the loft.

"'Luck is it?' the old man replied. 'Aye. Lucky we are right enough. Did you know they'll hang us if they catch us? I hope the lass is worth it.'

"The youth looked at me.

"'Oh, she is worth it. Come lass,' he said, holding out a hand. 'We have a ship to catch up with at Nantucket.'

"'Come with you? Never!' I said.

"'They'll hang you if you stay, lass,' the old man said.

"'But I did nothing…'

"'You busted an excise man's head, and caused his death…or do you think the crows saw it differently?'

"After a moment's thought I had to agree with him.

"'At least let me get some of my things,' I said.

"'Too risky,' the youth said. 'Tell Menzies what you

need and he'll fetch it.'

"I told the youth where to find my room.

"'And don't forget the axe'" I said as he was leaving. 'It will come in handy if I need to split some wood…or some wooden head.'

Fitz butted in, disrupting the flow of the story.

"And then she rapped me on the top of the head with her knuckles. Oh, she was a brazen hussy, even then. You should have seen her, sire…she…"

Megan passed Martin the jug once more.

"Ignore him, milord…he is as besotted now as he was then. I'll have no more interruptions…the story is getting to the part that will be hard to tell…unless you want to take over?"

This was directed at Fitz, who gulped and shook his head.

"No, 'tis your tale to tell."

Fitz took the jug, and swallowed enough of the brew to fell a lesser drinker, but his eyes were still clear when he handed it back to Megan.

She nodded, and restarted the tale once more.

"We left the town as quietly as we could. My every nerve jangled, but no one stopped us." "'The crows are down at the docks,' Menzies whispered. 'They think we mean to take to the water.'

"'Then let us take to their mounts instead,' Fitz said, and we finally left the town on three horses belonging to the excise men.

"'We may as well be hanged for horse-stealing as for murder,' Menzies said with a grim smile as we left New Haven behind.

"We had traveled many miles on dark roads before Menzies pulled us to a stop.

"'We need to rest up,' he said, 'The horses need a couple of hours respite before dawn. We will need to travel hard and fast by day if we are to reach Nantucket ere nightfall.'

"I was just about to vent my rage at the pair of them as

we dismounted, but I wasn't given the time. The Others came at us from out of the darkness…as fast as moonlight shadows in the wind.

"There were two of them…two gray savages, naked save for their war-paint. I had my axe in my hand in two seconds…but even then I wasn't fast enough. One of them went for Menzies, but the second one came straight for me.

"Things moved too fast for me. It was on me before I had even turned full around. I felt its cold breath on my face as it bent my head to one side to give it access to my neck. I even saw its eyes flare in anticipation, then I was pulled aside and an arm—Fitz's arm—came between the Other and me. In rage and frustration it bit down, hard, but while its fangs were clamped in his flesh, Fitz staked it through its black heart and they both fell away from me.

"On the other side of the horses Menzies was in hand-to-hand combat with the other bloodsucker. I raised the axe to go to his aid when I heard the voice from below me."

"'Here, lass,' Fitz said. 'I need your help.'

He was on the ground, his arm stretched out from him. The bite was a red, bloody tear welling darkly in the moonlight.

"'I hope you know how to wield that thing,' he said. 'Strike hard, I would prefer to only be hit once.'

"It took several seconds for me to realize what he meant.

"'Take your arm…I…I cannot.'

"'But you must,' he said through gritted teeth. 'I have seen men bitten before now. I would not end up like them. Now, strike…and strike hard, then go and help the old man. It seems I am going to be in need of some doctoring.'

"I looked into his eyes. There was pain there, and fear, but also something else, something of pity, pity for the situation he was putting me in. I believed I screamed as I raised the axe…he certainly did, as I cleaved his forearm from his body.

"I turned to call for Menzies, but the old man was already by my side, a bloodied stake dripping in his hand."

"'Make a fire, girl, he said to me as he knelt beside Fitz. 'And boil some water. And if you have any faith, say a prayer for the lad here. It is going to be a long night.'"

Megan stopped and lifted the jug to her lips, but she couldn't conceal the heavy tears that ran down her face. It was Fitz who took up the rest of the story.

"Aye, sire. It was a long night, indeed...and more pain and tears than I care to remember." Fitz scratched at the end of his stump. "But you should have seen Megan...she was magnificent. She held my head in her lap as Sawney stitched me up, and although I screamed and thrashed she held tight and never let me go...never mind how many curses I threw at her. "And it was she who threw my poor hand on the fire. She had Menzies turn my head away, but I could smell it...and I can smell it still. And when Menzies had finished his needlework, it was Megan who stood by me, and sang me lullabies until I slept."

Megan took up the story once more.

"Aye, he slept all right. He was in a delirium for four days...four days in which he had no more mind of his own than a newborn babe...four days in which he fought the taint of the Other in him. And on the fifth morning, Menzies tested him, with silver and bulb, and declared him man and only man.

"Even then we came close to losing him, for after the delirium he was weak and feeble. Indeed he was as pale as the Others we had dispatched. Old Menzies was forced to leave us together while he went off to forage for food. Left to our own devices we had nothing to do but talk to each other...he was too weak for any other activity.

"So we talked, and, slowly, something grew between us, a bond that kept us pledged together in all the years since. We talked about our hopes and fears for the future. He wanted an inn, a sailor's bolt hole in a hot sultry port in the Carib. I wanted somewhere more stable. He wanted to brew beer, I wanted to cook. I wanted to return to England..."

Fitz butted in again.

"You can see who won, sire. It took us long years of

sailing, and a few cargoes that were not wholly revealed to the excise men...but I figured they owned me an arm, and that some brandy smuggled through Penzance was only going partway to redress the balance. And finally, when we moved into the old inn at Far Sawrey, it was the happiest day of my life."

"You told me it was a Spaniard in the Carib that took your arm," Martin said accusingly.

"Aye, sire," Fitz replied. "But I was supposed to tell the Thane of Milecastle that I had killed an excise man, and been bitten by an Other? Either on its own is enough for me to be put to death."

"Then I will do my duty as Thane," Martin said. "For your stout service as my Quartermaster, I hereby pardon you for all previous crimes. When we get to your inn, bring me some ink and paper, and I'll make it official."

"Another good reason to get there," Fitz said, and coaxed his horse into a trot as he moved once more to the head of the line.

"Calm yourself, old man," Megan said. "It will be there, however fast you get to it."

But she was wrong.

They saw the red glow before they smelled the smoke, and Fitz was galloping away ahead before anyone could stop him. Martin took five men and followed him fast, but still couldn't catch him until they reached the courtyard of the inn.

Smoke was still rising from the ruins. All the ale barrels were in the yard in front, smashed and broken beyond repair. The building was completely burnt out...the roof having fallen in, bringing two of the four walls with it. A name was written in blood on the wall of the barn: ROLLO.

Fitz was on his hand and knees on the ground, pounding his arms in the dirt.

"Filthy, evil bloodsucking bastard...bastard...bastard."

Martin dismounted and put a hand on the man's shoulder, but it was brushed off as the innkeeper stood. He went to the cart in which Megan sat, climbed in behind her, and sat with his face in her shoulder. His shoulders heaved up and down, but there was no sound.

"Toby. Set up camp in the yard here!" Martin shouted. "Three hour watches, fifteen to a watch. Have a man on the big bellows at all times. Megan?"

The woman raised her head. Her eyes were red, but dry.

"Yes?" she said.

"Can you feed the men?"

"Aye," she said. "Give me ten minutes with my man here, and I'll be with you."

"Take thirty. We're not that hungry."

She managed a small smile and nodded. As Martin turned away, she was lifting Fitz's face towards her own. Soft words were muttered, and Martin moved away quickly, not wishing to intrude.

"There's nothing salvageable," Toby said as Martin approached him. "It must have been done last night."

"Rollo, or more truthfully, the Other he has become, did this, just to spite Fitz. It was no more than an act of cruelty," Martin said.

"Aye," said the smith. "But it means he was here. And if he was here, then the Boy-King's army must have passed this way. He is heading north."

Martin nodded.

"He is heading for the wall. Let us hope Milecastle still stands when we get there."

CHAPTER 2

NOVEMBER 10, 1745 THE FIRTH OF FORTH

Sean sat on a hillock and watched the sun come up over the smoldering ruin of Edinburgh. From here, some five miles away, the castle didn't look so grand, or so daunting. The fire had burned most of the night until a heavy shower of rain had finally dampened it down just before dawn. The plume of black smoke rose hundreds of yards into the air. It looked like a great crow hanging over the town.

Over to Sean's left was a wide expanse of water, a large estuary more than a mile across, rippling silver in the thin morning sun. Small islands clustered near the far shore, and there was a long range of wooded hills beyond...but there was no sign of a boat, or a ferry.

Not that I'd be able to use one anyway, Sean thought. For what would I say to an Other...be a good chap and give me a ride across?

Behind Sean to the west, just at the foot of the hillock, was the start of an oak and beech forest that stretched as far as the eye could see.

He had arrived at the hillock some ten minutes before, forced to stop as tiredness from the night's exertions started to take its toll.

He had lost the trail. Once, while running down the long street away from the Castle, he had caught a glimpse of Barnstable in the distance, carrying Mary Campbell over his left shoulder. But he had lost the man in the smoke and confusion.

He was nigh on a hundred miles north of the wall, and he had lost his guide and only friend in this wasteland. He had his cloak, a hunting snare, a tinderbox, and a long dagger tucked into his boot...that was all. At least his clothes were still in good order, and his boots were yet whole and waterproof. Which was just as well, as rain began to fall steadily in a constant drizzle.

All he had to go on was the names Campbell had given him...Linlithgow, Falkland and Stirling. He had heard of the last, but only vaguely...a memory from long boring afternoons listening to Menzies drone in the classroom. He had a feeling there had been a battle of Stirling Bridge long ago, before the Others. But he had never heard of the other two. He was at a loss.

If he had been a religious man, he would have prayed for guidance, but Sean suspected he might have other avenues to explore.

If there is any of you inside my head, Woodsman, he asked himself, I would appreciate some aid.

He tried to let his mind still, as if attempting to sleep, and gasped in shock as his vision filled with the sight.

The huge cave-system is packed full of Others. Sean's vision takes him through chamber after chamber, and all that can be seen are the tightly packed bodies, and their red eyes glowing in the darkness. He is taken among them, smelling the rank dead stench emanating from the bodies, seeing the earth, blood and fluids that encrust the torn and bedraggled remains of their clothes. Some of them are partially melted, like wax candles left to burn, then cool, their bodies stretched and malformed into grotesque parodies of man-and-only-man.

As Sean watches one of them pulls something from its clothes, something that looks like musket shot. Suddenly the Other's fingers explode in blue flame, and it starts to flap its arms around in the tight confines of the cave. Those surrounding it try to back away, but the press of bodies is too tight. The Other burns intensely for several seconds, the blue flame impossibly bright in the darkness, then the dark army shifts and the flame goes out under its weight.

Deeper and deeper he goes, down to a measureless depth where the air is damp and chill and tastes slightly metallic.

It is here that he finds the Boy-King in conference with a highland lieutenant and a squat creature in monk's garb.

"I have attempted to contact William of Rennes," the monk says. "But there is only fire and blood in the sight."

The Boy-King looks high and haughty, pale and wan with aristocratic cheeks and hair like fine silk. But there is a haunted look in his red eyes...something that might grow into fear, given time.

"And I have been seeking counsel from Baphomet...he does not respond. I fear the King of Kings has finally been sent to the true death."

"And what about the lassie?" the highlander says, "She is still yours?"

"Oh yes. At least that slave is still mine. Even now she is being taken out of danger."

"Baphomet? Gone?" the monk says, and crosses himself. "Then the bloodline is lost. We cannot make a new king of the babe she carries."

"The king is where the blood is," the Boy-King says. "And I am the blood. I have sent slaves to Edinburgh...we will know more by nightfall."

The highlander speaks again.

"Think you that it had anything to do with the 'Wolf' who sent Artus to his final death?"

The Boy-King shakes his head slowly. "I cannot yet see. But my blood-wife's father is dead...I have 'seen' him in the chapel. And there is one of the blood...a black-haired lad who is not quite turned. We will meet him anon."

"And what do we do now?" the monk asks.

"We go to Ross-Lynn, and thence to Edinburgh," the Boy-King says. "Before I can continue I must know what has happened to Baphomet. If it is as bad as I fear, then we must go to Stirling. My slaves will bring the Bloodwife there, and I will make the new prince myself. And then we will turn south once more, and I will avenge Baphomet in blood."

The Boy-King's eyes suddenly go blank.

"We are not alone," he says. "There is a Watcher

present."

His head swivels until he is looking Sean in the eye. Sean feels the draw, the magnetism of the gaze.

The Boy-King laughs.

"The young lover," he says, "Have you come to look for my bride? I fear she is out of your reach. But come...let me taste you."

There is a pull in Sean's mind and he feels himself spiraling down into the Boy-King's mind. But the woodsman within begins a song, something moves inside him once more, and the sight takes Sean racing away, backwards through the seemingly endless caverns before soaring out of a tiny cave mouth and up, up high into the cold morning air.

He is looking down on a landscape of high moor and stunted trees but has no time to look closely as he is whisked northward, faster than a falcon, higher than an eagle.

The sight is dizzying, and nausea starts to build inside, but the song strengthens and the air around seems to vibrate in time. The sick feeling recedes as they speed over the wall and north over a large forest. They speed faster, further, over hill and moor, until he is looking down on a large palace built of blood-red stone.

He arrives just in time to see Barnstable carry Mary Campbell inside, before the sight takes him eastward. He is drawn back through a dense forest, back along a riverbank and past a small squat cottage at a bend in the stream, back to rush through another forest to a hillock where a tired man sits and blinks and...

...Sean shook his head to clear the sight from it.

He rose immediately, and started down the hill, heading west.

This wood was thicker, darker, and wetter than anything he had encountered before. His boots sucked in heavy mud with every step, and wet branches dripped clammy water down the back of his neck. But at least his trail became more obvious...Barnstable, carrying a body, had made deep imprints in the mud that were easy to follow.

And after half an hour of trudging through the muck, Sean's spirits rose when the wood opened out to a marshy stretch of riverbank. There was even a path of sorts where reeds had been toughly chopped and laid on the sodden ground. Sean took the opportunity to clean the heaviest of the mud from his boots before carrying on.

He remembered what the sight had shown him...somewhere round a bend in this river he was going to find a stone cottage. So he was surprised when he turned the expected bend...and there was only more marsh. It was the first time the sight had failed him.

He followed the track, noticing that it would lead directly past where he had 'seen' the cottage. He was still wondering why the sight had failed when there was a shifting in his mind again, like a firework going off just behind his eyes. He blinked...

...and sitting on the riverbank is a small stone cottage; little more than four walls with a thatched roof. There is only one small door, and an even smaller window. A thin plume of smoke rises from a narrow chimney. Although the day is dull and overcast, the cottage looks like it is sitting in sunshine.

The building sits slightly higher than the surrounding ground, and has a channel leading from the river to the back of the house. In this channel there is a coracle tied up to a small wooden pier, and fishing nets and tackle hang to dry on hooks on the posts.

To the left of the house there is a small garden laid out in vegetables, herbs and fruit. There is a tree carrying large oranges...a fruit Sean has only seen once in his life...and a tall broad-leafed plant hung with a long greenish-yellow fruit that he has never seen and cannot identify.

The ground immediately surrounding the house shimmers. He steps forward for a closer look... and something inside recoils as his eyes begin to sting and he blinks...

...and pulled back from a fine spray of silver powder. But again, there was no cottage in front of him, only the uncut riverbank.

There was a mystery here and part of Sean would have liked to stay and solve it, but he had already 'seen' where Barnstable took Mary Campbell...it was a palace, but not this rough patch of ground. He resolved to move on...just as the woodsman's sight took over once more, and the cottage was in front of him again.

He could not pass by...his curiosity was aroused now. He stepped forward, feeling only a slight tingle and a sting in his eyes as he passed over the sprinkling of silver powder. There was a silver handle that felt slightly warm in his hand as he turned it and pushed the door open. A bright light exploded in his face and he fell, stunned, to the rough stone floor.

He came awake slowly. He was lying on a mattress of straw, and his eyes stung and wept.

"I am sorry, young sir," a voice said above him. "I thought you were one of the dark ones, but I see you are more than that."

Sean rubbed at his eyes until he was finally able to focus. "What did you do to me? And who are you?"

"Silver nitrate powder for the first, and Alexander Seton for the second. I am at your service," the man said.

Sean was looking at the strangest man he had ever seen. His hair was long, straggly and gray, both on his head and his chin, and his eyes were those of a very old man. But the skin of his face was as smooth and clear as that of a newborn babe, and his hands were free from wrinkles.

He wore a long black woolen coat with patchwork repairs at the elbows and pockets. Under that, he had a dirty shirt that had once been white, and a pair of black wool trousers coated in a multitude of stains. He was no more than four-foot-six tall, and the way he carried himself reminded Sean of old Menzies.

But the old doctor would never live in such a place. There was straw on the floor, and a small log fire burning in a corner. A long table took up the rest of the room. On top of it phials and retorts bubbled and hissed, and noxious fumes drifted in the air. There were burnt and fused patches on the floor that spoke of spilled fluids and experiments gone wrong.

Books were piled in every corner, books with strange titles in Latin and Greek. One particularly long title caught Sean's eye: Apologie Compendiaria Fraternitatem de Rosae-Cruce Suspicionis et Infamiae Maculis Aspersam Abluens.

Seton saw him looking.

"Ah, the estimable Doctor Fludd of Bearsted...a fine man. He would be most perplexed by your condition. Which daemon would he call in aid of you, I wonder, you who are such a mixture of the Boreal and the Austral?"

"I do not know what are you talking about, old man. Your words are unfamiliar to me," Sean said.

"The quest...the search for the true and real. The only reason to exist."

"You are an alchemist?" Sean said. "A seeker after gold?"

The old man snorted and spoke, as if quoting from one of his books.

"The extraction of the soul out of gold or silver by what vulgar way of alchemy is a mere fancy. But he who can, without fraud, gain or deceit, tinge the basest metal with the argent colors, hath the gates of Nature herself opened to him. And from there he can inquire into further and higher secrets, and with the grace of God, obtain them...That is what I do, and that is who I am, young sir. A humble inquirer into nature."

The old man had such a strange way of talking that Sean barely understood half of what he said. But there was no guile or pretence in the old man's stare, and he didn't protest when Seton lifted his head and looked deep into his eyes.

"Yes. The dark one is there," he said. "But there is also light. Tell me young sir...you have had dealings with the small men of the forest?"

Sean nodded as he pushed himself into a sitting position. "Aye, but 'tis a long tale, and I cannot stay to tell it. I have a geas to fulfill."

Seton's eyes went out of focus, and he spoke in a dull monotone.

"She is already out of your reach," he said. "For I see a great steed taking her northward. The Boy-King has requested her presence in Stirling."

Sean tried to stand, but his head spun and he sat back down before he had time to fall over.

"You are underfed, boy," Seton said. "When was the last time you ate?"

"In truth, I do not remember," Sean replied. "I have had little but fish and berries for three days, and only ale and pies in the days before that. In that time I have traveled hundreds of miles, killed men, Others, and a woodsman, and lost a man I loved as a father."

"Ah, a tale. It is many a year since I heard a new one. The last time I rescued anyone, I ended up in the Low Countries, married to a countess, then got myself chained in a cell."

He smiled to himself, and his eye took on a far away look before coming back into focus.

"But that is my tale, not yours...come..." the old man said, leading Sean to the tall table. "I will feed you, and in payment you will tell me your story."

"But I must be after her. I..."

Sean tried to pull away, but the old man's grip was remarkably strong and he was dragged to a tall stool. There was bread, cheese, fruit and berries piled there. Sean was sure they had not been there mere seconds before, but the smell of the bread, fresh-baked and still hot, had him salivating already.

"I will fetch some ale," Seton said.

By the time the old man returned, Sean had already consumed half the loaf and much of the cheese.

"Eat your fill," Seton said. "For I am old, and eat like a mouse."

Sean ate until his stomach was as tight as a drum. Between mouthfuls, he told the old man his story.

Seton made him go over the events on the woodsman's stone several times.

"They merged? His blood, your blood, and the dark one's blood. Three in one? I have scarce heard the like. The vulture, the scorpion and the calacant together in one vessel? You merely lack the serpent and you will complete the great work. You are greatly blessed, my boy."

Sean laughed, but there was no humor in it.

"Blessed? I am surely cursed...I have an Other in me."

"An Other? Oh...you mean a dark one. Yes you have a dark one, but you also have light, and balance. You lack merely the solvent that will finally release the quintessential elixir."

Sean laughed again.

"I do not understand your words, old man, but they sound very pretty."

"I am sorry," the old man said. "I read so much in ancient tomes that I come to sound like them. To simplify...you have the essence of earth, air and fire within you already. If you search out the essence of water, and let it in, you will be a complete being, privy to the secrets which God has wrought in this world, and all other worlds."

Sean shook his head.

"The essence of water? What is that?"

"I know not," the old man said, and it was his turn to laugh out loud. "I am still looking for it myself."

Sean laughed along with him, spluttering pieces of bread and cheese across the table. That sent them both into peals of laughter.

When they had calmed down, Sean asked the question that had been on his mind for some time.

"The dark one in me...can you remove it?"

"Remove it?" the old man looked shocked. "But why? You are near the Grand Arcanum."

"I care not for your alchemical fancies," Sean said. "I fear it is too strong and will overwhelm me."

The old man suddenly looked serious and nodded his head.

"That it may, for it is fire, and its nature is to burn. But remember boy...you are the Balance, and in the Balance is strength."

"But you have not answered me...can it be removed?"

"I am trying to tell you," Seton said. "It cannot be removed...but it can be controlled."

"I do not understand," Sean said.

"But you will," Seton said, "you will."

Seton's eyes became unfocused again, only for a second before clearing.

"And now you must go," he said. "You will need to be at Linlithgow Palace by nightfall, just to satisfy yourself that you are too late. I would tell you not to look in the Great Hall, but you are young and reckless...you will look anyway. Now go."

The old man shooed Sean away from the table and out of the door of the cottage.

"Come back and tell me how the story finishes," he said. "I love a good yarn."

The door shut behind Sean, and when he turned, there was only the unspoiled riverbank once more.

"Remember," he heard a voice whisper. "You are the Balance."

He turned to the track once more, but now he felt something he had not known since he found he was bitten...he knew hope.

The way was easier now, although the reed pathway petered out only a hundred yards from the 'cottage'. The ground underfoot was firmer, and the rain had slackened. It was no longer possible for Sean to follow the Constable's tracks, but as he climbed through the forest and away from the river he was soon able to catch glimpses of the red-stone Palace. It was still in the distance, framed black against the pinks and purples of the falling sun. He had been with old Seton longer than he'd thought.

Already his encounter with Seton was fading from his memory, taking on the quality of a badly remembered dream. All he could recall with any clarity was the last exchange between them.

He mulled over what the alchemist had said.

"You are the Balance." What did that mean? He suspected that the old man was trying to say that the man-and-only-man part of Sean was capable of holding both the woodsman and the Other at bay.

But how?

He had managed to make the sight come at will that morning…and during the fight in the chapel the night before he had had control over the fangs in his gums.

He was loath to give either aspect any further rein, but without practicing control, the Balance would never be achieved. He was still considering it when the path led him down through a copse of trees and out onto a wide-open expanse in front of the Palace of Linlithgow.

He had thought from a distance that the building was built from red stone, but as he got closer he saw that it was blood running down the walls, fresh blood that steamed in the slight chill in the air.

Sean circled the huge edifice, looking for a possible point of entry. Under the blood, the stonework was old and crumbling, but Sean was still staggered by its scope. He had thought Milecastle, and the wall it guarded, to be a marvel of engineering, but his home would be dwarfed by this structure.

A pair of tall spiked towers rose two hundred feet into the air, their tops nearly lost in the low cloud. The flow of blood that coated the walls seemed to originate from the highest points of these towers.

Beneath the towers, there were four storeys of wall topped with battlements and turrets, and carrying carved statues of demons and gargoyles that leered and glowered from every nook and cranny. The windows were little more than black holes, looking even darker amid the bloody wash on the walls.

There was no movement, but twilight was closing in

fast. He remembered the old man's words...You will need to be at Linlithgow Palace by nightfall, just to satisfy yourself that you are too late. The old man had read Sean right...he could not leave here...not without searching for Mary Campbell.

He strode forward towards a small oak door in the west side of the building. If he was going inside, he wanted to be searching rooms where there was still a chance of some sunshine.

He wiped the door handle with grass before pushing the door open...he didn't want to touch any of the red gore.

Luckily, the corridor beyond the door was free of blood. As his eyes began to adjust, Sean saw that the hallway led off into the black interior of the building. He slid the long dagger from his boot and, wishing he had a supply of the bulb, he stepped inside.

His first impression was of emptiness. The castle was quiet as a church. But where a church felt somehow alive, this building was an echoing, empty space.

He had entered what, in an English manor house, would have been called "the servant's quarters", but it seemed like it had been a long time since there were any servants here. Years of dust covered the floor, and great silver spider webs hung everywhere. When Sean looked back the way he had come, he could see his footprints crisply outlined in the dirt. If he were to find any signs of life, it wouldn't be in this part of the house.

He went in further.

After looking into his twentieth empty room he was on the verge of giving up. The only footprints he had seen were his own, and all the rooms had been bare, devoid even of basic furniture. The only living thing he'd encountered was a large, bloated spider.

Then he remembered the towers. The blood outside was pouring from them, and blood meant a living creature. He went up the next staircase he came to.

By the time he reached the spiral stairs that led up to the

tower, Sean was beginning to think that the Palace might be inhabited after all. He still had not seen any other footprints, but there had been a high-pitched whispering in one of the corridors, and a far-off wailing, as of a woman crying. He clutched the dagger more tightly as he headed up the stairs. They seemed to continue upwards forever. The air was cooler here, and damper. Thick mosses hung from the ceiling and green slime coated the floor. Strangely, Sean felt more at ease, reminded somewhat of the towers of his home...until he smelled the coppery odor of the blood.

He felt the fangs slide from his gums, and had to stop himself licking his lips. Disgusted, he stopped climbing, and tried to calm his thoughts.

I am the Balance, he said to himself, I am the Balance. The fangs retreated, and Sean spat the taste of blood from his mouth. He kept repeating the words as he started to climb once more.

Sean thought he was inured to any further atrocity the Others might commit, but the sight that met him at the top of the tower stopped him in his tracks and brought acid bile in his throat.

All round the rim of the tower...a circumference of more than twenty yards...were hung pale, naked bodies. They were hung upside down from huge butcher's hooks, and their wrists had been bitten so that the blood ran onto the walls below. They swung, like some obscene pendulums, back and forth, in a hypnotic dance of blood, spraying fine patterns of red rain across the top of the wall and down into runnels that led the blood away to other parts of the tower. Some of the bodies were blue, and obviously fully dead...but others were all too obviously alive, and the piteous moans reached him even above the rising wind. One of the bodies had turned and its fangs clicked loudly. But even their blood flowed and drained to merge with the rest.

A wind got up, and as one the bodies began to swing faster. Sean felt splatters of blood hit him in the face. Once more the fangs slid from his gums.

I am the Balance, he said. I am the Balance. The fangs

receded, but he had to fight off an almost overwhelming urge to lick the blood from his skin.

He was about to turn away when one of them spoke.

"Help us...please?"

But Sean couldn't find the source of the voice...whoever had spoken had used what little energy they possessed. He did the only thing he could do for them. He put the dagger to use, and sent them all to their final death.

By the time he headed back down the stairs his hands were soaked in blood up as far as the elbows. He was muttering to himself under his breath.

I am the Balance, I am the Balance.

But the fangs were sliding in and out of his gums, and his blood tasted sweet.

His only thought now was to get out of this hell and find somewhere he could spend the night in relative safety. He ran down the stairs, taking them two, even three, at a time. Then, once he was in the main Palace corridors, he ran full pelt. It was nearly full dark by now, and the whispering in the corridors had grown louder, more menacing.

He found himself in front of a stout oak door, one he didn't remember from his earlier wandering. He had taken a wrong turn somewhere in the maze of corridors.

The best thing now would be to retrace his steps and find his way out of the Palace before it was full night. But something called to him from the other side of the door, something that made the dark Other in him move and respond. He grabbed the handles and swung the heavy door open.

At first there was only darkness in the room beyond, a deep black that seemed sinuous and alive. Then the Other inside Sean moved, and it was as if daylight had flooded the room. Part of Sean knew it was nearly full dark, but he could see the whole scene in front of him in the minutest detail.

It was a long hall. I would tell you not to look in the Great Hall, but you will anyway, he heard Seton's voice say. A high ceiling arched overhead, with heavy, dark-stained wood paneling on all sides. A massive stone fireplace dominated the far end of the room, and dark portraits of Others, horsed and armored, lined the walls.

But it was the mosaic on the floor that drew his attention. It was done in blood red and black tiles, each no bigger than a fingernail, and it covered the whole floor some thirty yards long.

It was a serpent; a great, segmented, wurm with scales that flashed in the moonlight and eyes that glowed. It seemed to see into the depths of Sean's soul, and he was transfixed as sight took him and...

...he is in a high place, a rocky outcrop above a moonlit desert. He is one of a band of barbarians...hairy men with low brows and stocky, muscular bodies. They carry long spears with stone heads, and their clothes are little more than roughly sewn animal furs. When they communicate among themselves they use grunts and clicks, but Sean understands what is being said.

They are herding something ahead of them, something thick, scaly and wormlike that slithers on the ground and leaves a slimy trail behind it. It is almost twenty yards long...like a snake, but with a human-like face. Two long spiral horns spring from its forehead, and a long black forked tongue slithers from between its teeth. When it smiles its fangs hang over its lower lip.

The serpent cackles and giggles as it retreats from them. One of the barbarians gets too close, and the serpent strikes, so fast that Sean scarcely sees it. It latches itself to one of the Barbarians and begins to feed.

Sean moves forward and dives his spear deep into the man's heart as the rest of the tribe harry the beast closer to the edge of the cliff.

Blood drips from the serpent's lips and it smiles again.

"You cannot destroy me," it says. "My time will come again." The barbarians force it over the edge of the outcrop and down into the darkness. It makes no sound as it falls.

The tallest of the tribe raises his spear. The head on this weapon is different...it blazes with an intense blue light as the spear is thrust into the ground...and the rock of the cliff falls in an avalanche, burying the serpent beneath many tons of scree and debris. The tribal leader screams his defiance into the night...

...and it echoed in Sean's head as he blinked. Moonlight, as bright as any sun, washed over the mosaic, and the serpent seemed to writhe and squirm.

"The old one knows you," a voice said to Sean's left. He turned, and found himself facing an enormous, bloated Other. The thing was gorged with blood...so much so that its eyes leaked red and drips ran from its nose and ears. If it had been man-and-only-man it would have been over forty stone in weight, but Sean saw that it had left no tracks in the dust.

It wore a single long smock that covered it from neck to feet. The garment was covered in both wet and dry blood, and even at a distance of several yards the smell of it made gorge rise in Sean's throat.

Perversely, it had paid great attention to its appearance above the neck. It wore a long white powdered wig that was combed and set in perfect ringlets. Its eyes were shadowed with mascara, and its cheeks were rouged and polished.

It stepped backwards as Sean turned fully around, the dagger raised in front of him.

"Oh, you do not need that here," it said. "Not among brothers."

"I am no brother of yours," Sean said and stepped closer.

The Other fluttered its arms in front of itself, like a wounded bird trying to escape a cat. It moved away from Sean, backward out of the hall, faster than a man could run. There it stopped, and laughed loudly.

"Maybe not brother yet," the Other said. "But you are of the blood. Look at your hands."

Sean looked down.

The blood that so recently caked his hands and arms was disappearing...it was being absorbed into his skin. He felt a tingling glow, as if he'd put his arms near a fire, then a hot rush, like an orgasm. His legs gave way under him and he sat down on the floor, hard.

The Other came closer, but not close enough that it would be within reach of the dagger.

"See," it said. "You are of the dark. Can you not feel the thirst grow in you? A little taste like that should merely leave you wanting more."

I am the Balance. Sean muttered, but it was drowned out by the beating of a drum in his head, thudding loud in his ears and driving all else from his mind. He began to crawl towards the sound, then got up to his feet and walked. He pushed his way passed the Other, and soon he was running.

"Ah," the Other said behind him. "It seems we are called to the table."

The drumbeat was coming from somewhere underneath them. It was insistent and demanding, pulling Sean forward to a place where his thirst would be assuaged. His feet picked up small whirlwinds of dust as he rushed to the source of the sound. He pushed open a thick wooden door and threw himself into a long narrow room.

A small group of Others stood around a table. On the table a large man's body lay, and the drumming was coming from it...a great bass thump as his heart beat out its terror. Sean leapt forward, ready to bite and tear, to still the heart and feel the rush of blood in his mouth. He jumped on the table and bent over the body...only to find himself looking down into the terrified face of William Barnstable.

He threw himself backward off the table and retreated until he felt a wall at his back.

The compulsion to feed left him as quickly as it had come. I am the Balance, he said. And this time he felt in control.

The Others around the table were looking at him, puzzlement showing on their faces.

"He is unsure of his blood," a voice said, and the bloated Other seemed to float into the room.

"Why won't you feed?" it said to Sean. "For surely, the blood is the life?"

"I am not like you," Sean said through gritted teeth, but the Others merely laughed.

"You are as near as any I've ever seen," the Other said. "Why deny it?"

Sean looked at the prone body on the table. Barnstable had lost weight since the attack on Milecastle, but there was color in his cheeks. And his eyes no longer showed the blank stare of a mind-slave...they were the terrified eyes of a man surrounded by his worst nightmare, and unable to do anything about it.

"We are undecided about this one," the bloated Other said, motioning to Barnstable. "He brought the King's wife to us safely, and for that he should be rewarded. But he did nothing to save Baphomet, and for that he must be punished.

"What do you think?" it said, addressing the Others around the table.

"I have a thirst," one said. It was old, lank black hair hanging in front of a thin, almost skeletal, face. Its clothes, such as they were, hung off it in rags. It drooled from the side of its mouth: a pink- tinged, viscous fluid that hung in two long, ropy strands that reached almost to its chest.

"And I," another said. This one might be a female, but Sean could not tell. It was so caked with a mixture of blood and muck and, from the smell of it, shit, that only the red eyes showed it to be alive.

"No. Let us have some sport," yet another said. This one had been a minister of the cloth at one time. It's hair hung down its back, long and lustrous, and a neatly trimmed beard hung over a ragged dog collar. It might once have seemed almost pious—but the effect was spoiled by the old bloodstains that ran down the gray of the beard and onto the cassock below.

"Send them to the pit together, and see which prevails," it said.

The bloated Other smiled.

"That was my thought, and that will be my pleasure."

It moved to the table and lifted Barnstable as if he weighed no more than a feather. The big man whimpered, just once, then was silent.

"Bring the boy," the Other said.

Apart from the snare, Sean had only the Scotsman's long dagger. With it he managed to stick the old one in the belly, and poke another just over its left eye. The bloated one seemed to fly straight at him, pushing him down and pinning him to the table where he was subdued all too easily. He was lifted off the table and dragged, kicking and shouting, out of the room.

They were taken ever deeper into the bowels of the Palace, down into depths so black that Sean could see nothing but the feral red eyes of the Others shining in the darkness. The air became heavy and foul, like a bog on a hot day.

"Which one?" an Other said. "The dark or the light?"

"The light I think," the bloated Other replied. "Then we shall see how much the boy wants to live."

Eventually they stopped. Sean heard a sound, like flesh tearing, and then there came a loud moan from Barnstable, followed by obscene sucking noises as an Other fed.

"Ah. He is sweet," the bloated Other said after a while. Its voice gurgled moistly, as if speaking through a mouth full of liquid.

"You will turn together," it said to Sean.

"I will not turn," Sean said.

"Then you will die. One of you must feed, and the other must die. The one who wants to live the most will be the one who is allowed out of the pit. Throw them in."

Sean heard a metal grate being opened, then a thud as Barnstable's body was dropped. Then he himself was falling through the air.

He landed on a soft body and rolled away quickly. He still had the dagger in his hand—the Others had ceased to see it as a threat—and he held it in front of him in the dark. But there was no movement from Barnstable. Sean shuffled backwards until his back was to a wall. Something scurried away in the darkness, too small to be a man.

"You have some of our furry friends for company," the bloated Other called down from above, and Sean heard the smile in its voice. "It would be best to feed before they do."

"I will not!" Sean shouted.

"Ah, but you will," the Other said. "You forget, I have seen the thirst in you...the serpent has seen it in you. You are one of us. You just do not know it yet."

The metal grate slid closed overhead. Sean tried to judge the height, but could not get his bearings in the dark.

Barnstable whimpered.

"Be quiet, man," Sean said. "At least have the dignity to die in peace."

The big man moaned.

"I am bitten. I am bitten deep."

Sean scuttled across the room and put the dagger to the man's throat before he had time to move.

"Aye. You are bit. And I can end it for you here and now. So are you man enough for it, Constable? What do you say? Do you want to feel the cold steel?"

Barnstable started to weep.

Disgusted, Sean released him and went back to the wall.

"As I thought," Sean said. "Once a coward, always a coward."

"Grant?" the big man whispered. "It is you, is it not? At the table...when you leaned over me...I knew it was you...you have turned."

Sean heard the horror in the big man's voice.

"Oh, aye. I was turned saving Milecastle from the black bastards...just about the same time as you were slaying your Thane, betraying your duty and abducting a defenseless woman. Now be quiet," he said. "I have no wish to speak with you."

"But what are you talking about?" the big man said. "I remember nothing of what you say I..."

Sean was across the room and at the man's throat again

before he had time to finish the sentence. This time he let Barnstable feel the fangs slide against his flesh.

"What is it to be? The bite or the steel?" Sean said. "You have no other choices... you are already bitten. I can give you a quick death here and now if you wish?"

The big man went limp in Sean's arms. Sean could feel his heart beat strong and heavy. There was no compulsion to feed, but the fangs were sliding, wet and bloody, in and out of his gums.

I am the Balance, he told himself, but the hate he felt for the Constable was strong. He lifted the dagger, intending to draw it over the man's throat...

...and he is back in Milecastle, staring out over the wall at the dark army beyond. He realizes with a start that he is seeing the scene through Barnstable's eyes.

Something comes out of the blackness and into his mind...something black and foul that grabs his mind like a vise.

And from that moment on he only sees scenes flitting quickly across the surface of his mind, senses that melt and flow like dreams...no, like nightmare.

...he is in the Great Hall of Milecastle and the Thane approaches him, a question in his eyes. He stabs the old man, deep in the side, and leaves him on the stairs. Inside his mind he is screaming, in pain and rage...but the black thing has him in its grip and will not let go...

...he is carrying a young woman through the streets of Milecastle. Dark Others approach him, and inside he quails, but they part and fall in on either side of him, providing him with a guard. He sees Sean Grant, old Menzies, and a big man he doesn't recognize stare at him in disbelief as he passes. He wants to shout out, to tell them that he is not responsible...but the black thing has his mind.

...he is in a small chapel, and flames are lapping at the velvet drapes beside him, but he feels no pain. A man...Duncan Campbell...reaches past him towards the prone figure of his daughter, and the thing in his head commands, even stronger than before. He strikes out, as hard as he is able, and crushes the Scotsman's ribs with one blow, sending the man to the ground where he jumps, over and over, on the man's chest. He is disgusted with himself, and wails for mercy and peace...but the black thing has his mind. ...he carries Mary Campbell into a large blood-red palace and she is taken from his arms. He is led by a band of Others to a kitchen where he is laid on a long table. The voice in his head says sleep, so he sleeps. But even there the black thing has his mind...

... and Sean blinked full awake again.

He lowered the knife...just as the Constable went stiff in his arms.

"Ah, my young Watcher," an accented voice said from the Constable's mouth. "Now I will have my revenge on you for Baphomet."

Barnstable's arms reached for Sean, and instinctively Sean lashed out with the dagger. He rolled away in the dark, keeping the dagger in front of him.

He tried to will the Other inside him to see through the blackness, to show him his enemy, but Barnstable, or rather the spirit of the Boy-King, merely laughed.

"Who do you think controls the darkness? You, or I? Watch..."

It was as if someone had lit a candle. Sean saw the cell as if lit by daylight, and saw the figure of Barnstable move towards him. Then the light went, snuffed out as quickly as it had come. The Boy-King laughed again, closer now.

A hand brushed Sean's cheek. He jumped, and moved sideways fast, but again felt a hand at his neck.

"And where will you go?" the Boy-King said. "This body is ready for turning. Shall I allow it? Would you like to fight one of us in the dark?"

Sean stilled himself. Be ready for anything, Old Menzies had always taught him, and never engage an opponent in conversation.

Sean remembered how he had called the woodsman earlier, and tried to calm himself further.

I am the Balance he said, and called, not just for the

Woodsman, but also for the Other within. Once more the room lit up, and Sean saw Barnstable's eyes widen... just as the woodsman's ability on the hunt aided Sean's throwing arm. He sent the dagger straight and true through the big man's right eye.

"We will meet again," the Boy-King said, even as Barnstable's body fell to the ground.

Barnstable was still alive when Sean reached him.

"Finish me," he said, weakly. Blood was pumping from the ruin of his eye, and something in Sean lurched, but he sent it away.

I am the Balance," he said, and bent over the big man.

"Feed," a voice said from above him. "Feed, and be one of the blood."

"Never," Sean said.

He took Barnstable's head in his hands.

"Do you repent your sins, big man?" he asked.

Barnstable nodded. Tears streamed from his good eye. With one swift movement Sean broke his neck. The crack was loud in the confines of the cell.

"Quick. Feed now," the bloated Other shouted from above. "Before it is too late."

"I will not feed!" Sean shouted, and laid Barnstable down on the floor. He pulled the dagger from the ruined eye, wincing at the moist, sucking sounds as it came out. Then he slipped the blade in between the big man's ribs, making sure the heart was stopped in the full death.

"Then you will rot until you thirst enough to beg for release," the bloated Other said. There was the metallic noise of the grate being pulled shut, and Sean was left alone in the dark.

He sat beside the body, and said the words, then wept, there in the darkness.

Later Sean noticed that light was filtering into the room. At first he thought it was the sight of the Other helping him, but when he looked up he could see daylight coming in through a grille very high up to his left. Above him to his right, some ten feet off the ground, he could just see the metal grate through which they had entered the cell.

The room was some ten yards square, and the walls were smooth stone, almost like marble. It was going to be impossible to climb out, although Sean thought that, given a chance, he might be able to jump high enough to reach the lower grate. But it looked like it would be some time before he would be able to try—the Others would not be abroad during the day.

Barnstable's body still lay in the middle of the floor, staring sightlessly upwards with the one clear eye. If this was to be a long stay, then Sean needed to move it. He manhandled Barnstable to a corner of the cell and turned the dead face to the wall...the stare had seemed too accusing.

For most of his life Sean had hated the man, hatred made even worse by the murder of the Thane and the abduction of Mary Campbell. But now he had been inside the man's mind. He still felt the hate...but not the cold, all consuming rage that had previously filled him. Whatever the Constable's faults, he had not asked for the thing that had taken his mind, and he had not deserved the squalid death he had been given. He said the words again over the man's body, but left the dagger in its place...it would be well to be careful in this hellhole and he did not want any chance of the big man coming back.

He made a circuit of the cell, looking or any possible means of escape. It took him all of two minutes to realize that the only way out was the way he had come in—back up through the grate. He took a running jump at it, and found that he might be able to reach...if the grate was open.

For the time being, all he could do was wait.

The first day passed slowly.

At first he did not feel any hunger. The sun moved slowly across the floor of cell. He held his breath when the rays started to hit Barnstable's body, but there was no smoke, no fire. The man was truly dead.

Sean stood and placed his own hand in the rays, but again there was no smoke. The Other in him moved...he felt it in his mind. But Sean was in control. I am the Balance, he repeated to himself. The Other stayed down.

There was nothing for Sean to do except watch the march of the sun and wait for the night.

The night came, but the Others did not. Nor did they come on the second. Sean spent the nights keeping the rats from Barnstable's body and the days trying to find a plan that would allow his escape.

He had the dagger, a hunting snare and his cloak. He had searched Barnstable...not a task he would like to do twice...but had found nothing that would be of use to him.

He ran through countless scenarios in his mind, and he even tried to call the woodsman's sight for help. The sight showed him visions of bloody battle, of an army of the Protector's soldiers lined up in ranks on an open moor facing thousands of dark Others...but there was no vision to tell him how to free himself from the hellhole.

By the third night he still had no idea how he was to effect his escape.

It was full dark before the grate opened above him.

"Well, my young friend. Do you thirst?" the bloated Other said.

"Come down and find out."

In truth, Sean's lips were beginning to crack. He had managed to lick some moisture from the cell walls, but it had been bitter and metallic. He knew he was getting weak...he would have to escape soon, or die.

"He has not turned," he heard a voice whisper. From the tenor of it he guessed it was the old one with the long hair. "I can hear it in his heart."

"No. I am still warm," Sean said. "Come and see...my blood is sweet."

There was a rustling in the corridor above and the bloated Other spoke.

"Are you mad?" it said to its companion. "You saw how he slew the large one. He is a trained killer, this boy."

"But I have a thirst," the old one said, its voice a whining moan.

"Then come and quench it," Sean said. "For I am sick of this waiting. If I do not turn tonight I will end it myself with my dagger. You have had as much sport from me as you are going to get."

There was a scrambling in the room above, and a loud slap.

"No!" the bloated one shouted. "The King wants this one turned...we cannot feed from him!"

The grate slid shut once more, but Sean had a smile on his lips. He suspected it would be open again before too long.

He was proved right less than an hour later.

He heard the old Other muttering, even before the grate was opened.

"Just a little drink...that is all I need...just a sup. The King need never know."

"Come on down, old man," Sean whispered as the grate was pulled aside, "Come and drink from me, for I am tired of this mummery."

"Oh...I will give you rest," the old one cackled, and dropped down into the room.

I am the Balance. Sean said, and called on the night-sight.

The Other was making no pretence at stealth...it was coming straight for him. Moving fast, using the woodsman's speed and accuracy, Sean swung his hunting snare over its head before it had time to react. Still holding one end, he snapped his wrist, hard and fast.

The snare cut through the flesh as if it was a piece of cheese. The Other's head rolled on the stone floor, the shock in its eyes fading as it realized it was already full dead. Sean kicked the still standing body, tumbling it to the floor.

He jumped up and caught the edge of the grate, then

pulled himself up and out of the pit. Before starting up the corridor he slid the heavy metal cover back into place.

I am the Balance, he muttered to himself. The corridor ahead looked bright as day, although it was full night, and no torches were lit. Sean kept the snare in his left hand as he decided on a course of action.

He knew he was deep in the Palace. He was in the realm of the Others, in one of their strongholds...it was nighttime, and he was armed only with a snare designed for coneys. But he was free, from the pit, from his hatred of the Constable Barnstable, and from his fear of the Other within him. He smiled as he headed upwards through the building.

Eventually he found himself standing outside the large doors that led into the Great Hall. There were voices on the other side—three Others, one of whom was the fat bloated one.

Sean had a thin smile on his lips once more as he pushed the doors open and stepped into the room.

The great serpent on the floor seemed to writhe and squirm as Sean stepped onto the mosaic, and fangs slid from Sean's gums. But Sean mentally ordered them away, and when he ran his tongue over his teeth, they were normal incisors once more.

The bloated Other initially looked shocked, then laughed when he saw that Sean carried only the thin wire of the snare.

"Well, young sir," it said, "do you mean to talk us to death?"

I am the Balance. Sean said, and called on the woodsman's skills.

The Other who wore a dog collar was closest. Sean feinted with his left hand towards its heart, and instinctively it dropped its arms to protect itself. Sean had the snare over its head before it could lift its arms again. He leaped upwards and somersaulted over the Other's head, tugging the snare as he went. The head rolled on the floor even before Sean had tumbled and rolled back into an upright position. The filthy Other made a rush at him, trailing brown slime behind it. Sean let it come, and dropped to his knees as it closed, punching it hard in the belly. As it stumbled he slipped the noose of the snare around its left foot, rolling away and tugging hard in the same movement. The Other fell to the ground, its foot rolling some two yards from its body. It whimpered once and was still trying to stand when Sean dropped the noose around its neck and pulled tight, taking the head off cleanly.

He wiped the snare clean on his vest and looked around.

The bloated Other stood near the door. It was applauding, slapping its palms together with glee.

"Oh, he will be pleased to have you," it said. "Rarely have I seen such an efficient killer."

"I am no killer," Sean said. "An Other is lower than any animal...sending them to the final death is a mercy."

"No killer? Come boy...you know better than that..."

...and the sight returns.

Three bedraggled bodies, their clothes ragged and torn, lie underneath a hawthorn bush. Large white maggots crawl in and out of holes...in their faces, in their arms and in their bare torsos. The black sockets where their eyes used to be stare accusingly upwards...

Three Warden's men lie on a bare patch of ground. Ravens have found them, and one has an eye in its beak. The bird caws, and clacks shut the beak...the eyeball bursts moistly...

William Barnstable looks up, tears blinding his one good eye, just as Sean twists, hard, and breaks the big man's neck...

"They were all justifiable," Sean said.

The bloated Other laughed. It had moved closer to Sean, but not yet within range of the snare.

"Justifiable? Am I not justified in following my nature and feeding? Is the Boy-King not justified in seeking the throne of his fathers?"

Sean measured up the distance between them...he was still too far away.

"I will leave you now," the Other said. "No doubt we

shall meet again...the Boy-King has plans for you. Just remember to tell him that John of Falkirk kept his Palace for his return."

Sean jumped forward, but the Other was already far off down the corridor.

Its laughter echoed through the rooms as Sean chased behind it. But no matter how fast he ran, he was unable to catch it.

CHAPTER 3

NOVEMBER 15, 1745, MILECASTLE

The journey from Far Sawrey passed without incident. It took Megan several hours to persuade Fitz to leave the inn behind...the man had been prepared to stay there and rebuild the still-smoking ruin.

"We cannot rebuild while Rollo, and the Boy-King, are still in the land," she said. "I for one want revenge on the black bastards...they've taken our boy, our friend, and our livelihood. Are you grown so soft that all you want to do is hide your head in this inn?"

Those were the words that stung Fitz out of his melancholy mood. There was still a sadness in his eyes that had not been there before, but it had been joined by something new...a steely determination.

There was no sign of Others on the trek north...nor was there any sign of human activity. The only sign of the war was a broken cart by the side of the road, its axle broken and its contents— mainly clothing—left behind in its owner's haste to flee.

When they came to the field where Martin and Menzies had first noticed the disturbed earth Martin lowered his head...the memory of the old doctor was just too strong, and he did not want his men to see his tears.

The Hillman brothers kept up a steady flow of chatter all day. As if to prove that he too had some musical talent, Edward started to sing, "There was a young lady from Brest," but his singing voice was so bad that the men shouted him down, demanding that his brother gave them a song.

Edward took it in good humor, and Harold sang The Lay of the Thane again, then Greensleeves followed by a riding song about a fifteenth century raid into the Other's territory. The day passed merrily enough...until they came to Carlisle.

Even from a distance the stench was almost overpowering. No smoke rose from the chimneys, no noise reached them, and only the wind moved among the silent streets and houses. Martin remembered the black shadows that had flowed through the narrow alleys like a river, and the hairs tingled on his wounded arm as he mentally relived the battle and the slaughter that had so recently taken place. He shivered, though the sun shone on his face, and he turned his horse's head towards Milecastle, urging his men to follow.

Some of the men made the sign of the evil eye towards the town, but they knew better than to enter. The carrion eaters had dominion there now, and Martin had no desire to see what damage they had wrought on the bodies of the woman and children the Others had left there.

They gave the town a wide berth...it was obvious that the place was quite dead. A flock of carrion crows squawked noisily overhead as they skirted the city walls, then went back to their feasting.

"We cannot leave like this," Edward Hillman said, the horror showing bright and clear in his eyes. "There are people there, Christian folk who deserve to have the words said."

"Aye," Martin replied. "Mayhap you are right. But we are few, and they are many. We have not got the time."

"We should torch the place," Toby said, and Martin nodded.

"We will. After the Boy-King is driven off these islands forever, we will burn everything he has touched...there must be no chance of his kind ever getting a foothold again." The weather began to close in, and Martin knew that winter was not too far away. In some years the first snow would already be on the ground by now, and the biting cold of the rain as it started to spatter on their faces foretold of the short, damp days to come.

"Come, minstrel," Toby said to Harold Hillman. "Sing us something to remind us of summer."

The man with the squeezebox began to play a fast tune that marched the trotting of a horse, and soon young Harold's high, pure voice cut through the rain.

> Among the greenwood
> Walked a tall maiden fair
> The sun shone like gold
> In her long flaxen hair
> And the wee folk laughed
> As they took her away
> To the cave at the foot of the hill
> They plied her with wine
> And with sweetmeats so rare
> They danced her around
> With her feet in the air
> And the wee folk laughed
> As they caroused the whole day
> In the cave at the foot of the hill

They all knew this one and the band was all soon singing along, although the song ran to over twenty-five verses. Martin noted with a smile that Harold sang the polite version…there was no mention of fornication with the fairy king in this one. Maybe he would ask the lad for the tavern version later.

Despite the song Fitz was still morose, and Martin sensed a deep anger in the man, as if violence was only a heartbeat away.

He tried to talk to the innkeeper, but only got a grunt in reply.

"Leave him be," Megan said. "Even when we were at sea, all he wanted to do was to buy and manage an inn. He's spent the last ten years and more nurturing the best ale in the north."

"Aye," Fitz said, and spat on the ground. "And now it is gone…nothing remains but ashes and dust."

Martin was about to speak, but Megan shook her head, and they traveled in silence.

Martin found himself riding alongside the cart driven by old Barr.

"A man needs to be left alone with his sorrow," the old man said, and spat another wad of tobacco at his feet. "Now a woman...she needs to talk about it, preferably with other women. But leave a man alone and the black mood will pass sooner.

"There's another lesson for you."

Sudden tears sprang to Martin's eyes when Milecastle finally came into sight. He was surprised by how much emotion he still had left in him...he thought it might all have been burned out of him in his rage back in Derby. But the sight of his home made his heart lurch. He would never again be the boy he had been only short weeks before, but his heart would always remember.

He half expected to see his father standing on the walkway above the main gate, and old Menzies beside him, a flagon of ale in one hand and a pipe in the other. There were hot tears in his eyes that threatened to mist over his vision, but he brushed them away angrily. He was Thane, and his people needed to be led. He straightened his back and sat upright in the saddle as he led his men up the road to the castle.

The church bell rang to proclaim their coming, and Nat Cooper was at the gate to welcome them. He wore the uniform of Constable. His boots and belt were highly polished and the uniform, although not as black as it could have been, was sharp and clean. Cooper was obviously not a man to let his standards slip.

The big man had a broad smile on his face as Martin rode up to the gate.

"Well met, my Thane," he said, then his smile faded as he saw the new scars on Martin's head. "But I see you have been in yet another grievous fight."

"You should see his opponent," old Barr said, and

chuckled until Megan stopped him with a glaring stare.

Martin saw Cooper look along the line for Menzies.

"No," he said, "the Doctor is not with us. He gave his life for the Protector by stopping a breach in the walls of Derby."

Cooper removed his hat.

"For that I am sad, for I wanted to thank him for mending my leg...but you must tell me the story of it later. The town welcomes you home, my Lord. I shall prepare the Great Hall..."

"No," Martin said. "The Thane of Milecastle will not sit on the throne of Hadrian until the Boy-King is vanquished. We will billet the men in the inn and at the barracks of the Watch. And we will hold our counsel in the inn."

Cooper's eyes went wide, but he said nothing as Martin led his men into the town.

Ten minutes later Martin followed Fitz and Cooper into the dark empty inn. It was obvious that the place had been used since the battle, but it had not been cleaned, and trestles were strewn on the floor. Half-empty flagons of stale ale lay everywhere, and several mice scattered across the floor as the men approached.

"I'm sorry, Sire," Cooper said, "but what with getting the Watch back in order, and repairing the defenses I haven't had the time for..."

Martin stopped him with a wave of his hand.

"'Tis of no consequence. We have a happy circumstance…it seems we have an inn that needs an innkeeper...and an innkeeper that needs an inn."

He turned to Fitz.

"What say you, friend...can you make this place a tavern to be proud of?"

The bald sailor looked flabbergasted.

"Megan and I cannot afford it. We lost everything back in Far Sawrey and I have little more than the clothes I stand up in."

Martin interrupted him.

"This will cost nothing," Martin said. "Old Menzies is

owed a debt by this town. It falls to me as his Thane and his executor to repay it. "I can think of no better memorial for him...this is Milecastle's gift. It is a gift to a man that has shown care and affection to its Thane, its Doctor, and the Captain of its Watch. Now tell me...will you have it? Or must I get Nat here to find another man for the job?"

A broad smile broke across Fitz's face.

"Then I thank you for a favor we will never be able to repay properly. I will give you an inn that will be the talk of the whole country," he said. "The stone walls are more forbidding than I'd like, but a good fire and a few drapes will make the place more inviting. Now forgive me, Sire...I must fetch Megan. We have a party to prepare for."

After the visit to the inn Cooper led Martin on an inspection of the wall.

"You have been busy," Martin said. "The wall is fully restored."

"Aye. Men came from other forts along the line. We have manned four out of the twelve, and we are trying to keep a watch going. But until it is confirmed that the Boy-King is back across the wall, we are concentrating on protecting the towns themselves."

"Just what I would have done," Martin said. "And the bulb is fresh."

"But there is little of it left," Cooper said. "We must hope the dark army does not pass this way again, for we will be sore pushed to repel an attack."

"The Boy-King is heading north once more," Martin said. "But he seems to have lost his taste for battle."

Martin told Cooper everything that had happened since they left the town. The big man's eyes went wide when Martin spoke of the siege of Derby, and there were tears in his eyes as he heard of Menzies' passing.

The tale of the use of the smith's bellows put him back in better humor.

"I have been in the smithy at least four times in the past week...and it never occurred to me to use the bellows. There is a fine set there sitting and gathering dust."

"Get Toby and Edward Hillman to ready them," Martin said. "Young Hillman has shown an aptitude for construction…we should nurture it. And send men along the wall both east and west. We must have news of the Boy-King."

"And how long will you stay?"

"This will be our base," Martin replied. "We must send out search parties all across the north. The Protector must have knowledge of the Others before he sends Cumberland over the wall. I will ride out in the morning." "Then let us hope the innkeeper is as good as his word," Cooper said. "For your people want to celebrate your safe homecoming before you are away on your travels once more."

"Tell them there will be a party in the inn this evening," Martin said. "We have a new innkeeper to welcome."

Martin went alone into the Great Hall. The place lay dark and quiet. The fireplace was cold, and no torches were lit.

I will bring the joy back to this place, Martin vowed. And we will restore the Protector's law in the north.

There was a wavering in the shadows by the throne of Hadrian, and for a second it was as if the old Thanc sat there, smiling. But when Martin blinked he was alone in the dark, with only the soft cooing of a pigeon in the rafters to disturb the quiet.

He closed the doors softly as he left. To do otherwise would have felt like desecration of a tomb.

In contrast, the inn was full to bursting point. Apart from the Watchmen who were on duty, everyone else was crammed into the room. Ale flowed freely, cold pork pies were laid out in small piles on all the trestles, a pig roasted slowly on a great spit over a roaring fire, and there was bread and cheese for all.

"We found the hidey-hole where the innkeeper had stored his stock not long after you left," Nat Cooper said. "He must have been a prudent man. I believe we have enough ale to last the winter."

"Aye," Fitz said. He was walking past, carrying four flagons of beer in his hand. "And we'll have the spring batch brewing soon enough...there's malt and mash aplenty, and I found a sack of good Worcestershire hops out back. There is even a hogshead of strong Devon cider in the cellar. I would have liked to have met your innkeeper...he knew his ales."

"Aye," Martin said. "He took pride in them. He would be happy to know that his inn, and his beer, was in good hands."

"I will try to live up to his standards," Fitz said.

"Standards, is it?" Megan said as she pushed past them, her arms full with loaves and cheeses. "You'll be telling me next that you'll be needing a bath."

"What…is it March already?" Fitz called after her, and everyone in earshot laughed loudly.

"We'll make you an inn that will be famous across the whole of the north," Fitz said, and Martin saw something in the man's eyes that told him he should believe it.

"And have you decided on a cellar-man?" Nat said.

Martin saw the dark thoughts that passed over the innkeeper's face, but someone else spoke before he could say anything.

"That he has."

Martin turned to see old Barr standing behind him. The old man had a pipe in one hand and a flagon of ale in the other. It looked like it was his most natural position.

"I looked after the beer at the White Horse in Witcham and the Black Bull in Haltwhistle before you young pups were even thought of," the old man said. "And Fitz and I agree on the way beer should be."

"Strong, dark and heady…I like my beer the way I like my women." Fitz said. "Old Barr here has agreed to be in my employ—if the Thane can spare him?"

Martin smiled.

"An old officer of the Watch is welcome to do whatever he wishes in my town."

Barr bowed from the waist, taking care not to spill any ale.

"Then I will give you another lesson, young sir. Give respect to your elders...but never too much. Some of us have learned cunning enough over the years to take advantage of the good will of the young."

Martin laughed.

"I can see you and Fitz will be well matched...he will charm the customers while you pick their pockets."

"Shush," Fitz said in mock indignation. "Do not give away all our secrets on our first night."

The ale continued to flow, and music started up. The smith's man with the squeezebox was joined by a harpist, a drummer and a flautist. Jigs and reels, laments and ballads were sung with gusto by most of the company as the smith's men and the men of Milecastle traded songs and tales.

Nat Cooper, who possessed a deep bass singing voice that reverberated around the room, started a bawdy song about "The Virgin's Chastity".

The virgin and her partner
Went to bed to dance
Be careful sir, the virgin cried
You cannot use your lance

It had so many verses that the big man needed his flagon replenished twice during the rendition.

"Hey, Nat, We have never heard that one afore," Martin called out. The big man blushed and mumbled something under his breath.

It is his own composition, Sire!" one of the Milecastle women shouted. "The town has a new bard as well as a new innkeeper."

She went up to Cooper and planted a huge wet kiss on his lips.

"You can use your lance on me anytime, my fine Constable," she said.

Cooper lifted her high in the air and swung her down into a seat beside him.

"I have a woman back in Garstang," he said.

The woman cackled. "And I have a husband… somewhere in Ireland, I think. What does that matter? I am here, and I am warm."

"Don't fight too hard, Nat!" Megan cried out. "She might change her mind."

When the big man sat down Martin heard a commotion on the far side of the room, and turned to see Harold Hillman being pushed towards the musicians. He saw the boy talk to the man with the squeezebox. His heart sank as Harold started to sing "The Lay of the Thane".

Harold had added a new verse, about a triumphant return to Milecastle. Martin thought the whole thing mawkish and embarrassing. But the people of the town loved it, and demanded three repetitions while Martin blushed increasingly red. Soon renditions of the song were breaking out spontaneously among the gathering.

"A speech!" a voice shouted. "A speech from the slayer of the Dark Lord!"

Martin tried to dissuade them, but the clamor got louder until the men were pounding on the tables.

"Speech! Speech!" they called, until Martin climbed on one of the tables. The room went quiet when he lifted his arms.

"This is my home," he said, "and I welcome all my new companions. I hope you like our hospitality."

The throng cheered too loudly—some of the men were already very drunk.

Martin continued.

"Once we had many times like this in this room. And we will have them again, when we have driven the Others from these shores."

Again the crowd cheered, and Martin had to shout to make himself heard.

"And to ensure that we have more nights like this, Milecastle needs a new innkeeper. I have found you the man for it…Fitz, get up here and let them all see you." "They have all seen him already, Sire!" Cooper shouted. "He has taken payment from every man here."

"Aye. But ale does not come for free. I only take enough to make more ale!" Fitz called out.

"Then the inn will thrive!" Martin shouted above the noise. "Let the party start...the next round of ale is from the Thane."

There was a huge cheer, and as Martin sat down the musicians started up "The Lay of the Thane" once more.

Megan came and sat next to the Thane. The townspeople whistled loudly as she hugged him to her and planted a wet kiss on his mouth.

"I thank you," she said. "For the gift of this fine inn...and for the joy it brings to my old man."

More ale flowed, and dancing started. Martin found himself being whirled around the room in a reel so fast that his head spun and his legs threatened to give way underneath him.

At some point in the evening Martin found a quiet corner and tried to make himself inconspicuous.

I miss Old Menzies.

The old doctor would have loved a night like this...with the ale flowing and the talk free. Looking around Martin saw that there was little sign of the agony that had befallen the town so few days before. Part of him felt that the town should be mourning...for the Thane, for Menzies, for all those that had died.

To you, Father, he thought, and raised his flagon in salute. He drained it in one, feeling the warmth course through him.

"Another ale, young master?" old Barr said from his right. The old man was carrying a large pitcher in his arms, cradling it as if it were a babe.

Martin put his flagon in front of him and paired it with another from across the table.

"Take the weight off your legs, old man," Martin said, "and sit yourself down. I would drink with an Officer of the Watch."

The old man spat a wad of tobacco on the floor.

"Don't mind if I do," Barr said. "Don't mind at all."

The old man sat beside Martin and lit up a foul-smelling pipe while Martin poured their ales.

The impromptu band had fallen silent while they quenched their thirsts, so the men were able to talk in a near conversational tone.

"It is good to be back on the wall," old Barr said. "It is too long since I left."

Martin knew from the years of experience with old Menzies that there was a story coming and he wasn't disappointed.

"I walked the wall thirty years, man and boy," the old man started. "And I never saw an Other until last week in Derby. We kept the wall, we drank beer, and we made children. It was enough for me. But my wife had other ideas. She had dreams…of a house of her own, of a garden, of a shop where she could buy frills and lace.

"So when the Watch had done with me…just when I thought I might get some peace…she had me up sticks. It was just her luck that we ended in Derby."

The old man took a long pull from his beer, and Martin thought there would be no more, but after a puff of the pipe that sent a thick gray fog into the air around them, he started again.

"I had a daughter, you know. The sweetest thing you ever saw. After the lad took to the Wall she was the apple of the wife's eye. And when she married a doctor I thought my wife was fit to burst. It was because of her we moved to Derby. The doctor had a big house just inside the city walls, and we had a cottage just down the same road…and a garden. I do believe my wife was really happy. As for me…well, a city has many inns, and an officer of the Watch can scrounge many flagons of ale on a story of the night when he 'nearly' saw an Other."

The old man stopped to relight his pipe. A new cloud of gray smoke swam about his head for a second, as if his hair was on fire. Martin saw that the man's eyes had taken on that far-away look typical of people lost in a story's memory.

"And so it went on. My retirement continued apace, and my daughter was heavy with child. My wife was busy making enough clothing for an army of newborns, and the garden bloomed. Then, a couple of weeks ago, rumors began to spread, of trouble on the Wall and a Threat from the far North.

"I wanted to report to the wall and my wife wanted to go south to Bath, but the thing that sealed it was my daughter. She was too far gone to travel, so we stayed, while the town filled with soldiers and the rumors from the north grew wilder, yet more true."

Suddenly Martin did not want to hear anymore. The old man looked grim, his teeth clamped hard on the pipe, his knuckles white where he gripped his flagon. Martin put a hand on the man's shoulder.

"If the telling is too sore..." he began.

"No, young sir," Barr replied. "It is sore. But I need to tell someone."

There was pleading in the man's eyes, a need that Martin could not refuse. He realized that Barr had reverted to his Watch training, bringing a trouble to his senior officer. He was wondering if the old man even realized it when Barr started talking again.

"The lad came to visit. That was all the wife could think of, may God bless her...her boy was home. Never mind that the Boy-King and his army were rattling at the gates. Her boy was home and all was right with the world. Her small part of it, at least.

"The drums of war started to beat louder, and the town started filling up with soldiers. Rumors came from the north, of the falling of the Wall and the end of the Watch. I would have gone to man the walls, but the doctor took me aside, and asked me to look after the womenfolk...not just my wife and daughter, but other wives, other daughters. It was a kindness he did me...he knew I was too old for the barricades, yet he gave me a duty I could respect.

"I took the womenfolk to an old church near the south wall. By the time the battle started there were more than thirty of us…thirty women and children, and me…an officer of the Watch in his cups. "Oh yes. I was drinking…drinking for my lost youth, my lost pride…drinking to dull the noise of the preparations for the battle to come and the sound of chattering women and mewling babes."

Barr looked into his flagon, and made to push it away, then thought better of it and swallowed a deep gulp from it before continuing.

"I ran out of ale," he said. "'Tis strange how such a small thing can irretrievably change a man's life.

"I was only gone for ten minutes…just long enough to fill an ewer in a nearby inn and sample a pint of Winter Porter while waiting. But while I was gone all the joy left my soul for the remainder of my miserable life.

"The church was like a scene from hell. In my absence the south wall of the city had fallen, and the Others seemed to know instinctively where the weak and vulnerable would be found…and they had no compunction about desecrating the Lord's house.

"By the time I opened the church door there must have been twenty of them in there. They were rampaging through the women and children like a fox through a chicken run. I saw immediately that I was too late….there was to be no helping those poor souls.

"I smashed my ewer over the head of the nearest Other and shut them inside. The last thing I saw was my missus, an Other feeding from her neck, her eyes pleading for my help even as her life faded.

"Part of me…a large part of me…wanted to throw myself into the fight, to drag her away from the black bastards who dared to violate her. But I knew my duty. God help me, I always knew my duty. And I knew where the pitch was stored. "It took long minutes for me to round up some military help and get the pitch to the church. By this time Cumberland had repaired the breach in the wall, and I was able to recruit five men to help me set the fire. We had brands and stakes at the ready, and made to enter the church.

"But when we opened the door, there was naught there but the dead and the bitten. An officer, a short, fat, sweaty man, went to close the doors. Just then Jinny, my daughter, staggered forward out of the darkness. She was bitten in three places...but that was not what concerned her.

"'The baby...' she screamed. 'The baby is coming.'

"At first I moved forward, but that was the drink talking again. I was an Officer of the Watch, and I knew my duty. I closed the door shut in her face.

"'Burn it,' I said, turning to the soldiers around me. 'Burn it down to the ground.'

"'Belay that command,' the fat Officer said. 'There is a pregnant girl inside that church. Let her out. That's an order.'

"And do you know, some of them even moved to do it? I despair of some soldiers...they've got so used to obeying orders they have no mind of their own to decide when they should be disobeying one.

"I did the only thing an officer of the Watch could—I laid the fat soldier out with a single blow. Then I set to burning down the church.

"And just as the door caught fire, it burst open, and my Jinny tried to throw herself out.

"'The baby...save the baby.' She shouted, and, even as her clothes burst aflame, she was holding her arms out to me, pleading. I did the only thing I could—I threw a bucket of burning pitch over her.

"She screamed. She screamed something terrible. But I did my duty...I waited until the roof fell in. Nothing came out, either man or Other.

"The remaining soldiers wouldn't look me in the eye, but they were good men. They stood watch with me, making sure that the job was done.

"I waited there until dawn came to the sky, and I remember nothing of the time. I heard later that the fat soldier was threatening to hang me before his own men told him to be quiet, but I did my duty. I waited to be sure.

"And in the morning, I went to find my lad, to tell him what I had done. And he told me about a scouting party, about a wolf on the hunt for the Boy-King. I knew that was where I had to be, if only for a chance to see the Wall once more. And here I am. Your man, if you'll have me."

Martin clasped the old man on the arm.

"You have been my man ever since we left Derby," Martin said. "You are a true man of the Watch. And any officer of the Watch is always welcome in Milecastle."

Old Barr put his pipe away in the pocket of a stained waistcoat, and lifted the pitcher once more.

"Aye. I am your man," he said. "But duty is a hard thing, young sir. Do not let it rule you…for it can bring great pain."

The old man stomped away, but Martin stayed in the corner seat for a while, thinking of loss, and of duty.

His reflective time was ended when Megan found him.

"Here he is!" she shouted, dragging him to his feet. "Come, young sir. Tonight is a celebration for your homecoming. We cannot have you lurking in a corner."

And once more Martin was thrust into the raucous, drunken melee. Later, when the roast pig was little more than a pile of bones and dripping, and the bread was long since gone, Harold Hillman sang "The Wives of Henry" and "The Maid of Orleans," his high clear voice ringing strong in the rafters. Grown men wept.

Townspeople kept pouring fresh ale into Martin's pot until he was unsure how much he had drank.

His last memory was of Fitz and Cooper laying him down on his old bed in the high tower. The ceiling swam above him, so he closed his eyes, and let oblivion take him.

Martin dreamed of his father.

The old man came to him in the night and led him out of his room and down into the Great Hall. The Thane sat in Hadrian's throne, and Martin sat at his feet, just like they had done in all the years before.

They spoke for hours, of the life of the town, of Sean Grant, and of Martin's mother.

When Martin woke he remembered none of it, but his pillow was wet with tears.

The next morning he sat on his horse and hoped that he was not going to disgrace himself by throwing up over his saddle horn.

He had thirty men behind him, and one cart, driven by Fitz and Edward Hillman, containing four barrels of bulb-and-silver water and the large set of smith's bellows.

"We go to scout to the North," he said to Nat who was standing beside Martin's horse. The big man looked nearly as bad as Martin felt. "Look for us again in three days."

Nat nodded.

"Perhaps we might forego the homecoming party the next time?"

Martin smiled.

"I leave you the rest of the men...and the inn is now open. Keep the Watch alert. The party is over."

"Do not worry," Megan said, approaching across the square. "I will not sell them ale...well, not too much anyway."

"And I do not wish to drink anymore," Nat said. "Not for a few days anyway."

Martin led the men out through the North Gate. The sky was heavy and overcast, like a wall of slate hanging above them, but at least it was not raining. Megan and Harold Hillman stood on the wall, and they were still waving when Martin looked back from nearly a mile down the road. He felt a pang of loss as he turned his back on his home once more, and he had a premonition of doom, a blackness in his soul that told him he had a long hard road to travel before he saw the towers above the wall again.

"Where do we travel to, sir?" Edward Hillman asked him as they followed the road north.

"To the place where I learned that magic truly exists,"

he said, and smiled as the boy's eyes went big and round.

He had a vague idea where he was heading...he had walked this road with Campbell. Then it had taken them all day to reach the ruins of Newcastleton. But on horseback, and being able to use the road all the time, they reached it just after noon.

"Half an hour's rest," Martin said to Toby as they pulled up into the open ground in the middle of the ruined town. "Get the horses fed and watered...there is a stream to the North that should be clear fresh water. And make sure the men are careful. We still do not know where the Boy-King is, and his slaves could be anywhere."

Martin left his own horse with Edward Hillman and entered the ruin of the old church where he and Campbell had spent the night.

The place was as deserted as he remembered it. Only the fluttering of a small bird trying to escape broke the silence—he could not even hear the sound of his men in the street outside.

The remains of their campfire were still there on the stone floor. Martin bent down and sifted the ashes. Remembering the visions this fire had brought, he lifted some ash to his nose and breathed in.

The wound in his arm throbbed in sudden pain. There was no vision, no foretelling of the future...but there was a smell in the air, the faintest taint of something dead but still walking. It was a long way away, far to the east, but Martin knew what it was...it was the odor of the Others.

"Aye," a voice said beside him. "They are in the wind."

He had to look down to see the voice's owner. The smallest, fattest woman he had ever seen stood by his side. She was of the woodsman's tribe...that much was obvious from the emerald green of her eyes and the pointed tips to her ears. She wore a long fur cape, and from what Martin could see her whole body was covered in tattoos.

"I, Gwynneth, oldest of the stone," she said.

"My belly is full and my soul is empty. I am happy to meet another of Lennan's people," Martin replied, and the woman's face lit up in a huge grin.

"Greetings, killer of the gray shadow and Lennan-friend," she said, and hugged Martin around the waist. He felt the joints of his spine pop and stretch.

"You had best put me down, madam," Martin said, laughing aloud, "before you do me a mischief."

The bear hug loosened, but only slightly.

"Gwynneth is happy, for Lennan has a friend to remember him. And while you remember, his song will always be in the wind."

"I will always owe him for my life." Martin said. "And if he ever needs me, I will be there when he calls."

The small woods-woman smiled sadly.

"But Gwynneth's soul is full, for Lennan has gone with the wind."

Martin was shocked into silence.

"How...when..." he said.

Gwynneth put her hand to Martin's head.

"Easier to show," she said, and Martin's mind exploded in the woodsman's sight.

...Sean Grant is fighting a pack of Others just outside the walls of Milecastle. One of them latches onto him and manages to bite him in the shoulder, even as Sean sends many of them to the final death.

...Sean throws away bread and cheese, even though he looks thin and wasted from hunger.

...Sean attacks Campbell on a riverbank, fangs smiling from a bloody mouth just as Lennan shoots him with a padded arrow

... Gwynneth bleeds Sean in a cave high on a hillside

...Campbell lowers a silver cross into a bowl of blood as Sean screams

...Sean is tested on a long altar-stone in the middle of a circle of menhirs

...Lennan gives his blood to save Sean

...Lennan's body is burned on a pyre in a high place

...Sean and Campbell take their leave of Gwynneth on a high hilltop at night...

Gwynneth took her hand away from Martin's forehead. He almost thought he had caught sight of another vision, a glimpse of Sean in a red chapel, facing a tall Other clad in chain mail, but the scene faded too quickly.

"Sean is an Other?" he said. "The Captain of the Watch of Milecastle has been turned?"

Gwynneth shook her head.

"No. Not a dark one, but not man either...not now. He is a new thing under the Father...but fear not, you will see him, and ask him yourself. That not why I here."

She took Martin's hand and led him in front of the stained glass window so that they were in the sunshine.

"Old bones need warming," she said, before lightly stroking the arm that had been so recently ravaged.

"I come to tell you three things...what is, what was, what might be."

She counted off on her finger.

"...Peredur-An-Lennan will take the people of the Father away from this land...you will see us no more...the new king has no stomach for fighting the dark ones."

She spat on the ground at her feet to show her disgust before she counted a second finger.

"...Camp-bell has flown with the wind and sings with Lennan. He wishes to thank you for the gift of the gray-one's cloak. It warms him when he is far from the Father. He says you are to trust Sean Grant...things are not always true just because your eyes see them."

She touched a third finger.

"...the one you call the Boy-King is close by. He has brought his army to rest and sent his slaves away on a task. He is undefended when the sun is high. If you be quick, you catch him sleeping...send him to final death."

"Show me," Martin said, and lifted Gwynneth's hand to his forehead.

"Gwynneth likes quick learner," she said, and smiled again, showing the broken stumps of her teeth.

Once more visions filled Martin's mind as...

...he soars high above an ancient graveyard. The old

graves, and the grass around them, are torn and disturbed. He knows he is looking once more at the resting-place of the Others.

The graveyard sits on the edge of a tall hill. At the foot of the hill, in the valley, the flat ground near the river is similarly churned and broken over an expanse that seems to stretch for miles.

He is lifted higher, and the sight takes him up the river to its source, and over the hill beyond to join another river flowing fast on the far side. He races along with the current until the ground levels, the river flattens, and, at a bend, he sees a group of ruined buildings, with men and horses in a wide street. He blinks...

...and was again back in the church with Gwynneth.

"The Boy-King is there? In the churchyard?" he asked.

"The sight is true." Gwynneth said. "If you speed, you will catch him while he sleeps. Lennan's gift will aid you. It knows where he lies, and you will always be able to smell him. The gray brother will know."

"The gift...what is it?" Martin asked.

"Empty your soul." The old woman said. "Then you will be with the wind and will not need to ask."

He wasn't given time to inquire further

"You will go now," she said. "Go now, and send the shadow to sing in the wind."

There was a noise from the door of the church, and Toby the smith walked in. Martin turned to talk to him, and when he looked back, Gwynneth had gone...he had not heard her move.

"I heard voices," the smith said.

"I was talking to myself," Martin replied, and smiled.

The smith was not convinced. Martin saw him look around the church as if someone was playing a joke on him and would pop out from behind a pew at any moment.

In truth, Martin did not know where Gwynneth had gone, but he had previously witnessed Lennan in action. It did not surprise him that she was fast and silent.

"Get the men mounted," he said to the smith. "We're

riding out...and we need to go now."

"Where to?" the big man asked.

"East. We go east as fast as we can travel. We have a graveyard to find before nightfall."

The vision Gwynneth had provided for him was proved true some three hours later as Martin brought his men over the top of a ridge and they looked down on a graveyard in the lee of the hill.

"How did you know it was here?" Edward Hillman said, and Martin saw some of the men muttering to themselves. Several of them made the sign against the evil eye.

Martin said nothing. The truth would not help...none of these men had ever seen a woodsman. To them, the people of the forest were as supernatural, and to be feared as much, as the Others.

"We will have to add another verse to 'The Lay of the Thane'," Fitz said. "...how the young Thane found the sight."

I may have found the sight, Martin thought, but will it be of any use to me, I wonder?

"It matters not how I know," Martin said, loudly, so that all could hear. "We are here, and there are black-hearted bastards to kill."

He dismounted and called Toby and Fitz forward with him to the edge of the graveyard. They looked out over the stones.

Where the ground was disturbed old bones, brown with age, poked out of the earth. A skull, the black eye-sockets appealing for help against the desecration, stared at them from under a massive cross, carved in scrolls, knots and runes.

"And tell me, Sire," Toby said. "Just how did you know to come to this place?"

"One of the forest people visited me, back in the church," Martin said. Toby's eyes went wide, but Fitz didn't flinch.

"Their sight showed you this place, did it not?"

Martin nodded.

"And they said that the Boy-King himself lies sleeping under these stones. I need your counsel...the dark army lies sleeping in yon riverbed beneath us...and they are there in huge numbers...maybe even the whole army. If we attack, and they come at us, we will be overwhelmed."

"But you think there is a chance to give the Boy-King the final death?" Toby asked.

"Aye. We can end it here if we stand firm."

"Then we must try," Fitz said. "If there is even half a chance...we must try."

"Come, then," Martin said. "We must deploy the men quickly...there is not much of the day left."

Edward Hillman was left at the top of the hill with the horses.

"But I am needed to stir in the silver," he said. The lad looked like he was about to cry with frustration. "Toby needs me. If the silver is not poured right it will clog the bellows and make it harder to pump and…"

Martin took him aside and placed a hand on his shoulder.

"I need you here, man," he said, and the boy visibly straightened, his chest puffed out. "We may need to beat a hasty retreat and I need a man I can trust to keep the horses ready...we may need to move fast. Will you hold the horses for me...for all of us?"

The boy's eyes shone with pride, and he saluted, as crisp and efficient a salute as Martin had ever seen.

"I will not let you down, sir."

Martin returned to find Toby and Fitz manning the bellows, and one of the smith's men pouring silver powder into the water barrel and stirring it. Edward Hillman had thought of everything, and had supplied a cut-off oar from a rowing boat as a means of mixing in the powder.

"The men are deployed?" Martin asked.

"Aye, sir," Toby said. "We only await your order."

"Then let us go to it," Martin said. "While there is still light in the sky."

He made sure his pistols were loaded and cocked, and gave the order. Toby and Fitz pumped hard and a jet of water flew out over the graveyard. The air was suddenly full of the stench of the bulb.

At first it went as it had back at Thornton-in-Lonsdale. The ground heaved and began to burn in a clear blue flame. High screams rent the air, and a band of Others, about ten of them, pulled themselves out of the ground, only to be soaked by the spray from the bellows. They exploded, as if torched from within, pieces of burning flesh being strewn over the graveyard. The stench of death filled the air.

Close to the cart and out to a distance of some thirty yards, an area covering almost half the graveyard was well ablaze. Beyond that the ground was beginning to heave and boil as many more Others struggled free from their sleep, desperate to escape the fiery death.

Limbs poked out of the soil, only to begin burning, hands grasping for the sky even as flames burst over them and the flesh blackened. All over the site Others were thrashing free only to melt and burn as the silver, garlic and sunshine sent them to a speedy final death.

Suddenly a group of twenty or more broke free of the ground at the same time, just out of range of the main spray. They turned towards the cart, then fled as the bellows turned towards them.

"Burn, you bastards!" Fitz shouted. "Burn like you'll burn in hell!"

They pumped the bellows harder, and the jet of water shot out towards the group, taking the leaders full on and sending them down into a morass of steaming coagulated slime. The rest fled.

Ten of the escaping Others made it to the edge of the graveyard and were mounting the small wall at the far end when Martin gave the order to fire. The hidden musket-men rose out the long grass and sent volley after volley into the writhing, burning shadows.

"Another barrel!" Toby shouted, and the man on the cart started to manhandle a butt across the floor of the cart.

Martin sensed a movement out in the graveyard. A large stone, some eight feet square, moved to one side, and a band of six Others sprang up and out of a deep, stone-lined tomb. Their clothes gave off small wisps of smoke, and they carried their hands over their mouths to protect them from the fumes, but the silver had not reached them.

Martin recognized the thinner of the figures from the long white hair that streamed behind it...it was the Boy-King, and the ones with him were from his personal guard. Just then a second stone slid to one side and a tall figure, instantly recognizable, emerged. It was Rollo.

"Fitz!" Martin shouted, "The Boy-King...get the Boy-King!"

The innkeeper had already swung the spout towards Rollo, and had to re-adjust his aim. By then it was too late...the Boy-King and his guard had moved out of range of the main jet of water. Splashes hit them, but it bought mainly small wisps of smoke that they were able to quickly brush away as they sped out of range of the bellows.

Martin let off both his pistols. He hit one of the Boy-King's guards, a Highland Other which immediately started to blaze where the shot had punched a hole in its back. The Boy-King did not look back. With his remaining guards protecting him in the middle of the small group, he flew into the face of the rank of musket-men.

"Fire!" Martin shouted. "Fire!"

Four musket-men did shoot, and two more of the Boy-King's guards fell...the fat monk, and an ancient crone who had already got silver on her legs. She screamed as she burned, black and smoky like a badly made candle.

Martin yelled in triumph.

"Fire!" he shouted again.

But the rest of the musket-men lowered their weapons as the Boy-King and his three remaining guards burst into their midst, a frenzy of fangs and flashing swords. Within seconds six musket- men lay dead or dying and the Boy-

King was off and away down the hill.

There was more smoke rising from the escaping group, but the day was still heavily overcast, and the sun was not strong enough on its own to give them the true death.

The musket-men shook their heads as if waking from a long sleep.

"Shoot!" Martin shouted. "He's getting away!"

But the Boy-King was already out of range, heading off at speed to the foot of the hill.

And once more Martin felt the Other's presence in his mind.

"Ah...the Wolf is rampaging among the flock once more," the voice said. "You have got in my way once too often..."

The ground at the foot of the hill seethed, as if a massive tremor ran through the earth. The dark army rose up, a forest of hands grasping at the air. They groped upwards, the wrists coming slowly from the earth, then the arms. Finally their heads and shoulders pushed out of the soil.

Smoke rose from their bodies, but they came when their King called, out into the evening sun. Like a vast black blanket, they began to creep up the hill.

The voice in Martin's head laughed, long and hard. Martin knew he had to move, to get his men away, but his body was held as if in a vise as the black army got ever closer.

Then he felt it...the tickling of the long wolf hairs as they came on his arm. The contact with the Other was broken as quickly as it had come. Martin could still smell him, but was no longer compelled to obey him.

"Back!" he shouted. "To horse! To horse!"

Some of the musket-men were still dazed, still trying to shake off the Boy-King's spell, and it took long seconds to get the men mustered and moving. By then the bulk of the Boy-King's army had already risen out of the ground. Martin noticed with dismay that the last of the sun was leeching out of the sky.

"To horse!" he shouted once more, and this time the men all responded.

Fitz was trying to get the cart turned.

"Leave it," Martin said. "Get to a horse...we will have some spare."

"But the bellows..." Fitz said.

"Forget them. We can get other bellows...we have no other innkeeper. Now quickly. They will be on us in a minute."

Fitz rocked the last water barrel until it fell over, spilling bulb, silver and water over the cart and the horse that pulled it.

The horse snorted, but Fitz patted it on the flank as he undid the yoke.

"That should save you, old fellow," he said. "I can do no more."

He slapped the old horse on the side, and it trotted away sedately, then stopped, and began to feed on the grass beneath it.

"I've seen dead men with more sense," Fitz said, then turned back to Martin.

"We had best get going, sir," he said with a grim smile. "I think we may be out-numbered this time."

Martin also managed a smile as they turned up the hill.

"Mayhap if Megan was with us we would prevail."

"Aye..." Fitz replied. "Even the Boy-King would quail in his boots at meeting my wife when her ire is up."

Martin, Toby and the innkeeper were the rear-guard as they ran up the hill. When they got to the top Martin had a last look back.

The foot of the hill was already in darkness, but there was enough light to see that the bulk of the dark army were heading north, following the Boy-King and what remained of his guard.

The bulk...but not all.

A band of several hundred Others had made their way up the hill, and were even now almost level with the graveyard. They were led by the tall figure of Gord Rollo, with a turned dog loping along beside him, a dog with fiery red eyes and yellowed fangs that dripped stringy ropes of drool.

"I'm coming, Father!" they heard the tall figure shout. "Keep your neck warm for me!"

Edward Hillman was holding Martin's horse. His eyes were wide with fear, but he had not moved to get a mount of his own.

"Can you ride, boy?" Martin asked.

The lad nodded.

"I have been riding with the hunt since I was ten."

"Then find yourself a mount that suits you, but do it fast…there are Others almost upon us."

Martin got all his men mounted and turned them to face the advancing Others. As the dark horde came over the brow of the hill, the horsemen let off a volley of silver shot from muskets and pistols that brought blue flame dancing along the line of darkness. Without waiting to see the full effect of the shots, the men wheeled and sped off, following the setting sun.

The Others followed. They were not as fast as the mounted men, but they were faster than men-and-only-men would have been on foot…and Martin suspected they would not tire.

"I'm sorry, sir!" Fitz shouted.

They were galloping down the far side of the hill, as fast as they dared push the horses in the gloom. Behind them the band of Others was still coming on…more than quarter of a mile behind now, but showing no signs of flagging.

"Sorry for what?" Martin said.

"I went for Rollo…I should have gone for the Boy-King. My rage against him blinded me."

"Forget it," Martin said. "You were trying to kill Others, and you did a good job."

"But the Boy-King got away," Fitz said, and Martin

heard the frustration in the man's voice.

"And did you know it was the Boy-King?"

Fitz looked puzzled.

"No. Why would I...I have never seen him."

"Aye. But I have. In a vision," Martin said, and noticed too late that some of the men had overheard and were giving him the sign against the evil eye again. He decided to ignore them; he had seen too much this past few weeks to worry about their superstitions. "And I should have given the order sooner. It was the heat of battle, man...there was no fault." "Thank you, sir," Fitz said. "But it doesn't make me feel any better."

"Then maybe this will," Toby said, coming up beside them. "I reckon that yon crone that we burned under the silver was Hannah of Tyre. It is said she has been the nursemaid to six Blood-Kings, and was born even before the Others came to this land...we got one of the old ones."

"More than one," Martin replied. "We got the Monk."

"Aye," Fitz said, "I've heard of that one. He came from Rome, at the time King Henry was sacking the monasteries. He's been a plague on God-fearing Englishmen for centuries."

"So you see, old man," Toby said to Fitz, laughing as he galloped past them. "We are whittling them down. At this rate we should get them all by the turn of the century."

Fitz laughed, and Martin joined in, their spirits momentarily lifted. But all the time they were aware that the black Others came on apace behind them.

They galloped for as long as they could, but the time came when the horses needed rest.

"We cannot keep up this pace," Toby called out, but Martin was loath to stop altogether, and ordered them to slow to a trot for a while.

Edward Hillman drew up alongside Martin. The boy was a natural horseman—he and his mount moved as one.

"I have a new idea, Sire," the lad said. Fitz groaned, but smiled at the same time.

Edward was indignant.

"Do not scoff, Fitz...the silver worked, did it not?"

The lad looked so serious that Martin had to stifle a laugh as he spoke.

"Go on," he said.

"If you can find a narrow passage, I believe we can mount an ambush," Edward said.

"With what?" Fitz said. "We had to leave the barrels behind."

"Aye. But we have our canteens."

"Tell me your plan?" Martin said, and a thin, grim smile of expectation played on his lips as the boy outlined his idea.

Ten minutes later the opportunity presented itself as they rode through a gully between high rocks on either side. Martin sent Toby and Edward to prepare the lad's plan, and he positioned the rest of his men among the rocks on either side of the path. The horses were being held in a clearing fifty yards further back.

It was full dark now, and the sky was overcast. It was only just possible for Martin to see the high rocks on the far side, but he knew that Toby had his men ready and their muskets armed.

"Will it work?" Fitz said, and Martin smiled.

"Master Hillman is as bright as a button...I do believe he has found another new way to kill Others."

"Only as long as they come," one man said.

"They are coming," Martin said. "All we have to do is wait for them." He didn't add that he knew they were already close...he could smell them in the air.

They didn't have long to wait. The Others appeared out of the gloom, a thick line of blackness that seemed to suck in the available light. They were a rag-tag bunch...men, woman and youths, all in various stages of tattered dress mixed with mud and grime.

There were red tunics among them...soldiers who had been turned either at Nottingham, Derby or Carlisle. But these had no discipline left. They snarled and growled like wild animals, and they screamed in rage as they ran forward. There was no sign of Rollo, but Martin knew the Other would be there somewhere in the throng.

He let them come on until they were almost directly beneath them, then gave the order.

"Fire!"

A volley of musket-shot rang out, and the Others flinched...but the shot wasn't aimed at them.

A row of canteens, stretched out along a long rope, had been slung above the gully, and the shots found their mark. The canteens were holed and, spinning in the dark, sprayed water, bulb, and silver over the Others below. The scene was suddenly lit in blue, flickering flame as they began to burn and scream. Martin saw Rollo, several rows back, trying to put out a flare of fire at his breast.

"Silver shot. Fire!" Martin shouted.

Twenty rounds of silver shot slammed into the front rank of the attackers. Like small volcanic eruptions, blue explosions burst on their bodies. Some of them, the smaller ones, burned almost immediately. The rest panicked and fell back, burning, spreading the flame as they went. In the dim blue flickering light it was possible to see that the Others were at least eight-deep in the gully. If they had pushed forward at that point, Martin thought that they might have overran the musket- men but the panic spread as another volley of shot rang out.

As quickly as they had come, the Others retreated into the dark, leaving twenty-five of their company lying full dead in the gully.

Martin's men cheered as one.

"To horse," Martin ordered. "They will not give up...not yet."

"Do you have any other ideas Master Hillman?" Martin called out to the boy as they mounted.

"Aye, sir," Edward said, blushing. "But they will have to wait until we reach Milecastle once more...I have need of a seamstress for this one."

"Then we had best make sure we get you back there," Martin said.

Even as they mounted and wheeled south once more, Martin saw the dark Others begin to pour through the gully. He led his men away at a gallop.

"Yon trick won't work twice, Sire," Toby the smith said. "They may be dead, but they're not stupid."

Martin nodded.

"Aye. Our only hope is to outrun them. I fear it will be a long night in the saddle."

Half an hour later the horses began to tire again, and Martin ordered them to slow to a trot once more.

"By my reckoning we must be only ten miles or so from yon ruins we stopped in at lunchtime," Toby said.

"Aye. I agree," Martin said. "And we cannot push the horses like this much longer. It is our time to come up with a plan."

He was about to call Fitz over to join them when someone at the rear of the group screamed, and a shot rang out in the night.

By the time Martin and Toby fell back to the site of the shot, their rearguard had already gone, taken into the night by the Others. All that was left was a badly bitten horse, and a still smoking musket lying on the ground.

He ordered the men into a gallop.

By the time they reached Newcastleton they had lost three more men from the back of the group.

"We cannot go on like this!" Martin shouted, and Fitz agreed.

Martin ordered the men to a halt in the yard outside the ruined church.

"Fitz," Martin said, "take half the men, and Master Hillman here, and head for Milecastle...as fast as you can manage. The Protector needs to know where we found the Boy-King. Toby and I will hold them back as long as we are able."

"Sir, I…" Fitz began, but Martin cut him short.

"No arguments. Go now. We have no time."

Fitz nodded. Martin saw that Edward was close to tears.

"Fear not," he said. "I will see you soon…if your next idea is as fine as your last two we will be slaying many more Others together, you and I.

"Take our horses," he told Fitz. "And tether them a mile down the road. They will only get in the way if we keep them here.

"Now go," he said. "They'll be on us any minute."

"We will see you in the inn on your return," Fitz said, and saluted. "I will have a flagon waiting for you."

The innkeeper quickly chose the men to accompany him, and within a minute he had led half the men away to the south.

"Well, Toby," Martin said, "let us see how long we can delay the Others and give our friends time to make it home."

The Others began to pour into the yard just as Martin and Toby had fully deployed the men. They stood in a tight formation, two ranks of five men each, backs to the wall of the church. Each man had a musket loaded with silver, two pistols and his stakes. Martin did not expect to survive, but he meant to take as many of them with him as he was able.

"Fire!" Martin shouted. The air was quickly full of smoke and the stench of powder. The silver shot used at such short range tore through the ranks of the Others, but more were already leaping forward to take the place of the fallen.

"Front rank, fire!" Martin shouted.

A second volley hit the Others, blasting half a dozen of them to the final death.

"Back rank, pistols!" Toby called. The guns roared, and eight more Others fell.

"Front rank…!" Martin called, but by then the Others had closed tightly around them and it was down to hand-to-hand fighting.

The men in front of Martin started to club at the Others with their muskets, then attacked with their stakes. But these were not professional soldiers—before last week they had been bakers, butchers and cobblers. Although they fought well, they were not skilled enough, or fast enough, to have much impact on the Others. It was only seconds before Martin found himself face to face with a drooling creature.

He shoved his pistol into its face and shot it between the eyes with his last load of silver. Its head seemed to collapse into itself, and the creature fell away backwards...but there were plenty more willing to take its place. Grubby hands started to reach for him.

Martin felt the wolf hair rise on his arm, and the wound in his head throbbed painfully. He howled his rage to the sky, a scream so loud that the Others around him stepped back, confused. Martin dropped his guns, armed himself with a stake in each hand, and threw himself into the throng.

"No...Martin!" he heard Toby shout, but he ignored the voice. There were Others to kill, and there was a rage driving him.

There were still random gunshots in the yard, but the Others were rapidly overrunning the soldiers. Martin's men were falling fast.

Martin was only dimly aware of it. He was lost in a red mist, a frenzy where all that mattered was the stakes and the soft bodies of the Others. He gave them the true death, again and again. And as he killed, he howled to the sky.

Somewhere, out over the forest, his howls were answered as the wolf pack responded to one of their own.

Martin could smell the Others. They were like a bone that had been buried for too long, or a dog that had been rolling in a cowpat on a wet day. Among them somewhere was the smell he was trying to reach...the odor of the betrayer Rollo.

He pushed himself through the milling throng of Others as they tried to reach him with their fangs and their weapons. He was too fast for them, and they died the final death as he passed. He knew that the smith was behind him, and at least one other of his men, but Rollo was close now, and he howled once more as he pushed harder against the heaving mass of Others.

Suddenly they opened up in front of him, leaving a circle of clear space around him. Toby, and one of his men, pushed through to stand beside him.

The smith was panting heavily, and the man with him was holding a hand to a bleeding gash at his neck.

Rollo walked into the circle. He had a smoking hole at his breast, but seemed to be in no pain.

He looked at Martin and laughed.

"This is what frightens us? Look at him…" he waved a hand over the crowd, as if inviting them to share a joke. "He is little more than an animal. He…"

Martin snarled and threw himself at Rollo. He didn't make it that far…a bundle of hair and teeth leapt at him, and Martin rolled on the ground, trying to keep Fang's teeth away from his throat.

Something came into the circle, a gray shadow that was as fast as an Other. Martin felt the weight of Fang lift away from him as the wolf caught it by the throat.

Once more the Others were in chaos. Another gray wolf leapt high into the mob, and Martin threw himself among them beside it. He howled…and his gray brothers howled with him.

But the killing could not last. The press of the Others was just too heavy. The smith's man fell, badly bitten, only to be totally drained. Then one of the gray brothers barked in pain and went silent.

Martin fought harder. The fangs of the Others tried to bite but the leather of his coat held, although it was ripped and torn in places. He punched a stake into yet another heart, but it caught between the ribs of the Other as it fell. At almost the same time, Rollo caught him by the arm and pulled the other stake from his hand.

The second gray shadow fell, badly bitten, and Rollo killed it by stepping, hard, on its rib cage. The sound of its bones snapping was loud even above the noise of battle.

Martin tried to pull against Rollo's hold on him, but the Other was too strong. Rollo threw a punch at Martin's head that he didn't have time to avoid. The wound in his skull flared in white- hot pain and Martin's senses left him.

...he is flying in the air, soaring like an eagle over the smoking remains of a great castle. Mind- slaves of the Boy-King are steadily working their way through the debris, slowly, as if searching for something. Suddenly one of them bends and lifts a piece of burnt wood to one side. Beneath it he finds the golden chalice...battered and charred, but still with gold showing through. The slave bends and lifts something that is the size of a large apple. It is black, charred and still smoking. But among the burnt flesh a blood-red eye blinks.

The mind-slave lifts its head to the sky and howls in joy...

...and Martin found himself being lifted off the ground.

"Bring the other one!" he heard Rollo shout. "The Boy-King only wants the Wolf, but this one is also big and healthy...he will make good sport."

Martin felt the wolf hairs run along his arm. He wanted to tear and rip, gouge and bite. But his vision was blurred, and his body was not responding to commands. He was thrown over Rollo's shoulder and his head bounced against the Other's back, sending him reeling once more.

...he is once more in a high place, but this is not anywhere in the north. The sun is high in the sky, a blazing yellow orb that bounces bright off the sand of a great expanse of desert. A man, hairy and with a brow that hangs heavy over deep-set eyes, crawls along a dune on his hands and knees. His lips are cracked and weeping, and his skin is raised in large blisters, some of which have burst and are oozing pus.

Suddenly the dune gives way beneath him and he falls, screaming, into a deep, dark cave. His fall is broken by something soft that gives beneath him and the smell in the air is suddenly rank and foul.

A desert lion, days, maybe as much as a week, dead, lies beneath him, its body half submerged in a stagnant pool of dark, almost black liquid. The foul liquor steams and bubbles, but it is cool to the touch. The man drinks gratefully...and something black and vile whispers and laughs in the cave, something that is everywhere yet nowhere. Fire dances in the recesses of the cave, a fire that is red, but cold...

...Martin came up out of oblivion. He was in a tight cave, with four mind-slaves guarding the entrance. There was no sign of the smith, and even if Martin could have taken four men, he was still incapable of getting his body to obey his commands. Wolf hairs continued to rise along his arm and he raised his head to howl, but even that simple act was enough to bring the blackness back again.

...the man has drunk his fill from the stagnant pool, and is amazed to see the burns on his hands and arms begin to heal. He smiles, and fangs burst bloodily from his gums. The thing in the dark with him laughs loud and there is a hissing, as if a serpent is there with him.

"You will carry my power back out into the world," the thing says. "It is too long since I was abroad. I need to see what my creation has wrought. You shall be my emissary...the first king of a new kind. And together we will rule this world. Who knows...in time we may even rule the sky."

When night falls the Other, now no longer a man, crawls up out of the hole and runs smoothly across the desert, leaving only the merest indentation in the sand. The thing with him cackles again, and the Other smiles. He has a great thirst, but he will quench it soon...there is a great drum beating in the night, a beacon to guide him in the dark to a place where there are many waiting who will learn the joy of the blood...

...and Martin woke once more to the sound of a drum pounding. He had no conception of how much time might have passed, but they were no longer in the cave and he felt stronger…his head no longer felt like it might split.

Rollo still carried him over his shoulder, but by turning his head Martin was able to see that it was night once more. They were walking across a flat plain, following a drumbeat. Across the plain in the middle distance a high black castle sat on a rocky outcrop.

The dark army poured into the castle through a pair of huge iron gates. It was not long before Rollo led the band of Others through the gates, and Martin heard them clang shut behind them with a dreadful finality.

CHAPTER 4

NOVEMBER 20, 1745, STIRLING

Martin woke to sunlight falling on his face.

Waking was a slow thing...a gray dim light that only slowly got brighter and more focused.

"Ah...you are back in the land of the living, then?" a voice he recognized said.

He blinked, and looked up into the face of Toby, the smith.

Martin only had a vague memory of how he'd got there. The night before he'd been unceremoniously dumped into a black space, and the jar to his already wounded head had sent him once more into blackness.

"Where…" Martin started to say. His throat was too dry and he had to swallow hard and try again. "Where are we?"

"They say it is a place called Stirling sir," the smith said. "We are held in the cells beneath a castle. I have been in filthier places, but few that smelled worse."

Martin tried to sit up. At first the room spun, as if he had drunk too much ale. He was forced to close his eyes as a wave of nausea threatened to overwhelm him. He forced himself to breathe, deep and steady, and his stomach steadied. Finally he was able to look around.

The cell was large, nearly a hundred feet on each side. It was full of close-packed bodies, more than a hundred men, most of who wore the red tunics of the Protector's army. There were a handful of women amongst the crowd, but no old people, and, mercifully, no children.

The smith had been right about the smell. In his youth Martin had built many a dung-heap, but never one that smelled as rank as this. He guessed that many of the prisoners had been here for some time...and that many had stayed so long that they had died here.

On three sides the walls were stone, gray and slimy with condensation. On the fourth side there were heavy iron bars, and beyond that a group of mind-slaves.

There were at least ten of them, three of whom wore the red tunics. Martin searched the faces, wondering if he might know any of the men, but they were all unfamiliar, and for that at least he was thankful.

The mind-slaves stood, staring blindly into space. The only sign they were alive was the slow rise and fall of their chests as they breathed.

Suddenly the import of what the smith had said filtered through to his mind.

"We are in Stirling?" He remembered what he had seen of Cumberland's maps. "That is three days hard march from the spot where we fought in Newcastleton. I have been out that long?"

Toby nodded.

"Be thankful that you missed the journey," he said. "The Others are not fussy about their personal hygiene. And having to listen to the betrayer Rollo boast about how he would now sit at his King's right hand was more than I could take...it seems that the Boy-King has put a price on your head, and Rollo is going to collect it."

All Martin could remember was a vague recollection of a dream, something about Others and desert, but even that was fading fast.

"What happened? The last thing I really remember is the shadows attacking us in yon courtyard."

Toby leaned over and whispered in Martin's ear.

"You killed many, sir," he said. "And the wolves came to your aid."

In truth, when prompted, Martin did remember fragments. In his mind a great gray wolf howled and bit and ran among the Others. He fought to recollect more, but his head throbbed with red, almost blinding, pain and he found it hard to concentrate.

"And the rest of our band?" he asked.

The smith shook his head.

"There is no sign of any of the men we sent off with Fitz. For that we must be grateful...and hopeful. Mayhap they reached the safety of Milecastle. But of the group who were with us in the churchyard, we alone were spared," he said. "Spared?" someone said beside them. Martin turned to look into the face of an army officer. The man looked tired, his eyes dark pits of shadow, his hands trembling. There was a gray pallor to his skin, and his tongue looked almost black where it poked between the yellow ruin of his teeth.

"You will not feel like you have been spared when they send you out to the arena," the man said, and his fear showed in his eyes.

Martin pushed himself full upright, grateful that, this time at least, his legs did not betray him.

"Arena? They make their prisoners fight?"

"Aye," the officer said. "We've been kept alive to be used as sport for the black bastards. They took ten of us out last night. Your man here heard it."

The smith nodded.

"It's true, sir. Ten were taken out, then it sounded like there was a riot going on...and none of the men came back."

"They were sent out to fight," the officer said. "Each man is given a stake and sent out against a single Other. If the man wins, he is given a choice...fight again or be turned. There are no other options...none ever comes back to the cells."

"They'll get no sport from me," Martin said.

One of the mind-slaves laughed hollowly.

"Then you will die, my young wolf," it said. Martin recognized the tone of the voice...the Boy-King was speaking through this man.

"I refuse to give you the pleasure," Martin said.

The slave laughed again.

"But you do anyway," it said. "And I suspect the wolf-cub wants its sport, even if you do not know it yet." "Then come here in person," Martin said. "Then you will see what the wolf thinks."

"Do not be in such a hurry," the slave said. "Your turn will come soon enough."

Martin swore loudly, but the slave had the empty stare back again.

"He is gone, sir," Toby said.

"Aye. But I suspect he is here, in the castle…for otherwise how could he know that we are here? And if he is here, we may yet get another chance at him. Keep alert, Toby. I'll have need of your strength."

"Aye, sir. But you should rest awhile, for you are almost weak as a babe."

"I'll rest when the bastard is sent to his final death," Martin said grimly. "And not before."

"Aye, sir," Toby replied. "But while we are in this cell, it might be a long wait."

"Why do you call this lad sir?" the officer said.

It was Martin who replied.

"I am the Thane of Milecastle, and commander of the northern militia of the Lord Protector's army."

The officer looked at the smith, who nodded.

"Then you are the senior officer here," the man said. "I am John Turner, sergeant of Nottingham, and I am your man."

He saluted, and most of the other men in the cell stood and did the same.

"Well, Toby," Martin said. "It looks like we have a new command."

The day passed slowly. Water and bread was provided to feed them, but Martin did not feel hungry. His mind was full of images…Menzies on the pyre in Derby, Gwynneth and her strange tattooed body, the sight of the forest of hands as the dark army came up out of the ground, the Boy-King fleeing away from the graveyard, and the gray wolves coming to his aid against Rollo.

Then there was his vision from the journey here…the strange, almost animal-like barbarian being turned in the cave. He had a feeling that the vision had shown him something important, and he knew that the details were getting more vague the longer he put off thinking about them, but it would have to wait...his first priority was to get out of this cell.

"Will you eat something, sir?" a voice said, bringing him up out of his reverie. A woman stood over him. She was tall, with long hair the color of coals in a cooling fire. Her eyes were a light, pale green and when she spoke it was with a dancing lilt that reminded him of Duncan Campbell. She was offering him a chunk of bread. "You are not an Englishwoman," Martin said.

"No. I am Jean Munro, lately of Stromness on the island of Orkney, and I am pleased to make your acquaintance."

"And how came you here?" he asked.

"'Tis a long story, sir."

"It looks like we have time aplenty. Come. Sit and talk. Tell me your story...it will take our minds off our captivity."

"Watch that one, sir," a voice called out of the crowd. "She's a wildcat, and she'll have your balls for a necklace."

The woman blushed and her whole face went red. Martin saw the anger flare in her eyes, and her hand moved to her waist, as if looking for a sheathed weapon.

Martin laughed.

"They say I am a wolf," he said. "Let us talk together, cat and dog."

She sat beside him and he watched her as she told her tale. Most of the activity in the cell stopped as everyone went quiet and listened, but she didn't seem to notice...her eyes were unfocused as she replayed the story in her mind.

I was in the old cathedral in Kirkwall when they came," she began. "There were three hundred of us at prayer. We thought we would be safe in the Lord's house. But the Viking bastards have no religion worth mentioning when they're alive...even less when they are turned."

"Viking?" Martin said. "I thought they were vanquished centuries ago."

"As did we," Jean Munro said. "Their ancestors and

ours mixed their bloodlines generations ago...and there had been peace for many centuries. We even dismantled the brochs and used their stones for building houses and byres. We were unprepared.

"As you said...we thought they were vanquished. But they had merely been sleeping, and they came when the Boy-King called, promising death and blood. They came out of their sleep in the far North, where the sun is low and it is dark for six months at a time. They are like wolves in the night...tall and strong, their fair hair hanging in long pleats down their backs, their blue eyes cold as ice in the moonlight. Their bodies, even in death, ripple with muscle."

The woman broke off. There was something in her eyes that Martin didn't recognize. It was a mixture of fear, disgust, but, more than that, a strange far-away stare that spoke of attraction and desire.

"They came in their longboats just after the sun went down. It was a Sunday night, and many on the island were at prayer. They burned our churches with the people in them...they were not interested in feeding, only in plunder. Those of us in the cathedral did our best to barricade ourselves in, but we had grown soft. We were no match for such as these with their hard bodies and their lust for our hot blood. They battered down the door and took us, even as we called on our Lord for salvation. But the Lord did not hear...or he chose not to listen.

"We had no chance. They overwhelmed us in minutes. I was knocked senseless, and when I came to I was on their dragon boat. And five days later I was here, in this cell."

The story had ended too quickly, too abruptly. He hadn't been told everything, and there was something new in the woman's eyes that Martin didn't recognize...it looked like the devious cunning of a cornered animal. He made to stand and move away, but the woman grabbed him around the waist in a hug.

"No, please, hold me, sir," she said, and sobbed theatrically in his ear. "'Tis long since I have had a man to comfort me."

"I told you!" a voice shouted. "She'll have your manhood on a platter soon enough, sir."

Martin pushed the woman away to arm's length.

"In truth, you are comely," Martin said. "But I have Others to kill, and a duty to perform. I'm afraid your charms would be wasted on me."

She laughed.

"My charms seem to be wasted on all here. Mayhap I'd have better luck out in the arena."

Her eyes flared in green fire as she spun away from him and he watched, bemused, as she moved on to a large thickset redcoat. Within five seconds she was sitting on the man's lap and nibbling at his ear.

"I'll never understand women, Toby," Martin said.

"You don't have to understand them," the smith replied. "Just keep well away from them."

Everyone in earshot laughed, and for a moment at least they were able to forget where they were.

Toby told the story of their adventures, taking them from Derby to the ambush where they had almost trapped the Boy-King. The men in the cell cheered, but the mind-slaves did not even flinch...and cheers did not open iron doors.

"Toby. I want a search done of this cell...every inch of it. If as much as a rat can get in or out I want to know about it," Martin said.

Toby saluted.

"And get some strong men to test the strength of the doors, particularly around the hinges."

But the search was to no avail. And the iron bars proved too strong. Despite their obvious age they squealed when pressed, but held firm against all their efforts.

"The only way out is through the door," Toby said.

"Aye," Turner replied. "And I suspect ten more of us will be leaving that way soon enough." The officer was proved right just after nightfall. A band of Others arrived and took ten men away. Turner was one of them. He left with a straight back, but there was terror deep down in his eyes.

The screams started only minutes later. It sounded like the whole dark army was out there, tormenting the men who had been taken.

In the cell some of the men began to weep, and others among them were becoming noticeably nervous.

"We are in a dark place, Toby," Martin said.

"Aye, sir," the big smith said. "But yet we are still alive. And for that I am thankful."

Toby burst into song, at the top of his voice, loud enough to drown the screaming.

There was a young lady from Brest
Who could balance ten men on her chest
You could cover a city
With each of her titties And hide a small hill in her vest

The rest of the men in the cell took up the song. When it was finished Toby broke into "The Men of the Watch" and "The Old Protector's Victory".

All the Protector's men sang along, and when Toby had finished another took up with a new song, and another followed after that.

"Fine songs," Jean Munro said sarcastically when they were done. "I'll wager the Boy-King is quaking in his boots. Mayhap if you get called out next you can sing them into submission."

The night was long, and none of the ten who had been taken out came back.

In the morning Martin called the room to silence.

"Truly we are in the dark," he said. "Mayhap our Lord decrees that we are to die here. I ask you only that you do not yield. Let us show these bastards how real men die."

"You show them!" Jean Munro shouted. "For myself, I want to live...and I will live!"

Late in the afternoon they were again fed bread and water.

We will not last long if this is all they will give us, Martin thought.

As the sun began to go down the men started to get nervous once more, and this time Toby was not able to lift their spirits. They had nothing to do but wait for the Others to come, each man hoping that he would not be one of the ten called.

The sun had just fallen when the waiting was over. A small band of Others came into the cell. Martin, Toby and eight men were pulled out into the small room beyond.

"Let me come too," Jean Munro called out. "I cannot stay here any longer."

"Why not," an Other said. "She should provide some sport."

"Aye," another Other said, looking Jean Munro up and down. "For about ten seconds maybe."

The woman joined their group. Martin saw a sly smile on her lips as they were led out from the cells and up a long corridor.

Noise built all around, echoing off the rough stone walls. At the end of the corridor a red light flickered, and it was there that was the source of the noise…a roar that increased to an ear-bursting crescendo as they were dragged out into hell itself. The whole forecourt of the castle had been turned into a vast arena. Others lined three sides of a quadrangle, four or five deep. Some were dressed in fine, expensive clothing, in a grotesque parody of the tourneys of old, and yet others were already placing wagers on which of the ten would survive the longest.

High torches set at intervals around the esplanade lit the night in a red, fiery glow and sent black shadows dancing over the leering faces of the mob. The Others were already shouting and screaming, a cacophony over which Martin could also hear the beating of a great drum and the wailing of their bagpipes.

Directly opposite them, across the esplanade, there was a high platform, about a hundred yards away. The Boy-King sat in a tall, wing-backed chair, his guards all around him. He was laughing, in good humor. On a small seat by his left hand side Mary Campbell sat, stiff-backed, staring straight ahead. The Boy-King stroked her hair absently with his hand.

The tall figure by his right hand side was instantly recognizable...Rollo had indeed won his place in the personal guard. The traitor stood there as if he was there by right—indeed, as if he had always been there.

I'll see you staked and burned, Martin vowed. And I'll do it myself...for Menzies, if nothing else.

Out on the quadrangle a tall Other stood. This must be one of the Vikings Jean Munro told him about. It was big, almost a head taller than Martin, and it stood, legs apart, arms hanging loosely by its side. Long blond hair hung in twin braids down its naked back, and its muscles stood out proud under the thin, pale skin. Its eyes blazed red in the torchlight, and there was a feral grin on its face, as if it was anticipating what was to come. Yellow fangs slid in and out over its bottom lip, and there was blood in its mouth as it licked its lips and studied the ten prisoners, like a cat watching a sparrow.

The Boy-King stood, and a silence fell over the quadrangle. Although it was the first time Martin had gotten a close look at him, the Other looked just like he had in the woodsman's visions. He was thin, almost skeletal, and his skin was so pale as to be nearly white. He wore face powder and paint in the French manner, spots of rouge on his cheeks giving him a rough semblance of man-and-only-man. His clothes were fine purple velvet, with frills of lace at neck and wrists.

"If he tried to walk through Newcastle dressed like that, he'd have been lynched," Toby said.

"Aye," Martin replied. "He does like to preen and pose, does he not. Mayhap his narcissism will be his undoing someday."

As if to echo Martin's words the Other smoothed out his clothing before he started to speak. His words carried clear and loud over the esplanade. "We give you a chance!" he shouted, addressing Martin and his fellow prisoners. "Which is more than you have ever given us."

The mob howled and stamped their feet. The ground of the esplanade shook and the torches threw dancing shadows across the faces of the screaming horde. The Boy King shouted above the cacophony.

"Fight, win, and you can choose...to either fight again, or join us. Lose, and you will be bled dry."

The mob howled even louder. A chant went up, low at first, then rising into a crescendo in time with the beating of the great drum;

"BLOOD! BLOOD BLOOD!"

The noise echoed around the walls until it seemed the very stone was vibrating in time. The Boy-King raised his hand for silence.

"I think I will save my wolf for last...he will give the best sport. But who will be the first? Who wants to test their skill against my northern friend?"

Before any of the men could move Jean Munro stepped forward.

"I am first. This one…" she said, pointing at the Viking Other, "...sacked my town. I want revenge."

The Boy-King laughed.

"He will have you bled before you have moved, lass," he said.

"Give me a stake and I'll prove you wrong."

One of the Others threw a stake at her feet. She lifted it, saluted Martin, and went out to meet the Viking.

The Other didn't stand a chance.

It came forward, like a wrestler expecting to grapple with his opponent. Jean Munro rolled in a fast tumble that brought her inside its reach. Before it could grab her she had staked it and was turning in triumph as her opponent fell, full dead, to the ground.

The crowd went wild, and the Boy-King applauded.

"I knew not that we had an Amazon in our midst," he said.

Although he did not shout, his voice carried across the quadrangle. "What is it to be? Another fight, or the turning?"

She looked straight at Martin as she spoke.

"I choose the turning...I would serve my King."

"I'm sure I can find a use for you," the Boy-King said dryly, and the dark horde erupted in cruel laughter. Jean Munro climbed up on the platform, where the Boy-King gave her to Rollo. There was a thin smile on her lips as she was bled, a smile that stayed even when she fell into a swoon and was carried away.

"Next," the Boy-King called.

And so it went. One of the soldiers gave three Others the true death before he was killed and bled, but the rest fell, one by one, to a tall, lean Highlander. Soon there was only Toby and Martin left.

"It seems it is my time to die," Toby said. Before Martin could stop him, the smith stepped forward to meet the Other.

A stake was thrown at the smith's feet, but he ignored it.

"I need no weapon to deal with a black bastard like this," he said. The Other smiled, showing his fangs, and met Toby in the center of the arena.

The crowd cheered as the Highlander struck at the man's neck, but Toby was waiting for it. He grabbed it in a bear hug and the noise of its back breaking as he squeezed echoed around the arena. Toby dropped the Other to the ground and stepped on its neck, crunching its windpipe beneath his heel.

"Is that the best you've got?" the smith said. He lifted the stake and thrust it, hard, between the Other's ribs. The creature gave out a soft sigh, and fell in on itself like a burst bladder.

A soft moan ran around the arena. Martin felt like cheering as the smith lifted the deflated body and threw it into the throng. "Suck on that, you bastards," he said.

The Boy-King smiled.

"Are you working up a thirst yet?" he asked. "Would you like to be turned?"

"Never," Toby said. "Send on another. If I have to take you one by one, then so be it...I have all night and I'm not going anywhere."

Martin moved to step forward, but three Others grabbed him. He felt the wolf hairs rise on his arm, but forced them down...he would not give the Boy-King the satisfaction.

The Boy-King laughed.

"We too have all night," he said. "But I do not think it will take that long." He motioned with his hand, and a stocky Highlander jumped from the dais into the arena. The crowd erupted in a loud cheer.

"I meant to keep the Douglas for later...one wolf against another," the Boy-King said.

"Dinna fash yersel', man," the Highlander said. "I'll only be a wee while wi' this barbarian."

"Barbarian?" the smith said. "Have you looked at yourself?"

In truth, Martin knew he was looking at a figure of some power. The Douglas exuded it, and it showed in the swagger of his walk. His long pleated hair swung down his back, reaching almost to his waist. He wore only a kilt of heavy, dark tartan and above the waist he was naked. His torso, though pale, was heavily knotted in muscle, and old pink scars covered all of the exposed flesh.

"This is the Douglas' arena," the Boy-King said. "He has been fighting here for more than four hundred years. In all that time he has never been beaten."

"Then let us have to it," the smith said. "It is long gone time you had a new champion."

The Douglas smiled as he came forward. He walked straight into the smith's bear hug, and actually laughed as the grip tightened around him. "I've wrestled old Artus himself," he said. "And he had thrice your strength."

He began to return the hug, and beads of sweat rose on Toby's brow.

"Yield, man," the Douglas said. "Yield and we'll turn ye...ye will make a fine guard."

"Never," the smith hissed, and renewed his efforts to squeeze the life from the Other.

The Douglas laughed, a deep bellow, and squeezed back in return. Martin winced as one of Toby's ribs cracked, and bubbles of blood appeared at his lips.

"Again I ask ye," the Douglas said. "Will ye yield?"

Toby spat a bloody gob in the Other's face.

It was the last thing he ever did. The Douglas put his head under Toby's chin and, with one squeeze, drove the man's ribcage inwards and through his lungs. Toby imploded in a spray of blood and the Other laughed as it fed.

The crowd stamped its feet and chanted in rhythm...Douglas, Douglas, Douglas.

"Are you quenched, man?" the Boy-King said when the Other lifted its head from Toby's lifeless body. "I have a cub for you to break in for me."

"Aye," the Douglas said, wiping blood and tissue from his face. "Bring him on." He tossed Toby's body into the crowd where it was torn to bloody pieces in seconds in a frenzy of bloodlust.

Martin had no time to mourn as he was pushed out into the arena and the crowd howled even louder.

"Do you want the stake?" the Boy-King said.

"Aye," Martin replied, taking off his long leather coat. "For although I do not have my friend's strength, I have twice his speed. Say goodbye to your champion...he is in sore trouble."

The Boy-King laughed again.

"My wolf eats cubs like you," he said.

"I am no wolf," Martin said.

"So you say. But the Douglas will show you otherwise."

Rollo threw a stake at Martin's feet.

"Who is next after the champion?" Martin asked him. "Please say it will be you...we have many scores to settle, you and I."

"I am ready," Rollo said with a smile. "But the Douglas will see to you first."

Martin walked forward to meet the Douglas, and the level of noise rose even higher.

The Other waited for him in the center of the quadrangle. Blood spattered his upper chest and across the lower half of his face.

"Yer pal was sweet," it said. "But he didnae have much in him. I still have a drouth."

Martin said nothing. He circled the Other slowly. He knew that he could not allow himself to get in close...the Douglas was too strong.

The crowd screamed its displeasure.

"Come, laddie," the Other said. "Are ye here tae fight or tae dance?"

Still Martin circled. The Other watched him closely, its eyes flickering from the stake to Martin's face and back again.

"Dae ye mean tae make me dizzy? Or are..."

Martin threw the stake straight at the Other's heart, but the Douglas was too fast and swatted it away just before it touched his skin. The stake landed nearly thirty feet away, and Martin would have to get past the Other to retrieve it.

The Douglas jeered as Martin turned and ran across the quadrangle away from him.

"This is yer cub? He has a yellow streak up his back."

The crowd howled in laughter...until they saw Martin's intent.

Martin grabbed hold of one of the tall torches that lit the arena and began to swing on it. If he could get the pole out of the ground he would effectively have a lance...a weapon against any Other.

He got the pole swinging and was beginning to believe he might succeed, but he wasn't given enough time. The Douglas was almost on him and Martin had to retreat again.

"Come, laddie," the Douglas said. "Just a wee hug...that's all I ask."

Something landed with a soft thud at Martin's feet, and he chanced a look down. Someone had given him a weapon...a coney snare.

By the time he had bent and lifted it, the Other was right on top of him. Martin was grabbed in a bear hug. His arms were pinned at his side, and the Other smiled as it squeezed. "I have you now," the Douglas said.

Martin head-butted the Other just above the nose, gaining him a momentary respite where he was able to get his arms free.

"No. I have you," Martin said, and slipped the snare over the Other's head, pulling it tight around its neck.

There was a sudden frenzy about the Douglas now. He began to squeeze tighter, and Martin felt the bones of his back begin to pop.

Martin knew he had only this one chance. He pulled on the noose and saw the wire dig deep into the flesh of the Other's neck. Something gave in his ribs, then Martin screamed in triumph as the Douglas' grip began to ease.

He crossed the handles of the snare and gave one final pull...and the Douglas' head rolled from his shoulders. Martin kicked the body over and lifted the head by the long hair plaits.

"This is how I treat Others," he said. He spat in the dead face and tossed the head into the suddenly quiet crowd.

The Boy-King stood and applauded. He did not seem concerned at the loss of his champion.

"You are feisty, my cub," he said. "And you have won the right to choose. What is it to be...the fight or the blood?"

Martin stood square in the center of the quadrangle, the snare dangling from his right hand.

"Send on your best," he said. "The Thane of Milecastle will not bend the knee."

"Ah, but the Wolf might, for he is of the night, like ourselves."

"There is no Wolf. There is only man."

The Other laughed again. "We both know better than

that. But let us see if we can bring the beast forth to vouch for itself."

He waved his hand and two Highland Others jumped from the platform.

They were too cock-sure. They came at him separately...and Martin took them quickly and efficiently. Both were finally dead before they even knew the snare had caught them.

"Have you got nobody faster?" Martin asked.

Over the next two hours they sent fourteen more against him, and they all were sent to the final death, although the thirteenth nearly managed to reach Martin's neck. The crowd roared and stomped their feet, sending the torches trembling, but Martin managed to punch the Other hard in the face and gain himself a second. It was time enough to put the snare to use once more. He tossed the head towards the platform, but he was weakening and it fell short.

"It is nearly time, my cub," the Boy-King said. "It would be best if you joined us of your own free will."

"Never," Martin said, and spat in the dust at his feet. There was blood in his spittle and he feared that something was broken inside him.

The fourteenth managed to knock him over. It raised a foot to stave in Martin's ribs...and the wolf in him rose up, faster than thought and completely unbidden. He grabbed the foot and pulled the Other to the ground where he tore its throat out with his teeth. He howled his fury to the sky...and the Boy-King clapped his hands in glee.

Martin threw himself forward. He could smell them. Even above the stench rising from the gathered throng he could pick out their individual scent ...the betrayer, the daughter of Campbell, and the leader of the Others. He leapt onto the pedestal, intent on tearing and gouging...and his legs gave way beneath him as a grip took hold of his mind.

"Quiet, my pup," the Boy-King said in his mind. Martin

felt the thick hairs rise on his arms once more, and talons seemed to grow from his fingers. The Boy-King's grip on his thoughts loosened slightly, but he was too weary.

"Come and sit at the feet of my lady," the voice said. "She is in need of a new guard...after tomorrow, if the stars go right, she will carry a prince of the blood."

Martin screamed inside, but his body betrayed him. He crept, on all fours, to Mary Campbell's feet and lay there, quiet.

"Behold," the Boy-King said. "My lady has a new pet."

The gathered horde roared in laughter.

"Lie still, my cub," the voice said in Martin's head.

Hot tears ran unbidden down his cheeks, but he was unable to move to wipe them away.

CHAPTER 5

NOVEMBER 20, 1745, STIRLING

Sean could have wept at the sight of Martin's humiliation...but Others did not weep.

He had almost given himself away when tossing the snare to Martin. Any indication now that he was not what he seemed could prove disastrous. He forced himself to watch as the Boy-King addressed the crowd.

"My friends," the Other began. "You can see how I have tamed the cub. In the same manner we will tame the Protector. But first, we must ensure the bloodline."

He held a chalice above his head. Sean was dismayed to see that it was the same one he had thought destroyed back in Edinburgh.

"Agents of the Protector tried to stop us," the Boy-King called out. "And they thought to destroy Baphomet." He put his hand in the chalice and drew out a small, bloody mass. As he raised it above his head the blood ran thickly down his wrist, and the Other smiled as he licked himself clean, like a cat after a kill. "The King of Kings will not be sent to the final death that easily," he said, his mouth red.

The crowd cheered loudly. The Other next to Sean looked at him strangely until he joined in with the cheers.

The Boy-King shouted above the noise.

"And later, when the moon is up, and if the stars are in the rightful place, we will see the turning of a new prince." The crowd howled again.

"And maybe we will give my son a new pet," the Boy-King said, and ruffled the hair on the top of Martin's head.

The crowd of Others around Sean laughed loudly, and they were still laughing when the Boy- King took his entourage out of the arena. The crowd began to disperse, and Sean went with them, trying to give the impression that he was on an errand of some import, adopting a haughty look and hoping that no one would examine him too closely.

Martin's mind was in turmoil. He remembered fighting the Others' on the esplanade, but only as a memory of blood and meat left uneaten. Somewhere out in the darkness his gray brothers waited, ready to howl at his release, ready to join him as he led the wolf pack in a hunt.

But when he raised his head to howl all that he could produce was a strangled moan.

"Look, my Lord," a tall Other said. It was a voice Martin knew from another time, another place. "Your new pet has something to say."

The Other knelt beside where Martin lay, curled at the feet of a tall dark throne. It put out a hand, as if to stroke the top of Martin's head. Martin sniffed. It was meat. It might smell as if it had been dead for some time, but it was meat, and Martin hungered. He growled, and snapped his teeth forward, just missing the outstretched fingers.

"It seems my cub needs to be house-trained," it said. Martin remembered that voice. There was hurt there, and pain. But most of all, there was hatred. Martin wanted to rip, to tear, to bite, but the Other put a hand on his head, and it was like being in a strong cage, one with no exit.

"Be calm, my cub," the Other said. It stroked the hair on the top of Martin's head and began to speak, almost distractedly.

I had another cub once.

He was my birthing gift from my father…a huge gray timber wolf from the forests of the frozen north. We used to run together, my wolf and I, through the streets of Rome and Paris, Prague and Warsaw. My father was ruler of the strongest countries in the world, and soon he would take Europe. I was on the Grand Tour, sampling the tastes of the old countries while there were delights yet to be had.

I was young, having only five years in the night, but my wolf taught me the ways of the hunt, and the joys of blood that has been pursed until it is filled with sweet terror.

We were in Bucharest...an old city, but with older things still prowling through it. There are brothers of the blood there who knew the King of Kings when he was a mere youth, and a great dark one who may even be speaking true when he says he can remember when all men lived in caves, in fear, and quaking in terror at the coming of the night.

My wolf and I coursed through the city, and the blood was so sweet. But there came a day that I shall never forget. We were asleep, cuddled together like twin brothers, when my cub woke in frenzy. He was tearing and gouging...most uncontrollable in his rage. I grabbed him tight, there in the dark place away from the sun.

And that's when I felt it...the hammer-strike to my heart.

I knew even then that my father had gone to his final death. And I vowed that I would have my revenge, and that I would reign in his place...a reign of terror such that the world would never forget.

We bided our time, my wolf and I, while I sought allies in my quest. But allies are hard to come by for a King without a throne, and I was in need of a grand gesture that would prove my intent.

And so it was, in the year 1666 of the false god, I took my wolf and myself to London, for there was a new Protector in the land, and I wished to pay my respects.

The voice stopped, but the hand kept petting Martin's head. Somewhere deep inside himself Martin cried out in disgust, but he was paralyzed...locked inside the wolf and held by his Master's will.

"It is an old story," an Other said, a tall Highlander on the Boy-King's left. "It will end differently this time."

"Aye," the Boy-King said, "for I am older, and wiser, and the cattle have grown weak in my absence."

He started to stroke Martin's head again.

The last time we crept into London under cover of night, just my wolf and me. It was no different to us than

Vienna or Berlin, the only difference being the squalor and sickness that pervaded everything.

We ran through the streets like moonlight shadows, unseen by the populace, unlooked for by the meager guard posted on the river. But we did not feed, although my wolf was hungry. I was saving him, you see, stoking his need, in order that the protector's blood might be all the sweeter.

We ran the length of the city, from Dockland to Westminster, and wherever we passed the cattle quaked in fear, although they knew not the cause. And finally we came to what passes for a palace under the regime of the Protectorate…a poor, squalid, tawdry effigy of the gothic magnificence of the continent.

He was there…the one who called himself Protector…the son of the one whom had staked my sire at the Bloody Tower. The wolf's blood was raging by now, so I let him have his head…a mistake I will not make again.

Before he had gone a yard a cross-bolt took him in the shoulder, and another in the flank. From being hunters we had become hunted, in the blink of the eye. My wolf was sore wounded, and we fled, my wolf and I, pursed by many horsemen.

The city was in uproar, and on another occasion we might have reveled in the chaos and bathed ourselves in the cattle's blood. But my wolf was greatly pained, and the horsemen were gaining on us. I took my cub in my arms, feeling the heat as his blood spilled over me, and I ran, ran like the wind, with the protector's guard screaming at my back and crossbow quarrels hissing past my ears.

I could have made it back to the boat waiting at the docks, but I could not leave my cub, no matter that he was slowing me down or that I was growing weaker by the stride. He licked his own blood from my hands as I raced back to the east of the city.

I was barely thirty yards ahead of my pursuers as we ran into the warren of hovels and shacks to the north of London Bridge. The wolf was like a dead weight in my arms, and I could go little further. I used up what little charm my exhausted state would allow and persuaded my pursuers that I had taken a left turn, while I darted right into a dark alleyway, and right again into a quiet and empty shop that smelled of yeast and flour.

I laid my wolf on the floor. The swift companion was nearly spent. His haunches shuddered and trembled as if a terrible ague had taken him, and his tongue was hot and dry as it rasped against my hand. I bent beside him to give him a final peace, when the first flaming firebrand came through the window, followed by three more in quick succession.

The air itself seemed to explode, and in less than five seconds the place was a roaring inferno. My cub thrashed in distress, and when a burning ember alighted on its nose it could stand no more. It burst out of the bake room and was immediately surrounded by jeering guardsmen. I had to watch as they kicked and stamped my cub to a bloody mess. They then pissed on its body, and flung the bloody pelt onto the fire.

I stood there, the fire raging around me, and for the only time in my life in the dark, I wept bitter tears.

"It is near time," the tall Highlander Other said.

"We are nearly done," the Boy-King replied. "My cub should know why he has been chosen."

And finally the flames and the heat got too much, even for me. My cloak began to burn and I flung myself out into the night, a ball of smoke and fire.

The guards, the cowards who had been so keen to stamp on a wounded and dying animal, fled before me as I fled through the city. And behind me, London burned.

It was near dawn when William of Rennes found me. I was little more than a charred, blackened mass of meat and bone. But Baphomet's blood runs strong in me, and although it would take long months of pain. I would be myself again.

Even as the boat turned away from the red sky over London, I was taking a vow, that I would return, and that I would take one of the protector's guards to be my pet, and I would show him the same courtesy my cub was shown.

"So here I am," the Boy-King said. "And look, the serpent has sent me a cub…a Protector's guard…and one who so wants to be a wolf."

"It is time. She is ready," the tall highland Other said.

The Boy-King took Martin's head in his hands and dug his fingers deep into the head wound until the pain caused Martin to thrash and scream.

The Boy-King stood, and licked bloody fingers. "So sweet," he said. "And it will be sweeter still when you are turned. I will have a new cub…and together we will hunt the Protector down."

The Other lifted a foot and kicked Martin, hard, on the side of the head, sending him into unconsciousness in a sea of red pain.

Sean had left Linthithgow just after dawn without having gotten close to catching the bloated keeper of that blood-soaked castle. Many times he had thought of setting the place alight and sending its occupants to the hell they deserved. But that would have drawn more attention to himself, and he had done enough of that already.

Instead, he had called on the new part inside him, the part he had inherited from the woodsman. With the newfound skills he was able to track the progress of the one who had taken Mary Campbell north. The trail had led him steadily north and east and, earlier that evening, he had entered the castle.

Mary Campbell was inside…part of him could sense her presence, even through the four-foot thick walls. He knew that by entering the castle he was bargaining on the dark one inside him to fool the Others, but that was a risk he had to take. He had to get to her before the Boy-King performed his ceremony of king making.

All evening he had managed to mingle with the Others. Being so close to them turned his stomach, and on several occasions he was near to exploding in rage and violence. But he kept repeating the phrase old Seton had given him.

"I am the Balance," he told himself. It didn't stop the

rage inside him, but it was enough to give him some sort of control.

He had almost given himself away when Martin was brought out into the quadrangle, and it was all he could do to stop himself from jumping in and joining the fight once it began. The Others around him were in a frenzy, and he had managed to get the snare to Martin without being noticed, but any more help was impossible.

Now he had to get both Mary Campbell, and his Thane, out of this nightmare, or let the Boy- King perpetuate his hellish bloody bloodline.

"I am the Balance," he said to himself, and gave the Other inside more freedom, using the scent of blood in his nostrils to pinpoint his goal. He caught Martin's spoor straight away. His friend was near, somewhere within fifty yards. The smell of blood almost over-whelmed him, and Sean swayed slightly, nearly colliding with a tall, tartan-clad Other.

He snarled and showed his bloody fangs, and the Other bellowed a huge laugh.

"The arena is a bit too strong for you young ones," it said. "You'll have to learn to control yourself better if you wish to see your second century."

It clapped Sean on the shoulder and, still laughing, went on its way. Sean could still smell it long after it had passed out of sight.

And there was another smell in the air...far away yet, but coming ever closer, the slightly acrid stench of garlic.

He was not the only one who had noticed it. The activity around him became frenzied as the Others and their mind-slaves sealed the castle against attack.

Somewhere in the night he caught the spoor of Mary Campbell but it was blown away in the wind.

Out beyond the castle walls the stench of garlic filled the air. A single bugle blew a long, fading note, and a drum took up a martial beat. Cumberland had brought his army to Stirling.

Martin woke in darkness. At first he was disoriented, thinking he was back in his own room in Milecastle. Then the smell hit him, the stench of fresh blood, and he knew he was a very long way from home.

The last thing he remembered was fighting in the arena. His head throbbed, as if he had drank too much ale, and there was a heavy feeling deep in the pit of his stomach. Panic began to grow in him, and it took all his training to fight it down and check his body for bites. He let out an audible sigh when he discovered his skin was unbroken.

"Not yet, dearie," a voice whispered in the darkness to his left. "I thought we might have some fun first."

Martin's eyes were beginning to adjust to the gloom and he could just make out a figure heading towards him. He scuttled away backwards, but came up hard against a rough stone wall.

"Now is that any way to treat a lady?" the voice said, and it laughed, a deep throaty chuckle. "And one who was so polite to you earlier."

And now Martin recognized the voice. His eyes finally began to see through the darkness, but he didn't need them to tell them that Jean Munro was the source...or rather, the Other who had once been a woman of Orkney of that name.

"Did you get what you were looking for?" Martin asked. His hands frantically searched for a weapon, but there was nothing within reach as the Other stepped in close and put its face nose to nose to his.

The creature was still recognizable as the woman he had spoken to earlier, but her hair was now blood red, and that was matched by her eyes. Where once they had been green they now shone like hot coals.

"Oh, I got what I wanted," it said. "What I've always wanted...power over puny little men like you."

"Come closer, my lady, I'll show you that I'm not what I seem," Martin said.

"Oh, I intend to see everything you have to offer," the Other said, and stretched out a hand to stroke at the front of

Martin's breeches. "The King wants you turned, but he wants you whole," it said. "Otherwise I could have had more sport. But at least you will be my first feeding."

"They say a maiden always remembers her first," Martin said.

The Other was about to reply, but Martin gave it no chance to speak. He drove his right hand forward, heel first, straight at the point of the Other's nose, forcing bone backwards towards the brain. Blood gushed, hot and heavy, against his face as the Other fell away from him.

The blow would have killed a man-and-only-man, but the Others did not die so easily.

The thing that had been Jean Munro smiled and smeared blood across its lips.

"Yours will taste sweeter, my pretty," it said, and came forward with the speed of a striking snake. Martin only had time to get his hands up near his neck before he was pinned hard against the wall, rough stone grating on his back.

The Other began to writhe suggestively against him, and its tongue rasped against the skin of Martin's right hand.

"I can feel your heart, little boy," the Other said. Martin grabbed it round the neck and began to squeeze, but the Other took hold of his wrists and started to pull his hands away, opening a path to his exposed neck. Martin tried to push back, but he was as weak as a newborn, and the Other laughed as it lowered its fangs to his skin.

"It's nice to see I'm not the only one with woman problems," a familiar voice said, just as the Other was pulled violently away.

A sudden splash of blood from the Other's ruined nose caught Martin across the eyes and he was temporarily blinded. When he rubbed the slick redness away he saw Sean Grant and the Other rolling on the stone floor of the room.

They were like a pair of rabid dogs, and Martin could scarcely discern who was who, let alone who might be winning, until there came a loud crack of bones breaking, and Sean Grant stood away from the still body of the Other.

"You shouldn't mess with wildcats, my Thane," Sean

said. "That's my job." He looked back to the body, and gasped, turning his head so that his friend would not see, but he was too late...Martin stepped back in puzzlement as the fangs slid bloodily from Sean Grant's gums.

Once more Martin raised his arms in front of him.

"You are turned. You are Other," he said, but Sean shook his head.

"No, my Thane. Not Other, but no longer man-and-only-man. I have our friend Lennan to thank for that."

Martin remembered his encounter with Gwynneth back in the church of Newcastleton and nodded his head as understanding came.

"Aye. I have seen it. It seems we both carry the woodsmen's legacy within us."

Now it was Sean's turn to look puzzled, but Martin lowered his hands and stepped forward.

They embraced quickly.

"We will have time for stories later," Martin said. "First, we have to get out of here."

"Aye," Sean said. "For Mary Campbell is somewhere in this castle, and we must find her before the Boy-King does any more deviltry."

"There are also more than fifty true men-and-only-men in the cells below," Martin said. "If we can free them, we will have more chance of escape ourselves." "There is more hope than you know," Sean said, just as the boom of cannon reverberated in the room. "It seems that the Protector has brought the war north."

The scene in the castle esplanade was one of chaos and nightmare. Hordes of crazed Others and their mind-slaves screamed and ranted as cannon shot rained from beyond the wall, and, even as Martin and Sean emerged into the open, a fine spray began to fall, a rain that caused the Others to shriek as blue flame started to burn among them.

Martin gave a grim smile.

"It seems that Master Hillman is near," he said. "For surely only he could have thought of this."

He pointed upwards, to where the sky was full of large kites. Water bottles hung from harnesses slung beneath, and it was from these that the silver and garlic water was falling. Martin was pleased to see that the concoction seemed to have no effect on Sean.

It was however bringing a new form of hell to Stirling Castle.

"Come, man," Martin said. "We must find Mary Campbell before this turns into a rout and she is lost in the confusion."

"Oh, I can find her," Sean said. "It is as if I am a compass and she is a magnet...I am drawn to her."

Martin fell in behind Sean as he pushed his way though the shrieking throng. A tall Other made a grab at Martin, but Sean spun on him, showing newly exposed fangs and hissing loudly.

"This one belongs to the King...would you sup at his table before him?"

The Other backed off, and the crowd parted before them as a wind got up, the kites soared overhead, and the deadly rain fell ever more heavily. Small fires burned all across the esplanade, and the smoldering bodies of Others were beginning to fall and melt at their feet.

"Hurry!" Sean shouted over his shoulder, making for the nearest doorway. "I fear we are too late. The ceremony has started."

Sean led them through a series of hallways, stopping only to snap a tall wooden candlestick in two and pass one half to Martin.

"Not much of a weapon," he said.

"Enough for these bastards," Martin replied, and they smiled grimly at each other.

"Are you fit enough for a fight, my Thane?" Sean said, and Martin laughed.

"As fit as I deserve to be," he said. "I've already sent many to the final death this night...a few more should be little trouble."

In truth Martin felt weak and tired, but he was in the company of his closest friend, trying to save the daughter of a man he was indebted to, and with a chance of meeting the Boy-King face-to- face. He would find the strength from somewhere.

"We're here," Sean whispered as they came to a heavy oak door.

The air around them seemed to get suddenly colder, and Martin felt a stab of icy fear before reaching out to help Sean push the door open. The scene that met them would be etched in Martin's mind for the rest of his days.

Two large black candles that burned with a blood-red flame provided the only light and the smoke from the heavy tallow rose thick and black to hang in a rolling cloud above their heads. Four Others stood at the corners of a large table, across which was draped the limp body of Mary Campbell.

Her eyes were wide open, but they stared, sightless, at the ceiling. Her naked body was smeared with thick, congealing blood, and the taste of copper stuck at the back of Martin's throat.

Even as the pair of them burst into the room, the Boy-King took something red and dripping from the golden chalice before him and raised the bloody mass over the girl's mouth.

"Let the life of Baphomet be the life eternal, and let the blood go on, in line never ending, till the ends of time."

A slow stream of blood and gore dripped between Mary Campbell's open lips. Martin gasped in disgust as she licked her lips, and gasped again as he saw the fangs that emerged to hang on her lower lip.

The Boy-King turned towards them. His eyes blazed with a light even brighter than that of the candles, and his cheeks, although yet pale, looked strangely flushed, as if he had recently fed.

"Ah, the young suitor and my wolf cub," he said. "Come to take the girl away from all this evil."

He laughed, a cruel thing, and the three Others joined

in.

"But I'm afraid there will be no last-minute rescue. Baphomet has seen to that. The deed is done."

He pointed at the prone girl, and Martin was dismayed to see her eyes change color until they blazed deepest red.

"No!" Sean shouted, and jumped forward, his stake raised, aimed straight at the Boy-King's heart.

The Other didn't flinch. In fact, the corners of his mouth rose in a wide grin that showed his fangs.

"Protect me, my cub," his voice said in Martin's head, and, without thinking, Martin reached out and grabbed Sean as he passed, pulling them both to the floor.

At first Sean thought he'd been tripped from behind, and was about to shout a warning to Martin when he realized that it was Martin himself who had attacked him.

They rolled on the floor together, a bundle of flailing arms and teeth. Sean felt Martin's teeth try to bite through the leather of his boots, and had to kick out hard to prevent his attacker from climbing further up his legs.

The Boy-King stood over them and laughed out loud.

"The biter and the bitten...which will prevail? I wish I could tarry and see the result, but I fear we must leave this place. It seems Cumberland has come knocking, and I am not quite ready to receive him."

He took the gold chalice in his arms, dropping the bloody mass he held into it.

"Once more the King of Kings has brought forth a blood-heir. But there is no time to rejoice. Not yet."

He motioned at the three Others, and the tallest one lifted Mary Campbell across its shoulder as if she weighed no more than a child.

"Adieu, my young friends," the Boy-King said. "I will no doubt see one of you again, and I look forward to finding out which of you is the stronger. I do believe the victor will prove to be an able companion to me once I have taken the throne."

Sean was vaguely aware of the Others leaving the room,

and he just managed to catch a glimpse of Mary Campbell's hair as it swung behind the Other who carried her...it was already beginning to turn red from the roots.

Sean struggled, attempting to follow them, but he had his hands full trying to keep Martin from tearing his throat out.

The thing he fought bore little resemblance to his friend. It snarled and salivated, teeth bared, and it fought...not with the cool precision of an Officer of the Watch, but with the naked frenzy of a rabid dog.

Sean had an opening where he could have taken his attacker by the neck and snapped it, but he held his hand...he could not kill his Thane, even in this debased state. But by delaying his strike he gave Martin an opening of his own, and had to bring his arm up in front of him to stop teeth tearing at his cheek.

He forced Martin's head back and managed to roll over, pinning Martin with the weight of his body.

"My Thane!" he shouted, then had to hit Martin hard in the face to prevent himself being bitten.

"Martin!" he called. "It is me! We should fight Others, not ourselves."

But there was no recognition in his Thane's eyes as he lunged upwards, knocking Sean off balance and bringing a scream from Sean as he was bitten, deep, in his left hand. Unbidden, fangs came from his bloody gums, and it was all he could do to stop himself from feeding.

He threw himself sideways, away from Martin, and managed to get the table between them as the snarling creature came forward once more.

The smell of blood was even stronger now, and Sean felt the Other move inside him. It would be so easy to give it rein, to let the bloodlust take him...indeed, he felt the joy in it ready to take hold in his mind.

But that would make me no different from my poor Thane, he thought. I have a duty...to myself.

"I am the Balance," he said out loud.

Martin growled at him, but Sean kept moving around the table, keeping it between them. "Remember the fisher wife?" Sean said, circling. "Remember the night on the wall when Campbell's light came from the North?"

Martin leaped on top of the table and seemed to be readying himself to spring.

"This is not who you are. Remember Barnstable," Sean said, and thought there might be hope, for deep down in Martin's eyes, there was a spark of what might be humanity.

"Remember your father," Sean said, and a single tear ran down Martin's cheek.

Martin raised his head towards the ceiling and let out a howl that echoed around the room and rang in Sean's ears.

"Sean?" he said, and it was almost a sob. "Help me."

He stretched out a hand before he fell, insensible, on the table.

Sean looked down at the prone form, then towards the door.

Mary Campbell insensible in the hands of the Others, my Thane insensible in front of me. I have a duty to my Thane...and a duty to Mary Campbell. And I cannot fulfill one without neglect of the other.

He sighed loudly.

One is here, the other is not. And I have a duty to my friend. That must make my mind up for me...for now, at least.

He lifted Martin in his arms and made for the door.

The castle esplanade was a scene from hell. Everything was lit in dim blue sparkling flame that burned in small patches everywhere he looked. Others were fleeing in all directions, but wherever they ran, the silver and garlic got them. Partially melted Others tried to drag their still burning bodies away, but the kites seemed to cover the sky, and there was no escape.

Sean scanned the bodies littering the area, hoping that

the Boy-King may have been caught in the falling death, but he knew it was not so. Mary Campbell was already outside the castle, and was heading north...he sensed it.

And even as he thought it, the Boy-King once more spoke in his mind.

"Ah, the suitor won. Tell me," the Other's voice said as it crawled in his head, "...did you feel the blood rise? Does it still quicken in you? Enjoy your warmth, little one, for you will soon…"

"Run, run while you can!" Sean sent back, interrupting him. "For know this...wherever you go, I will hunt you down."

And with that, he closed his mind against the Boy King. I am the Balance he thought. As if from a far distance he heard singing, a woodsman's song, and the Boy-King was excluded from his mind, like a candle being snuffed out. Sean imagined he heard a howl of anger, and allowed himself a grim smile.

The garlic rain from above was slackening now, but it had done its job well, for there was scarcely an Other left standing in the castle forecourt. He picked a way through the foul mess, and was heading for the main gate of the castle when a small figure jumped into his path.

"Put him down, you foul bastard," a youth proclaimed, and pointed a small tube in Sean's direction. Sean was suddenly sprayed with a mixture of silver and garlic.

He spluttered as the garlic got into his nose and stung his eyes, and he stumbled, almost dropping Martin.

"How do you like that, then?" he heard, and was hit with another spray of the garlic. "Die, you bastard!" the youth shouted, then stepped back as Sean shook off the liquid. The boy looked so shocked that Sean burst into a loud laugh.

"A good try, boy, but an Officer of the Watch does not die as easily as an Other."

"Grant? Is that you?" a voice asked to his right. "Surely this is not the same boy who left my inn with my best boots and sword?"

Sean turned to see Fitz at his side.

"Aye, it is me. Well met again, innkeeper, although we are both a long way from home."

"We are that. But I am no less pleased to see you for all that. And the Thane? Is he...?"

"He lives," Sean said. "But he is sore afflicted and is in need of doctoring."

"Then come," Fitz said. "It looks like the battle is already over, and young Hillman here has saved us a sore fight."

The youth blushed. He carried a water sack on his back and a bellows, like that of a bagpipe, under his arm from which he directed a stream of water through the small pipe, hosing the steaming remains of Others at their feet.

"It was a simple idea," he mumbled. "All I needed was the kites, and it was Megan who made them and..."

"Aye, a simple idea," Fitz said. "Like the inspiration for yon sack you carry...so simple that everyone else was too intelligent to think of it."

He ruffled the boy's hair.

"Come. Megan will be looking for you."

"The smith?" the boy asked. "He was with the Thane. Have you seen him?"

"A big fellow, built like a bull?" Sean said, and the boy nodded.

"He fell in the arena," Sean said, and sudden tears sprung in the boy's eyes. "But he died like a true man rather than become an Other, and he did not give them an easy time."

The boy turned away and wiped his eyes, but when he turned back there was only a grim determination showing.

"Martin told me that there are more Protectors men down in the cells..." Sean began. The innkeeper interrupted him.

"Aye. They were the lucky ones. We got them out."

"Then come," Sean said. "My thane grows heavy."

The three of them went down through the great gate. All around them soldiers were hosing down the remains of

Others, each using a water sack fitted in similar manner to that used by the boy. Vast pyres were being built of the mind-slaves killed by the cannon shot.

"We did not get them all," Fitz said. "Nor even the half of them. But we have given the Boy- King a sore beating."

"Mayhap," Sean said bitterly. "But I couldn't stop him begetting his heir."

"Shhh," Fitz said, putting a finger to his lips. "It seems we have many tales to tell each other, we two. But rumors will spread too fast this night. It would be best to keep them for the comfort of our tent."

Sean nodded grimly.

"Aye. And maybe old Menzies has a cure for what ails my Thane."

Fitz looked at Sean, and seemed about to say something, then thought better of it.

He clasped Sean on the shoulder.

"Come. I can have a flagon of ale and one of Megan's pies in your hands in less than five minutes. Then we'll see what can be done for our young Thane."

"The old doctor is dead?" Sean said.

He was standing at the entrance of a large tent. Inside Megan was applying a cold compress to Martin's head, while Fitz and himself stood and tried not to think about how helpless they were.

"Aye. He died an officer's death," Fitz replied. "And your Thane avenged him...a bit too strenuously for the liking of some."

Sean heard the sharp tone in the man's voice.

"Hush," Megan called out to them. "I have a sick man here."

Fitz drew Sean out of the tent and over to a heavily laden cart where he drew back a tarpaulin and uncovered a beer barrel.

"If we are to tell stories we'll need something to loosen our tongues."

He drew two flagons from the barrel and sat Sean down

on the tailgate of the wagon before beginning to speak.

"It started, for me at least, when your Thane and old Sawney turned up at the door of the inn..."

They swapped tales for an hour, while the Hillman boys fetched and carried for Megan. Sean was surprised to see that the sun was coming up by the time Megan came over and joined them. She took Fitz's ale and downed it in one gulp.

"The fever is passed," she said. "But it is a shame to see such a young man go through so much pain."

She turned to Sean.

"He asks for you," she said. "But do not tire him further. He needs to rest."

"As do we all, madam," Sean said with a smile and gave her his own flagon as he passed by her into the tent.

He expected to find Martin yet abed, but instead the young Thane was pulling on his boots and was already fully dressed.

"The innkeeper's wife will not like it, my Thane," Sean said.

Martin turned to him and he had a grim smile on his face, a face that looked ten years older than Sean knew it to be.

"And when did you ever pay attention to anything you were ordered to do? Do you expect me to lie like an invalid when the Boy-King is so close?"

Sean held up his hand and showed Martin the teeth marks imprinted there—still red and raw looking.

"You are not yourself, Sire."

Martin winced. "The wolf is strong in the presence of the Boy-King. It comes when it will, and leaves again as suddenly. I am sorry. As you say, I was not myself."

He laughed again, but this time it was hollow and full of pain.

"I have not been myself since my encounter with the old gray one. But once the Boy-King is sent to the final death, then mayhap I can rest. But I have men to lead, while

I still can…Fitz!" he called, and the innkeeper came at a run, still carrying a flagon of ale.

"Sire?"

"Who is in charge? Is the Duke himself here?"

"Yes, Sire. His command post is some two miles to the west. He has called a briefing of officers two hours hence…I will attend."

"No," Martin replied. "Sean and I will go."

Sean was aghast.

"No, Sire. I must be gone. They have too much of a start already. I must be after them…and soon."

"I had thought to keep you beside me," Martin said. "For you saw her…we are too late…she, and her unborn child, are already turned."

"But so was I," Sean said. "And her father would not give up on me. I will not give up on her, not when I have breath left in me."

"Sean," Martin said. It was almost a sob, and Sean heard the need in his friend, the need and the uncertainty.

He put a hand on Martin's shoulder…

…and they are together in a circle of high stones. A small figure stands before them, and Sean realizes with a start it is Lennan.

"We are all with the wind," the woodsman says.

"I fly with it, you stand steady in front of it," pointing at Sean, "And you…" pointing now at Martin, "…fly before it. All three are with the wind. Remember its song, and we will sing it together."

Sean feels Martin move forward, but already the scene is fading and only the sound of Lennan's singing remains. He reaches out to Martin…

…and they were in the tent once more, the sound of Lennan's song ringing in his ears.

"Lennan?" Martin said, and Sean realized they had both been privy to the same sight.

"Yes," Sean replied. "I carry his song with me. It has sustained me in many a dark place."

"The song…" Martin said, his gaze far away. "I had

forgotten the song."

"It seems Lennan knew that, even from wherever he is now."

"I pray, young sirs, what are you talking about?" Fitz said. "Have you both lost your senses?"

Martin shook his head as if to clear it. He seemed stronger somehow, and his eyes were clear and bright.

"I will not forget it again," he said in a whisper, almost to himself. He ignored Fitz and looked deep in Sean's eyes.

"Lennan guides you still?"

Sean nodded.

"Then go...seek out Mary Campbell...that is your duty now." He managed a small smile. "Your Thane orders you."

"Then I accept your command," Sean said with an answering smile, already moving to the tent entrance.

"Follow me north, and follow quickly," he said. "For the end of this mummery is coming soon...I can feel it."

He didn't wait for Martin's reply. He left the tent for a cold morning, one that got colder still while he provisioned himself for a journey.

By the time he left the camp, his gaze set to the North, the first snows of winter had already started to fall.

CHAPTER 6

NOVEMBER 21, 1745, STIRLING

Martin sat alone in the tent long after Sean had left him, the sound of Lennan's song still ringing in his ears.

How could I forget, he thought as he felt new strength course through him. He was still full of self-disgust at how the Boy-King had taken hold of his mind, but he would not suffer it to be done again…not now that he had the song once more.

And if it works for me, why can it not work for others?

"Fitz!" he called once more.

The innkeeper arrived at a run, with Megan close behind.

"You should be abed, young sir," she said.

"Only if you come with me," he replied.

Fitz chuckled.

"It seems the Thane is quite well."

"Better than I have been at any time since Derby," Martin said. "And I'm ready to chase the Boy-King to the ends of the Earth if need be."

"Mayhap we will get the chance," Fitz said. "The Duke sent a message…he has no time to hold any more meetings. We have orders to break camp immediately. We are being sent north as an advance party, to harry the dark bastards wherever we find them. The Duke will bring his army on behind us, razing the country as he comes. It seems that the Protector has declared that this land is now English soil, and he will have no Others on it."

"Then let us get to it," Martin said. "We should not keep the Boy-King waiting. And send for Harold Hillman…I have a new song for him to learn."

As they broke camp, Fitz told Martin of what had passed since they were parted at Newcastleton.

"We got back with reinforcements the next morning, but there was nothing in Newcastleton except for the smoking remains of Others. We thought we had lost you forever," the innkeeper said as he tied the tarpaulin over the cart, making sure that the beer barrel was secure.

"And when the Duke brought his troops north the next day, we joined with him," Megan continued. "We never expected to see you, or young Grant, again."

"Aye," Fitz said. "So I was surprised to see Sean carry you out of yon hellhole. You haven't told how that happened, Sire."

Martin shook his head.

"It can wait until we have ale and pies and a hot fire," he said. "For now, let us gather what men we have, for if I know the Duke, he will be moving out soon, and it wouldn't do for him to catch us on the road."

By the time Martin led his troops out of Stirling the snow was falling heavily. Only an hour had passed since Sean had departed, chasing the Other's army, but already the rough track had gone from view under the white blanket.

"Harold...strike up the tune," Martin said, and as the lad began to sing, Martin felt his heart lift.

How could I have forgotten the woodsman's song? he thought.

But now that I have taught it to young Hillman, it will always be there.

Indeed, it seemed to be working its magic on the troop...Martin had never seen a band so happy to be heading to war.

"'Tis a fine air," Fitz said beside him. "Indeed, it lightens a dark place like no other song I've heard."

"It does more than that," Martin replied. "I believe it is all that stands between myself and damnation."

It was only half an hour before they found evidence they were on the right trail. Three bodies lay directly in their path…Others, their pale bodies partially melted and eaten away.

"Looks like these were caught by young Edward's rain in the castle," Fitz said as he knelt beside them.

"Aye, but that wasn't what killed them. One of our band goes before us," Martin replied, pointing out the stakes that stood proud from each breast. "Our Captain of the Watch has been doing his duty."

Over the course of the day they found five more bodies, each staked in the heart. The last was almost totally snow-covered, only the dark of the stake showing above a white mound. The snowfall had become so thick that visibility was down to ten yards. To make matters worse, they seemed to be traveling in a valley that tunneled all the falling snow straight at them. Martin's leather coat was already encrusted with an inch or more of half-frozen slush, and his face felt stiff and numb.

"We must hole up, sir!" Fitz shouted from his left. This is folly…we'll find nothing but a gully to fall into!"

Martin signed, but knew his quartermaster was right. He peered through the white, as if willing it to part and show him the way.

"Form a circle," he said. "Carts and horses to the outside…And see if we can get some fires going. It could be a long night."

It was only as he tried to dismount that Martin realized how near he was to total exhaustion. He nearly fell as his knees gave way beneath him, and it was only Fitz's strong arm that kept him from toppling.

"Nothing that some strong ale won't cure," Fitz said, loud enough for the nearest troopers to hear. He led Martin to the largest cart and helped him sit on the tailgate. Harold Hillman appeared under Megan's watchful eye as preparations were made for the night's camp.

Soon two large fires roared in the center of their makeshift encampment and everyone except those unlucky enough to draw first sentry duty was huddled around the flames. The falling snow hissed and spat, but for now the fire was winning.

Martin was slowly beginning to feel stronger, although the second flagon of ale threatened to go to his head.

"We made good time today, Fitz," he said.

The older man wiped some foam from his lips as he replied, "Aye sir, but if this snow keeps up its likely we shall see Christmas on this very spot."

"No…" Martin said. "The end will come sooner than that…don't ask me how I know…but I can feel it. Besides it looked like we took care of more than half of them in Stirling alone. Mayhap we have him on the run."

Fitz looked grave, and he took a long pull of his beer before replying.

"His army is not as small as you think, Sire," he said. "There is news to which you are not yet privy. Let me get another beer for us both…'Tis a short tale but a sad one."

Martin stared into the fire while waiting for Fitz to return. None of his men spoke to him, and the Hillman boys were both somewhere on the opposite side of the small camp.

They're scared of me.

The thought struck him forcibly…he had seen that look in men's eye before.

I'm turning into my father.

He laughed out loud, and Fitz gave him a quizzical look as he handed Martin a new flagon. Martin motioned for the man to sit.

"Tell me your news," he said. "And you'd better make it quick. One more beer and I'm apt to lapse into sleep."

"It must have happened while we were in Milecastle," Fitz began. "Even possibly while we were carousing at your homecoming revels.

"Cumberland sent Old Barclay to the east, with nigh on three thousand men. He gave orders that the force should push north as fast as they were able. I believe he was hoping to catch the Boy-King on the run…but Barclay was the one who was caught."

Fitz stared deep into the fire, and there were tears in his eyes as he continued.

"It happened in Berwick. An old soldier like Barclay couldn't resist billeting his troops in the castle and barracks. Unfortunately the Boy-King…or one of his lieutenants…knew it.

"In the dead of night, Others poured through in three places thought to be the prison, the cellars and the river gate. You can imagine the carnage. It is said that old Barclay was the last to go down, and that the Others lay full dead in a heap around him. But he did fall…and by the morning the Boy-King had nigh on three thousand new recruits…twice more than the number he lost last night in Stirling."

Fitz took another long draw on his beer and toasted the fire. "To Barclay. A fine soldier, and a good friend."

Many of the company, Martin included, joined in the reply. "But how do you know?" Martin said, "…if they were all killed?"

"Not all, sir," Fitz said. He drank from his flagon, but it was nearly empty.

"Take mine," Martin said. "I'm dead on my feet. But I will not sleep until you finish the story."

Fitz took Martin's flagon, but only stared into the pot as he continued.

"We were preparing to leave Milecastle to search for yourself and the smith when Thomas Barr staggered up to the gate…it is from him we have the story."

"He survived, then?" Martin asked. "Aye," Fitz said and spat into the fire. "But not for long…he was sorely bitten. I offered to do it, but it was his father who made sure he was put to a final rest. And after it was done, old Barr took himself off to the wall. His body was found just as we were leaving…he had looked out over the wall one last time, then near blew his own head off with a musket."

Martin woke to a cold, clear morning. Last night's snow

glittered like tiny gems in the morning sun, and a brisk wind blew down the valley in which they had set up camp, shifting the snow into soft drifts that coated the landscape in a shapeless blanket.

He broke his fast with a lump of bread and some hard cheese, washed down with ale…only half a flagon…his head told him that he had taken too much last night.

The troops were already breaking camp by the time Martin finished the ale.

"A fine day for traveling," Megan shouted wryly.

Martin smiled as he shouted back.

"If it is too cold for milady, there is a warm bed back in Milecastle waiting for you."

"Only if milord comes with me," she called back.

Some of the men, new to the troop, were bemused to see Fitz laughing as loudly as any of the men.

"Come, young Hillman. Sing me my traveling tune," Martin said. Once more the boy took up the Woodsman's song, and once more it worked its magic as the troop headed out, northwards, in search of prey.

Sean Grant spent the night in a high cave overlooking a long, deep glen.

Yesterday he had been able to follow the Other's trail north even going as far as catching up with some stragglers from the horde. But they had been unable to tell him anything more than he already knew.

He is going north…he has something he must do…and Mary Campbell is of vital importance to his plans.

He had pushed his mount hard, but when the snow got too heavy he'd been forced to seek refuge. Somehow he'd known exactly where shelter would be.

He had slept little. The cave was barely large enough for himself and the horse, and long before morning the hot animal smell was becoming overwhelming.

The view as the sun came up more than made up for any discomfort he'd been feeling. The whole length of the glen lay deep in snow with only the trees at the bottom of the valley showing as dark sentinels. Overhead the sky was a pale, duck-egg blue, without a single cloud, and high above a pair of buzzards soared, warming themselves for the day's hunt.

My soul is empty Sean whispered soundlessly. And without warning, the sight once more filled his mind.

He is in a castle, in a room of rough-hewn walls with only a single window almost impossibly high above him. A massive fireplace stands cold and empty, and in front of it, naked on a large wolfskin, lays the Boy-King and his bride.

Mary Campbell, her hair now impossibly blood red, turns to the Other and smiles broadly, her fangs sliding bloodily over her lower lip. She is hugely pregnant, her belly swollen and her skin stretched so tight that the child can be seen struggling beneath it.

The Boy-King strokes her belly, and, leaning over, bites her, hard, around the nipple, drawing blood. They both smile as he bends once more and begins to suckle.

"No!" Sean shouted.

The Boy-King looks up, smiling still.

"Ah, the young lover," he says. "Do you still covet my bride?"

He runs a white hand down to between the woman's thighs, and she opens her legs to receive it.

"Does she stir your blood?" the Other says, bending once more to suckle. When he lifts his head his lips are smeared red. "Or is it her blood that stirs you?"

Sean felt the fangs slide in his gums, and suddenly he became aware of the hot pounding of his horse's heart.

"Join me, and one day, my young lover, all this will be yours," the Boy-King says, and laughs, a cold thing with no mirth it.

Mary Campbell smiles as she runs a cold hand over her breasts.

Sean sat in the mouth of the cave, sweating despite the bitter cold. The beat of the horse's heart pounded through him like a great drum, and the vision in his mind of Mary Campbell's naked form inflamed him further until he could take it no more.

The horse tried to shy away from him, but he caught it hard in a strong grip, feeling the course hair against his lips as he bit deep into its neck.

The Boy-King laughs again, and his eyes flare, blood red as the child inside his bride kicks excitedly.

Hot blood coursed in Sean's mouth, and a fever grew inside him, but even as he made to swallow, new sights took root in his mind…of Duncan Campbell lying on the floor of the chapel in Edinburgh Castle, of Lennan's drained body on the altar stone in his people's village, of the friends he had lost…Menzies, the old Thane, and finally, of Mary Campbell herself, on the night he had first seen her, the night he had pledged his life to her safety. He flung himself away from the animal, retching, and spilling a bloody trail on the ground at his feet.

The horse bolted…off and away down the hill, but Sean barely noticed. He sat down on the cold cave floor and cried bitterly…while in his head the Boy-King's laughter rang and echoed.

It was a long time before Sean became aware of where he was. The sun was high in the sky and a deep cold had made its way into his bones, so that when he finally stood and stretched he felt brittle, like fresh ice.

I am the Balance, he repeated in his mind. It brought him some calm, but it couldn't remove the taste in his mouth.

At least I had the sense to unload the saddlebags, he thought ruefully. He knew he would have to follow the horse and catch it, but for now he needed ale…several mouthfuls of ale to wash away the foul taste in his mouth.

Only after he had gargled and spat three times was he able to taste beer rather than blood, and he took a last long swig of ale before shouldering the saddle-bags and heading down the hill, following his horses panicked trail.

He didn't have far to look. The beast had stopped at the small stream and was drinking, its head down. It let Sean mount as if nothing had happened, even though Sean could see the twin punctures at its neck.

Almost as if I were a different man, he thought.

And maybe that is not so far from the truth.

He turned the horse around till they faced north and once more put himself on the trail. He knew that resisting the Boy-King would be hard, but now he held Mary Campbell's face in his mind, from the night he slept beside her and her eyes filled with tears as she stared blindly at the stars.

Martin led his troop north for three days. They had long since lost sight of any trace of the Others, nor had they had any sign of Sean's passing, save a solitary pile of horse-droppings…and that had been nearly two days ago.

He was feeling progressively stronger…in body at least. Fitz's ale and Megan's pies were beginning to knit his battered body back to its fighting condition. But his mind was another matter altogether.

At night Martin dreamed, fiery fantasies of mayhem and bloodletting. And in the dreams he was not human…he was a wolf…a huge, gray, terrible wolf.

He had told no one, but Fitz and Megan knew something was wrong. One or the other of them was by his side at all times, and in truth he was glad of their company. Their tales of warm sultry days in the Carib seas did much to dispel both Martin's mood and the biting cold through which they traveled.

But even the pair of them couldn't sustain his mood forever, and more and more Martin's daylight thoughts turned to his incarceration in the castle, and his humiliation before the Boy-King.

I nearly killed Sean, he thought. I cannot allow it to happen again.

When those thoughts struck him he got Harold Hillman to sing the Woodsman's air once more. By the end of the third day he guessed that both Harold and the rest of the troopers were heartily sick of the tune. But it was the only thing standing between him and madness.

Just let me stand before the Other one last time, he thought. I will not be cowed so easily again.

The end of the third day found them in a narrow clearance in the midst of a forest. They had been traveling along an ancient cobbled track, old enough to have been there when Hadrian oversaw the building of the wall.

Martin organized the sentry duty then joined Fitz and Megan by the newly kindled fire. "The men are restless," Fitz said as he bit into a pie. "They say there is no purpose to this."

"No purpose!" Martin stood and began to shout. "No purpose? Have you forgotten Carlisle and Derby…and Milecastle? Those men did not all die in vain. We will harry the bastards until Cumberland catches up. Then we'll put the Boy-King to the final death."

Martin's blood was up, and at first he didn't realize there was laughter all around him.

"See…I told you that would wake him up," Megan said.

"Aye. You had the right…as usual," Fitz replied. The quartermaster passed Martin an ale.

"Welcome back, Sire," he said. "We feared the black mood had taken hold too deep."

"Deep enough," Martin admitted. "But not so deep that it can't be cured by ale and good company. Young Hillman!" he shouted, and for the first time in many days there was a smile on his face. "Give us a song…a different song. Just as long as it's not 'The Lay of the Thane.'"

Before long the clearing echoed with loud voices raised in song, and for a while Martin forgot his cares and lost himself in the pleasures of ale and friendship.

But all too soon the troops fell into sleep and there was only the fire for company. And then it was difficult to keep the wolf at bay. Even when he dosed himself with nigh on a gallon of ale, the dreams still came, and in the morning he had a hangover to go with the return of his black mood.

He saw the look of concern pass between Fitz and Megan, and he heard the troopers groan as he called for

Harold Hillman. But when the lad struck up the tune, at least he was able to mount his horse and lead out the men.

He'd been worried he might not even get that far.

Sean finally found he was on the right track on the fifth day.

Night was close when he came upon the old keep. He was dog-tired, but the smell of blood immediately woke him, all senses tingling, as once more the Boy-King's voice filled his mind.

"I found you something that might be more to your liking," the Other said.

The keep's door was open, and Sean knew that the source of the blood-smell was there, and it was close. Part of him wanted to get closer to that smell…much closer.

I am the Balance, he told himself again, and he almost believed it…but his legs didn't. They took him up towards the door so that he could look into the darkness beyond.

There was a body on the floor inside, and Sean's heart leapt, for at first he thought it might be Mary Campbell. His legs had taken him even closer to the door, so close that he was able to push it further open.

A young girl lay on the stone slabs. From the look of her she was no more than fifteen. She was naked and her heartbeat pounded loud in his ears. He felt saliva pool in his mouth, and spat it out in disgust.

I am the Balance, he whispered, and all compulsion left him.

"I will not be Other," he said out loud.

The voice of the Boy-King replied in his head, "What makes you think you have a choice?"

The girl's eyes flashed open…blue to start with but slowly filling from the bottom up with a deep blood red.

"Are boys more to your liking, then?" the Boy-King's voice said from her mouth. Like a cat the mind-slave came up off the floor and leapt for Sean's throat.

His training and instinct took over. He had a stake in his hand in less than a second, and in another second the twice-dead body was falling away from him.

"What a waste," the Boy-King's voice said, and a smile played on the girl's lips, even as the life went out of her eyes…blue again. Blue and cold.

Sean fell on the body, staring deep into the already glazing eyes.

"Where are you, you bastard?" he screamed.

And a connection was made.

It is as if Sean has caught the tail feathers of an eagle. He flies over a winter landscape with a dizzying speed, northwards and eastwards, over hill, forest and river until he is looking down on barren moorland. Even as he looks down, pale hands are beginning to push up through the dank ground, a forest of hands, an army of Others rising for one more night.

Jesu help us. There are thousands of them. Tens of thousands of them.

"Now do you see?" the Boy-King's voice said. "We have not even begun."

"I killed your Baphomet once," Sean replied. "And I will do it again."

The Boy-King laughed, but this time Sean caught something else in his tone…the first hint of fear.

Sean was still looking down on the moor below.

"Where are you, you bastard!" he screamed, and focused his mind on that of the Boy-King.

Once, when just a boy, Sean had fallen into the cesspit in Milecastle. Looking into the Other's mind felt just the same. He sensed the Other trying to push Sean out, but he pushed further.

His mind filled with fragmented visions…a pale Other sitting on a tall throne…Mary Campbell in the throes of childbirth…a black fleet of tall ships speeding north against the wind under a night sky…and a horde gathering on that barren moor.

"A name. Give me a name!" he screamed. Blackness began to seep into his mind, shutting off the visions, but still he pushed. It felt like his head was trapped in a vise, but, just as the link with the Other finally broke, Sean got the place name. Just one word, but it was enough.

He staggered out of the keep and back into sunlight. His head pounded, worse than a porter hangover, and he had to hold down a bout of nausea in his stomach. But he was elated. He had beaten the Boy-King. And he knew where the Other's army would be gathering.

He took half an hour to leave a message at the keep…but thought he might have a quicker way of contacting Martin.

An hour later Martin awoke from a deep sleep. At first he didn't know where or who he was…it had seemed in his dreams that he was Sean Grant, traveling under a starry sky. And in his dream he had talked to himself, of the Boy-King, and the gathering of a great army.

When he awoke he could only remember one word clearly:

CULLODEN!

Chapter 7

NOVEMBER 27, 1745, THE PASS OF GLENSHEE

It was two days later before Martin led his men to the keep to find Sean's message, but by that time couriers were already well on their way back to the Duke.

"How did you know?" Edward Hillman asked, standing in disbelief at the crude sign nailed to the keep's door.

CULLODEN. TELL CUMBERLAND HURRY.

"I just knew," Martin said.

Several of the men made the sign of the evil eye, but Fitz clapped Martin across the shoulder.

"A soldier who doesn't trust his hunches is no soldier at all," he said loudly. "And where now, sir?" he continued. "Do we wait for the Duke?"

"No," Martin said. "The Protector wants us to harry the Boy-King. And harry we shall. My Captain of the Watch is north of us, and it is time we were reacquainted."

"North it is, then," Fitz said. "Although I don't suppose there'll be any inns in the godforsaken country."

"'Tis just as well we brought enough ale with us to fuel an army, then!" Megan shouted.

Martin's mood had been lifting ever since he had received the dream, and now he felt filled with a new purpose.

"Keep the ale ready, milady," he said. "For we will be riding hard, and will be in need of it at journey's end."

For the first time since leaving Stirling he didn't need the Woodsman's song…not as sung by Hillman, anyway. The air played in his head, and, to his wonder, he found he could call it up at will when he remembered Sean's words.

I am the Balance, he told himself. And for once he believed he might be able to keep the wolf at bay.

"Lead them out, Fitz. And no slacking. Let us see if we can pass my Captain on the road."

Sean traveled north as fast as he was able through the thick snowdrifts, but still there were no signs of any Others.

He passed several keeps that showed signs of recent habitation, but all were now quiet and empty. Not so quiet that he wished to spend a night in any of them, though. He slept in the woods, with the practiced air of a watchman…always alert, even when both eyes were closed.

There had been no more voices…no more attempts by the Boy-King to seduce him.

Mayhap I have given him a fright, he thought, and snorted with amusement. His horse snorted back at him, making him laugh aloud. It sounded out of place in the stillness of the clearing where he'd spent the night.

He felt like he'd been alone forever, in a world bounded only by trees and snow. He had no idea whether Martin had received his message, and at times he thought his mental encounters with the Boy-King were no more than figments of his imagination.

Alchemists and serpents, woodsmen and severed heads that talk…I am living in one of Campbell's stories, he thought.

But that thought always brought him back to his quest. He knew one thing, at least…he had little option but to stay on his path north. Mary Campbell was in the hands of a great evil and he had promised to save her.

The depth of snow had been getting less for several miles when he realized he was coming down off a high plateau. He descended through thin cloud that slowly evaporated to reveal a rolling vista below.

To his north, some thirty miles distant, a vast loch stretched away into the mist, while over to the east the land fell away to a long open moor. Even as he gazed in that direction Sean knew…that was where the Boy-King was.

And if the Other is there, Mary Campbell will be close by.

He did not have a plan, but if he meant to try to pass for

an Other again, he would have to travel on foot from here on. A flesh and blood horse would not let an Other ride on it, and it would give him away immediately.

He unsaddled the horse and slapped its flanks. At first it would not leave him and he had to hit it hard.

"Get off with you!" he shouted. "Or shall I give your neck another bite?"

Almost as if it understood, the horse finally bolted. Sean watched it as it fled...uphill and back along their trail. If Martin was indeed following him, he'd be one horse to the better. Leaving his saddle atop a large stone outcrop, Sean shouldered his saddlebags and headed down the hill.

Two horses met up with Martin's band less than a day later. On the second was a messenger from Cumberland. The carrier was flushed, and looked almost exhausted, but Fitz pressed food and ale on him, and by the time Martin had read the letter he delivered, the lad looked almost human.

Martin folded the letter, and shouted, so that all his men could hear.

"The Protector means to finish with this Maid once and for all," he said. "And we are to be the vanguard. He brings his whole strength north...and he wants us to make sure that the Others are held here until he arrives. What say you, men? Shall we ensure that the Maid is suitably prepared?"

His men roared and cheered, but there was tension in Martin's face as he turned to face Fitz.

"Cumberland is near on a full day behind us," he said. "And I have orders to press on to Culloden. If what I fear is true, we have just been ordered to hold back the whole dark army. One hundred men against how many thousand?"

"Let us wait until we see the lay of the land," Fitz replied, clasping a meaty hand on Martin's shoulder. "Besides, Master Hillman looks like he has a new way of killing them in mind."

They had made camp beside a pool at the foot of a long, roaring cascade, and Martin was aware that Edward Hillman had been sitting, knee deep in water, for more than an hour now. He was holding a shoulder pack, one of those modified to hose the garlic mixture, under the cascade, and playing with a hose that served as an outlet. Martin noticed that he was managing to send a fine spray of droplets clear across the pond, without having to pump the shoulder bag.

The boy looked up excitedly.

"Let me guess, Master Hillman," Martin said. "You have an idea?"

"Yes, Sire. If you can find us a running river, I believe I can provide you with a weapon that will fire constantly."

"Aye, young master," Fitz said. "But it is a lot of effort for such a small gain." The look Edward Hillman gave Fitz was almost pitying.

"You don't understand. If the river flows fast enough, we can power the big bellows to fire even further than a man can pump…and we won't need to transport barrels…and…"

Martin stopped him. He could already see the weapon in his mind's eye…and young Hillman did seem to have a truly remarkable knack for putting Others to the final death.

"Tell Fitz what you need, and make it so," he said, bending to lift the lad from the water. "And get yourself dried off and warmed up. Megan will kill me if you catch the pneumonia."

Martin left the pair to it, and went to call the troops to horse. He noticed as they broke camp that young Hillman was ensconced in the back of one of the carts, in earnest conversation with two older troopers who looked at him, first with amusement, then with wonderment and respect.

They had only traveled a mile or so when they came across Sean Grant's horse traveling slowly towards them.

At first Sean kept his mind on heading east, towards the moor, but every time his attention wandered he found himself veering north, towards the large body of water, as if he was being drawn there.

Mary Campbell was to the east, of that he was

certain…he could feel it. But something in what he had become was minded to go north, and kept turning him that way, like a compass needle.

I am the Balance, he said, but that only made it worse…he found himself walking north with no memory of having set himself in that direction.

He focused his mind on Mary Campbell, trying to remember every detail of her face, her hair, her eyes…but when he remembered to look at the trail, he found that he was once more heading north.

It looks like someone wants to speak to me.

Someone…or something.

Sean unsheathed his sword and allowed himself to be taken.

If it is a fight the Boy-King wants, then 'tis a fight he will get, he thought grimly.

But in truth, the compulsion he was under did not feel like the work of an Other. It had none of the blackness he associated with the Boy-King's forays into his mind…none of the feeling of invasion. Instead it was like being a child led by the hand by a doting parent.

He was led in this manner for the better part of a day and a half and night was beginning to fall on the second day when he passed through a thick coppice of trees and found himself standing on the shore of a vast stretch of water.

Barely a ripple broke the still, black surface, as if a sheet of glass lay there, covered by the thinnest film of liquid.

As suddenly as it has come the compulsion disappeared, and Sean looked down to find himself ankle-deep in the shallows. A sudden quiet fell over him, as if all nature had just drawn a breath.

Out in the blackness the water rose in a gray swell…something huge was coming to the surface, then a long neck rose up and a huge head turned to look at Sean. Once more pictures filled his mind…pictures from his recent past.

He is standing on the wall of Milecastle as Duncan Campbell brings a sickened daughter to the Gate.

He is sleeping beside Mary Campbell as she lies on her back beside him, her eyes filling with tears.

He is fighting for his life back in Milecastle, and in the melee he doesn't notice that he has been bitten…no more than a scratch, but enough to seal his fate.

He is lying on a stone slab as Lennan, the Woodsman gives him blood and life that Sean might live.

He is in the cottage of a strange little man who calls himself Alexander Seton

The memory vision stops, but not before he hears Seton's voice, as if it comes from a great distance.

You only lack the water to complete the great Arcanum.

He still didn't know what the phrase meant, but he believed he was about to find out.

The water serpent's head bent closer, so close that Sean could feel the heat of its breath, could smell the heavy fishy odor that emanated from it.

Suddenly Sean remembered a previous vision, of a serpent not unlike the one before him. And then came a further memory…of the coiled mosaic in Linlithgow Palace. Panic began to rise inside him.

I am the Balance, he told himself.

"No," a voice said, a voice he knew had come from the serpent. "But you will be."

A black wave rushed towards him. Sean closed his eyes and fell into darkness.

"We were first-born," a voice said in the blackness, "Earth, air, fire and water. And all that is, was and will be is part of us and we are part of them and all is all together. In the days when the stars were young everything sang that it was so. But nothing lasts forever, and the Balance is fleeting.

"We quarreled, there in the dark, my brothers and I. We quarreled because we could. And because we could, we were sundered, each to his own and his own to each, and my song washed into the seas like tears on a rainy day.

"And now the Balance is given sparingly to those that have the eyes to see, the heart to sing, the mind to live.

"Welcome to the song."

The voice fell quiet. Darkness surrounded Sean like warm velvet. Feeling no fear, he drifted to sleep, rocked by the pounding of his own heart.

Martin stood on a small hill overlooking a huge expanse of moor. To his left there was a small waterfall formed by the joining of two streams cascading over a rocky outcrop.

"Will this suffice?" he said to Edward Hillman.

He watched the lad peruse the site in the same way that old Menzies used to study a chessboard. The boy pursed his lips, then nodded.

"Give us an hour," he said. "And you'll have your weapon."

They had approached the moor an hour before, wary and quiet, but there was no sign of the Others, or of them having been there. As Martin turned away from Edward Hillman he almost bumped into Megan. She was staring out over the moor, cold fear filling her eyes.

"He's here," she said. "I can feel him, here in my heart."

"Rollo?" Martin asked.

She didn't reply, merely nodded, and spat on the ground at her feet before turning away. Her tears had stopped, leaving her eyes clear bright and cold.

"I hope she never looks at me that way," Fitz said at his side, his voice almost a whisper. "I believe I might just die on the spot."

"Aye," Martin replied. "And be happy to go."

The quartermaster stared out to where his wife had looked seconds before.

"Is she right?" he said. "Do you think they are there?"

"Sean Grant said so," Martin replied. "And the word of an officer of the Watch is good enough for me."

"And it usually is for me, as well, Sire," Fitz said, but as he scanned the bleak expanse of mud and heather, there was doubt in his eyes. "But why even the Boy-King would choose this place is beyond my understanding." In truth, Martin agreed with him. The scene before them was one of bleak desolation.

The sun had begun its journey down to the west, but it was all but invisible behind thin, slate gray cloud. The light was flat and no shadows were cast; a damp gloom seemed to hang everywhere. Even the cascade was silent now, its previous wild rushing stilled by the dam and sluice system that Hillman and his helpers were building.

After Martin had got his band arranged in a tight circle of men, wagons and horses around the base of the hillock, he went to see what Hillman was building.

The men already had a water wheel functioning in the gorge beneath the falls. It was spinning so fast it was almost impossible to see the individual paddles.

"Very pretty, sir," Fitz said. "But what use is it?"

"Watch and learn, old man," Hillman said. "It is obvious you were an innkeeper, not a miller, else you would know the power of falling water."

The two men working with Hillman carried a contraption of wood, string and leather strapping over to the water wheel and began hammering the pieces together.

"You see," young Edward Hillman said. "You can turn the circular motion of the wheel into an up and down motion with a series of cogs and wheels…and with the up and down motion you can create pressure and…"

Once more Martin was struck by the way Hillman made him think of the old doctor. Menzies used to make his eyes glaze over in exactly the same way.

"Just show me when it is done, Edward," he said. "If it is as good a trick as the kites were, then we'll all be happy."

"It wasn't a trick. It was science. And…"

Fitz clapped the boy on the back.

"The Thane knows," he said. "He is pulling your leg."

The boy looked at Martin, cautious, unbelieving.

"Away with you, young Sire," Martin said. "If you have found a better way to kill Others, then I will make you a Captain of the Guard."

The boy's eyes went large, and he had a broad smile on his face as he turned away.

"Do you truly mean that, sir?" Fitz said. "You might see

the cold fire in Megan's eyes again if you play false by the boy."

"Oh, I meant it, to be sure. A Captain of the Guard's job is to kill Others. And young Hillman is passing good at it."

"It's not fair," a small voice said.

Both men looked over to where Harold Hillman was helping to fill the barrels for the bellows.

"Edward gets all the glory. And all I get is donkey-work pumping water."

Martin laughed.

"A Thane can have several captains, but he only has need of one minstrel," he said. "Come down from that cart and sing me a song. I'll decide later which one of you will get to sit at my right hand."

Harold Hillman's face lit up in a broad smile. He jumped from the cart. The sudden movement caused the cart to sway slightly. There was a loud crack, and the whole wagon fell to one side. Two barrels of garlic and silver laden water toppled to the ground and smashed, emptying a small flood down the small slope towards the moor.

The first, burning, Other came up out of the quagmire less than five seconds later.

Sean came awake slowly, but he was still deep in the velvet blackness.

"We were still young when the blood-lust came on my red brother," the voice said, continuing as if there had been no pause.

"The fire was consuming him, and the rest of us had no defense against its power. So we called on the Maker, and the Maker made us flesh, so that we were neither one thing nor the other and we had no Balance. But the maker saw that my red brother's fire was quenched, and it was good.

"And for millennia all was as it was and we were together in the flesh. And many things rose and lived and fell again to be with the maker. And our red brother was quiet and it was good."

Then came man."

Somewhere out in the deep black Sean could see a pale gleam, like the moon seen through a cloud.

"My red brother and man were natural brothers in blood, and the fire grew once more.

"And since then the Balance has become ever harder while the fire grows ever stronger. But the Maker is kind, and he gives the Balance where he will, in order to quench the fire, for a while at least.

"Welcome to the Balance."

The pale gleam blazed suddenly brilliant white, banishing the black. Sean fell forward, face first into bitingly cold water.

"Others!" Fitz shouted, and leapt onto the cart containing the remaining bellows and barrels. "To arms!"

The encampment was a sudden flurry of activity as men groped for weapons while other troopers tried to calm horses suddenly panicked by the commotion.

Martin jumped up beside Fitz and took the other side of the bellows. Together they turned and pointed the weapon down the slope.

They faced a scene from hell. Martin thought he'd seen the full scale of the effects of the garlic and silver, but it was now doing its worst under the damp soil. The things that pushed their way to the surface were already fused and melted...squirming, wormlike things like giant maggots... maggots that popped and hissed as the blue flame burned over and through them.

But already Others further down the slope were pushing themselves from the soil, coming up out of the ground with wet, sucking, noises that Martin could hear even above the rising screams of those dying for the second time.

"Aim over the top of the burning ones!" Fitz shouted.

Martin nodded, and together they started up the bellows, and the screaming went up a notch.

The next ten minutes passed in a blur of noise and gunfire, with Martin and Fitz emptying eight barrels of garlic and silver into the moor. Thick greasy smoke hung in the air, and the stench of death stuck in the back of Martin's throat.

He looked over the top of the bellows and saw Fitz smiling grimly back at him.

The ground for more than thirty yards beneath them was a sodden mass of mud and molten flesh that steamed and bubbled as it cooled. There was no trace of any Others…none that moved at any rate. Martin looked around his troopers…he had not lost a single man.

Harold Hillman stood in front of Martin, tears streaming down his face. "I'm sorry," he said. "It's all my fault, I broke the cart, and…"

Martin stepped down from the cart and gathered the boy to him.

"The cart broke. You did not…if it is anyone's fault it was mine for not having the cart checked. Now come. A victory in battle calls for a song, not tears."

Soon Harold Hillman was leading the troop in song.

"That was well done, sir," Fitz said. "Mayhap Megan will look kindly on you, after all."

"I hope I have time to see it," Martin said, looking towards the sky. "For I fear night is nearly on us…and there is plenty more room out on that moor for more of the bastards."

Sean spluttered and coughed as he swallowed a mouthful of water, and managed to push himself up onto his feet at the second attempt. He stood in little more than a foot of water. The loch stretched away from him, flat and featureless. Sean was shocked to see that it was getting dark. He had no idea how long he had been standing in the water, but he had no sensation of cold. In fact, he had no sensation of anything.

From the corner of his eye he caught a flash of white reflected in the water below. It was only when he put out his hand to investigate that he realized that what was being reflected was his own face.

He studied the back of his hands. If they were anything to go by, his face was white indeed. He turned both hands over. His palms were brilliant white, and completely unlined, as if he was carved from the finest marble. But his skin was warm, and, testing, he found he still had a heartbeat, although he was unsure if his blood yet ran in him, for he could see no sign of veins.

A strange calm had settled on Sean. For the first time since his experience with the woodsmen he did not feel on edge. He could no longer sense the raving of the Other inside, but he felt strong…strong and fearless.

"My soul is empty," he whispered, and for the first time began to realize what the woodsmen meant when they said it. The air around him tingled and rang in a low bass note, counterpointed by a tuneful whistle that rose up from the loch itself. Behind him the trees hummed, dancing in the wind, and Sean laughed in joy as he saw it. The laugh stilled as he turned his head eastward.

There was a discordant crash in his ears, a ripping scrape like metal upon metal. And even as Sean looked, a red haze seemed to rise up from the East, a haze that pulsed and grew. It was from this that the disruption came, and Sean immediately moved towards it. The Boy-King was there, and Mary Campbell. But more importantly, the Balance was disrupted. And he knew how to fix it.

Martin addressed his troopers just as the last of the daylight was leeching out of the sky.

"The Protector is coming," he said. "And he will rid the land of the Maid once and for all."

The men cheered as one, and the sound echoed around the moor.

"He asks that we, his eyes and ears in the north, keep the Maid warm till he arrives. What say you men? Shall we begin the revels early?"

Again the men cheered.

"Master Hillman. Are we ready?"

"Aye, sir," the lad said.

"Then let them come!" Martin shouted. Once more a cheer went up, then silence fell on the moor as the sun finally dropped over the horizon and night came to Culloden.

They stood, tense and expectant, while the darkness deepened around them. At one point a shot rang out, followed by a sharp volley of four shots before anyone had time to think.

"In Jesu's name, man. Why did you go and shoot a crow?" a voice suddenly called out, and a ripple of nervous laughter ran round the circle.

That went some way to lower the tension and, after an hour with no further incident, Martin had the men stand down.

"Are you sure it's safe, sir?" Fitz said.

"By no means," Martin replied. "But they're apt to shoot each other if we keep this up. Post double guards by all means, but get the rest of them fed. It could be a long night."

Ten minutes later Martin walked up to the hill to see what manner of thing young Hillman had built.

The water wheel was still in place beneath the cascade, but now it was joined to an outlandish contraption of wood and rope. The wheel seemed to be turning an axle as thick as a man's arm. That axle in turn was attached to a bewildering array of cogs and wheels that ended in a plunger that was currently pounding up and down twice a second inside an empty barrel.

"I'm loath to ask," Martin said. "But what does it do?"

Young Hillman looked up from his kneeling position beside the barrel. He looked exhausted, but there was a huge grin on his face.

"We're nearly ready, Sire," he said. "Give me five minutes. I just have to attach the inflows and the hose for the outflow and you shall have a demonstration of the power of water."

The boy stepped over towards the axle, and pulled a lever next to a large cog. The water wheel kept turning, but the plunger in the barrel stopped abruptly.

"Is it broken?" Martin asked, suddenly realizing how little he knew in the face of the lad's invention.

"No, Sire," Hillman said. "'Tis merely a safety device to stop taking someone's hand off. It works by taking one of the cogs out of the system temporarily and..."

Martin tuned the boy out...not by intent, but he suddenly felt like he was once more at his lessons with old Menzies, and the sudden intensity of emotion of the memory almost brought him to tears. He was clearing his eyes when he became aware that young Hillman was watching him warily.

"Sire?" the lad said.

"It's all right," Martin said. "I'm not about to go Berserker on you."

The young man looked so distraught that Martin had to laugh. "Forgive me, Master Hillman, I am a mite distracted at the moment. I will leave you to your task...else that five minutes might turn to twenty." The boy looked relieved to be dismissed. Martin was about to ask another question, but young Hillman was already back at work, deeply engrossed in hooking a hose to a faucet attached to the barrel in which the plunger stood.

"How goes it?" Fitz asked when Martin returned to the line.

"Oh, it goes well," Martin said. "I'm still not sure what it does, but it goes very well."

Fitz was about to reply when the first droning notes of the Others' pipes drifted across the moor. Out in the dark a drum took up the beat, and another joined in. Soon the night was pounding with the throb of drum and screech of pipes.

Martin felt the rage build in him...the need to rip and tear.

"I am the Balance," he told himself, and began to hum the Woodsman's song. Once more it was enough to keep the wolf at bay, but the drums beat louder still. Battle was coming, and Martin prayed to the heavens that he be allowed to see it through as man and only man.

He would not have long to wait to find out if his prayers would be answered.

"Here they come," a voice yelled out along the line. Martin jumped up beside the bellows once more and Fitz joined him. "One more time, old man?" Martin said. "One last time," Fitz said. "We can only hope," Martin replied. Then there was no more time for talk.

Sean was aware that he was running faster than he ever had in his life, faster than any man had ever run, faster even than the swiftest deer.

He was on his third hour heading east, yet he felt no strain, no tiredness. The red haze he could see to the east was closer now, and the sense of 'wrongness' bit deeper.

"I'm coming for you," he whispered. And, as if his desire had made it so, he found himself once more inside the mind of the Boy-King, looking out over the blackness of a dark moor.

"Ah, the young lover returns," the now familiar voice of the Other said. Sean felt a probe in his own mind, but he cast it aside as if it was no more than a fly in his ear. He felt the Other try again, so Sean let him in, let him see what the "Grand Arcanum" had made. The Other recoiled, and Sean was aware of his surprise.

"I am beyond your power now, milord," Sean said. "Mayhap it is your turn to bend the knee."

"A conjurer's trick will not save you," the Other said.

"Oh, it is no trick. Come to me and I'll show you." At first Sean sent out his compulsion, and the Boy-King actually turned, and began to move away from his bodyguard.

Sean smiled grimly, as he felt the panic that gripped the Other. The Boy-King strained against the leash that was slowly drawing him in, and pressure grew inside Sean's mind. But he managed to get the Other to move ten yards towards him before the strain got too much.

"I'm coming for you," Sean sent, imaging the loudest cry he could muster.

Just before the link between them was broken he saw the Other stagger and fall, and felt the fear that had suddenly lodged in the Boy-King's dark heart.

Martin and Fitz were ready to start pumping the bellows. From out of the moor Others started to appear...rank after rank of them, coming forward. Not with any sense of military discipline, but each with its own ravening hunger driving it on.

Fitz made to pump the bellows, but Martin stopped him.

"They're not in range yet."

"Yes, they are," a voice said. Martin turned to see Edward Hillman signaling to a man standing beside the water wheel. Martin heard the plunger scrape against the side of the barrel, and then there was suddenly an arc of water stretching out over the moor. Others in a thirty-yard swathe started burning immediately, their flesh boiling off them in waxy lesions. They fell where they stood. More of them, panicked by the burning, ran back into the spray, and they too started to fall in their droves.

Almost before it had started, the Others fell back into the darkness, leaving their fallen brethren to burn and decay on the sodden mud. Edward Hillman leapt around behind the ranks of troopers, almost unable to contain his joy.

"Edward," Martin said. "Don't bother ever explaining anything to me. Just build it."

The water wheel was still turning, and the water still arced out above them.

"Better turn it off," Martin said. "We don't want to use up all the garlic and silver."

"Oh, that's all right," Hillman said. "We turned the valve off. That's just water...but the Other's don't know that."

Martin saw that Hillman was right...the water was spraying out over a huge swathe of moorland, and the

Others had pulled away from it. Now they merely stood there, staring at the troopers in naked hunger, but unwilling to move any closer. "We had better watch our positions, Fitz," Martin said. "Hillman is not only smart, he's also developing cunning."

"More than cunning," Hillman said, and signaled once more to the man at the wheel. Martin saw the man pull two levers, and the height of the arc of water immediately doubled.

The Others fell and burned in their hundreds. Two minutes later the moor was once more empty. The pipes and drums had stopped, and there was only the thwup-thwup of the water pump.

An area of land almost a hundred yards square lay sodden yet burning. Of the bodies of the Others who had fallen there was no trace, just a gray bubbling mass of twice-dead tissue.

"Now we can turn it off," Hillman said.

Sean was still moving east, but a niggling doubt had settled in his mind. The red haze still hung before him, but now there was a new sound among the new music he heard, a dissonance off to the north.

He turned slightly in that direction. Although night had fallen he could see everything sharp and clear, as if the sun still shone in the sky. He was ascending a slight slope, that when he looked north he was looking down across a stunted wood. Far beyond the wood a thin strip of silver glistened as an estuary showed up in the moonlight. And over the estuary hung another red haze...smaller than the one that marked the Boy-King's position, but pulsing, and growing with each pulse.

The wrongness was there as well, and Sean sent it out a thought, seeking to find a cause, but all he could discern was a formless hunger, and a desire to rip and tear. He felt suddenly warm, cocooned in deep red velvet that held a slow burn. It was seductive, and Sean felt drawn down deeper, to a black core where something lay, waiting to be born…his thought had taken him to the Boy-King's child!

Even as he pulled away from the connection, even as he changed direction and started to move north, he heard the last thought of the child ringing in his ears.

Father. I am coming soon.

Martin stood for long minutes and watched the smoke rise from the smoldering morass of the moor.

"What do you think Fitz…five hundred?"

There was wonderment in the old innkeeper's eyes.

"And more," he said. "I do believe the Other's will never again be capable of attacking as a armed force. We have found a way to stop them." Martin had been thinking the same thing…with one of these 'water cannons' every hundred yards along the wall the land would be safe and secure. He wasn't about to start celebrating yet, though.

"They will not be so unprepared to meet us again," he said, remembering the siege at Derby. "Make sure the men have a full supply of shot…he will send the mind-slaves soon, for garlic and silver will not stop them."

Martin was proved right ten minutes later when the pipes ands drums took up their battle rhythm again, and pale figures began to come out of the dark, first in tens, then in hundreds, an army of the enslaved.

"My God," he heard Fitz exclaim. "There are thousands of them."

And now it really begins.

"Wait for my order," he called out along the line. All around the circle of carts men were praying. Some even went as far as to clutch Bibles in their hands, as if the power of the Lord would somehow leech through into them.

"Young Hillman!" Martin shouted. "Keep the cannon ready. I fear we will have more use for it ere too long."

He saw that the pale attackers had drawn closer.

"Fire at will!" he called, and the air filled with the noise of gunshot and the stench of death.

The defenders circle was tight enough that the men were two ranks deep, three in places. They were able to pour volley after volley into the approaching mind-slaves.

But all they were achieving was the slowdown of the attack. The enslaved came on over the bodies of the fallen, and Martin knew that the Boy-King cared not how many fell…he had no concern for the lives of men-and-onlymen…there were always more recruits available.

Smoke hung heavy over the defenders, and the acrid stench of gunpowder and burnt flesh caught in the back of the throats. The nearest of the attackers was now no more than ten yards from the defensive line.

Martin looked over at Fitz. The innkeeper was stoking his old blunderbuss with what looked like a pound of shot. His face was streaked with powder and sweat, and there was a grim, hard resolve in the set of his features. Martin realized that the same expression could be seen all around the circle, and the same one was probably on his face.

The innkeeper fired the blunderbuss, and, without even looking at its effect, immediately began to reload.

Martin saw what had happened, though. Five of the attackers had fallen, their flesh torn to shreds. The ranks behind merely walked over the fallen as if they did not exist.

"How can we fight such as these?" he said, having to shout to be heard above the cacophony.

"With heart and soul," Fitz said, grimly. "There is no other way, no matter who, or what you are fighting."

Martin wished for the stout defense of his wall at Milecastle, but all they had were the wooden carts and their horses. And soon the defenses would be sore tested, for the attacking line was only five yards away. They were dying in vast numbers, but still they came on, inexorable, relentless, driven.

"If you have any tricks up your sleeves, now is the time," Fitz said.

Sean Grant ran with the wind, bounding over both heather and rock alike, as fleet as a March hare, as sure of his footing as a mountain goat.

At one point he discarded his leather coat and let it

fall… it was merely slowing him down. The red haze of the 'wrongness' drew him on like a beacon, northwards. He knew that his quarry was near the estuary, and he was proved right when he came round the side of a small hill and found himself looking down on a squat black watchtower overlooking a small harbor.

There was a black boat moored at the dock, and it itself carried a red haze that sent a dark chord singing in Sean's head. But the focus, the thing that had drawn Sean here, was centered in the black tower. The red haze hung heavy over it, fading and glowing in time with the heartbeat of the child inside.

Sean leapt forward, and was at the main door of the tower in a blink. He raised a foot to kick in the door.

"NO!" The Boy-King screamed inside Sean's head.

"YES!" Sean screamed back, and was gratified to be given the sight of the Boy-King falling to the ground, blood pouring from eyes, nose and ears.

Sean followed through on the kick and knocked the door off its hinges, where it fell to the floor with a crash that echoed in the suddenly still night. He stepped over, and into the blackness beyond.

The first of the attackers was now pressed up tight against the cart beneath Martin. Fitz had taken to using the blunderbuss as a club, wielding it with such force that it caved in the heads of any that were unfortunate enough to come within his reach.

All along the defensive line hand-to-hand fighting broke out, and at the far edge of the circle from Martin and Fitz one of the carts suddenly overturned. The troopers fell back, and a horde of shambling mind-slaves filled the gap.

"Milecastle!" Martin shouted, and leapt from the cart, his musket raised like a club.

He took the first one in the ribs, and felt bones break as he hit it again, but the second blow snapped his musket in two, and he only had time to step inside a flailing punch before he was in the middle of a rolling melee.

Rage grew in him as he punched and gouged, and once more he felt the ripple of thick hair erupt and spread up his arm. His nails became talons as he reached forward, meaning to rip the throat from the pale thing that faced him.

And suddenly the glazed look left the mind-slave's eyes and it backed away from Martin, screaming in fear.

But the rage still held him and Martin grabbed the retreating man by the throat. His grip was tightening when the man spoke.

"Please. Don't kill me…Please."

"I am the Balance," Martin said.

His grip loosened.

"I am the Balance." The wolf's hairs receded as fast as they had come. He opened his hand and freed the man from his grip.

All around the circle those suddenly released from the thrall of the Boy-King were fleeing in terror and confusion. Some, clearly driven mad, continued fighting, but they were easily quelled, and in a matter of minutes the moor was once again quiet apart from a forlorn wailing of a lost soul out in the darkness.

Martin held his hand in front of his face. He remembered the hairs, the talons. But now there was only his own grime-covered skin.

"I am the Balance," he said, and gasped as the hairs once more sprouted on the back of his hand. He felt tension grow in him, then ebb as he brought to mind the Woodsman's tune.

I control you. You are merely part of what I am, he thought.

If there was anything inside to answer him it kept quiet. Fitz looked at him…a puzzled look.

"It did not happen this time," the innkeeper said. "I told you it was the stress of losing the old man that set you off in Derby."

Martin realized that Fitz did not know about the wolf's re-appearance in Newcastleton or Stirling.

If we live through this night I will allow him to get me

drunk…then I'll tell him…if I can.

"Make sure the men are restocked with shot and anything else they need. And get that cart back on its wheels…I don't know what happened to the mind-slaves, but there is still an army of Others out there."

While Fitz went to carry out his orders Martin inspected the troopers. Miraculously, they had suffered no fatalities. There were three wounded…one broken leg from a man under the cart when it toppled…one broken nose from a punch, and one with a badly bitten leg. None were life threatening.

He found Harold and Edward Hillman with Megan. They were helping to serve the troopers with ale or water.

"Pardon me, milady," he said. "But I must take our cannon-maker back to his work. We need to be ready."

"Take him, then," Megan said. "But woe betide you if he comes to harm."

"No Other will harm him," Harold said. "For he would just bore them to the final death with his toys."

"They're not toys…" Edward began, but was unable to continue as Megan cuffed both boys around the ears.

"Get off with you both," she said.

The boys ran off laughing.

"They are fine boys," Megan said.

"Aye. And they need a mother," Martin replied.

"She already has a son," a voice they both recognized called out from the dark. Martin knew who it was even before he turned.

Out in the dark, just beyond the churned up mess that marked the range of Hillman's cannon, Gord Rollo stood at the head of a vast throng of Others.

Sean strode through the blackness inside the tower as if it was fully lit by torchlight. The sense of wrong was so strong that it buzzed in his head and vibrated through his teeth, sending a throbbing through his skull. He was close. And getting closer.

"My King has given me the honor of finally ridding him of an irritation," Rollo said.

"Come closer if you have an itch!" Fitz called back. "I will be happy to scratch it for you."

Rollo merely laughed.

"I will clasp myself to you one more time, old man," the Other said. "But first we must find out if you yet remember how to fight us."

Rollo raised an arm, and once more the pipes and drums echoed across the moor and the army of Others began to move forward.

"This is madness," Martin said. "The water cannon will destroy them."

"That it might," Fitz said. "But there is an awful lot of them."

"Then let us have at it," Martin said grimly. "Master Hillman…start it up once more. Let us test their taste for garlic and silver."

The arc of water shone in the moonlight like a silver bridge. The first splash hit the ground just in front of Rollo, forcing the Other to step backwards. Martin smiled, and was about to call out a mocking jeer when he saw that Rollo was watching the cannon's spray closely, assessing its trajectory and timing the sweep as it panned from left to right.

He saw immediately what the Other was searching for.

"Fitz. To the bellows. There is a spot on our left where the cannon is no more than a fine spray."

Rollo had noticed it too, and was directing the throng of Others in that direction. Soon they started to push through the thin sheet of falling water. Small flames and lesions burst from their skin, and their feet smoked where they trod on the sodden ground, but they kept coming on, even after they came into range of Martin and Fitz's bellows. By sheer force of numbers they were forcing their way closer to the small circle of defenders. Soon they were close enough for Martin to see the bloodlust in their eyes.

The ground floor of the black tower proved to be silent and empty, but Sean already knew that what he sought was above him. He could feel the wrongness of it pressing down on him like a dead weight.

He took the stairs two at a time and burst through the door at the top.

"Always in a hurry," a voice said. "And look how pale you are. You must remember to feed, my boy, or you'll never reach your maturity."

He was in a bedchamber, one dominated by a huge, ornate four-poster bed. Mary Campbell lay on the bed, on top of the covers. Her belly was swollen and distended, black veins crawling over it as if it was a piece of living marble. She was naked, but Sean did not see that. He saw only her hair, now full blood red, and her eyes, filled with crimson gore that ran in runnels down her cheeks.

At each corner of the four-poster stood a guard...four ancient Others in full highland regalia. Each rested their crossed palms on the hilts of heavy broadswords, and their eyes stared at Sean with a cold disdain. They did not move as Sean walked into the room.

"A boy should be more circumspect in a lady's chambers," the voice said. Sean turned to his left. Standing by the fireplace was the huge bloated Other Sean had chased through the palace at Linlithgow.

"Lord Falkirk," Sean said. "I refuse to take lessons in manners from such as you."

The fat Other looked down at the blood and gore smeared over his clothing. "If I had known you were coming I would have made myself more presentable."

Sean unsheathed his sword. "I fear you will not have long to worry about your appearance." He moved forward.

"Longer than you," the Other said, and moved to one side. Sean found himself looking down into a familiar golden chalice, and there, in the midst of a lump of gore and gristle, a single, red eye started back at him. Sean felt a cold grip take hold in his mind.

You are just in time, it said in his head. The blood of my blood will be hungry after his birthing.

The garlic and silver rain was felling the Others in their hundreds, and most of the rest were soon dispatched by Fitz and Martin.

"This is no way to fight!" Martin called. "Surely this cannot be their only strategy?"

"I fear not, sir," Fitz replied. "Look!"

Beyond the veil of water six larger shapes loomed, approaching fast. Even before Martin had time to distinguish what they were, six horses pounded through the spray in a tight wedge. Each of the horses was covered head to toe in heavy swathes of cloth, but even then the red-flaring eyes showed they were full turned. And atop each horse sat a heavily swaddled figure, hunched close to the horses' neck.

"Fitz!" Martin shouted in alarm.

"I see them," the innkeeper said and together they turned the bellows. But they were too late.

The defending troopers only had time for one volley. Two of the horses stumbled and fell, but their riders rolled with the fall like acrobats and kept coming. Martin and Fitz were able to turn their weapon on the two prone horses, but they were unable to stop the rest of the attackers from crashing through a cart like it was matchwood. Troopers tried to jump on to the attacking horses, but they were moving too fast.

"They are after the weapon!" Fitz cried. Martin saw that he was right. Without a thought he abandoned the bellows and threw himself after the last horseman. He was vaguely aware that a trooper had jumped up beside Fitz and that they were trying to turn the bellows around, but they would be too late…the Others were already halfway across the circle.

Two other horses were brought down in a rapid volley of shots, and one of the riders was doused, flamed and staked in a matter of seconds, but there were still three horses and five Others in the band that smashed into the small group of defenders around the weapon.

Martin caught up with one of the unhorsed riders. It

never knew what had hit it. Its neck was broken and it was staked before it hit the ground. Another horse fell, its leg taken from under it by a large axe. When it fell, it took six troopers to keep it down, and the spray of blood from its heart covered them all in thick red gore.

Martin saw the first of the water cannon's defenders fall, his hand bitten off by the savage teeth of one of the horses. He put on an extra burst of speed when he realized that it was Edward Hillman who had stepped into the man's place.

The boy's face looked as pale as an Other as the great horse bore down on him, and Martin thought for sure the boy would be killed in an instant. But when the horse opened its great mouth Edward pumped the water sac under his arm and sent a long draught of garlic and silver straight down its gaping throat.

The beast exploded, as if blown out from the inside.

Martin had no time to stop and wonder, but he did register the grim smile on young Hillman's face.

The defender who had tackled the last horse was not so lucky. The horse trampled over him and had reached the water wheel in two strides. It made one quick turn and kicked the wheel into pieces just as Martin rolled under it and grabbed it by the neck.

Woodsman, if your gift was a true one, I have need of it now, he thought. And his prayer was answered. His hand became rough and hairs sprouted once more, but it was the talons he used to tear the beast's heart from its body. The animal fell on him, but it weighed little more than a child, and he was able to push it away. He stood, splattered in blood and gore, and surveyed the carnage the attack had wrought.

The attackers had all been put to the final death, but the damage was done…the water wheel lay in pieces. Young Hillman was already on his knees, assessing the damage.

"I can fix it," he said as he turned to Martin. "Keep us alive for five minutes and I can fix it."

"If I can get you those minutes, I will," Martin said, but in truth he was not sure they would last that long.

The throng that had been held back by the water were even now inching their way forward, and Fitz had only just managed to get the bellows back around facing the attackers. Martin strode quickly over to where Fitz was getting ready to send the first spray over the moor.

"Young Hillman needs five minutes. Can we give it to him?"

Fitz looked out over the moor and rubbed his mouth with his good hand. He looked for several moments, then shook his head.

"They are too many."

Martin nodded grimly.

"As I thought."

He jumped up into the cart beside Fitz and called out into the dark. "Rollo. Gord Rollo. In Stirling you wanted to fight me in single combat. Are you still man enough yet for a chance?"

At first there was no reply, and the Others kept coming forward. Martin wondered in dismay whether Rollo had been one of the Others dispatched in the earlier attack.

But a hush fell over the night, and the Others parted as Rollo stepped forward.

"Come down then, young wolf, and let us have at it," the Other said. "I have seen you fight… I have nothing to fear."

Martin stepped forward, but was stopped as Fitz put a hand on his shoulder.

"He is mine by right," the innkeeper said.

"That he is," Martin replied. "But you would kill him quick and we need five minutes. I can keep him dancing for a while. And if he takes me, then you can offer yourself next. Either way, we will get Hillman his time."

Fitz nodded.

"Just don't make it easy on him," the innkeeper said. "The bastard broke Megan's heart, and I'll never forgive him for that."

Martin clasped Fitz on the shoulder, nodded once, and jumped down out of the circle. He removed his long coat and took a single stake from the harness around his neck before passing it and the coat back to Fitz. Then he took vital seconds in rolling up his sleeves before stepping out onto the moor.

The eye held Sean in its grip.

I have memories of a time when the works of man were no more than daubs on a cave wall. The blood of my blood was made in the home of the red serpent, where my father's father's father was given dominion. For centuries, nay, millennia, the Blood Kings have waited, waited for the stars to be right so we could take our place above the cattle.

And now, when we are on the path of victory, you come, with the blood inside you. I know you frighten the blood of my blood. But you do not frighten me. I have met your like before.

Sean was powerless to stop the visions that rose up in his mind.

They are in the desert, three of them, of Arab blood, but with skin as pale as alabaster, their eyes blue pools with no white showing. They have been following a sign, a blazing ball of light in the sky. For three months it has been leading them on, far from their home in the high eastern mountains. They travel light, wearing only thin robes and carrying their gifts…of garlic, silver and stake.

A new king would be born, the signs had foretold it…and they intended to be at the birthing.

Eventually their travels bring them to a small town deep in a dry rocky waste. The people of the town are all enslaved, their expressions dull and lifeless as they gather around a small stable. The three make their way to the center, where a child lies in a manger, still bloody from its birth. Four soldiers in bronze armor stand around the child, while a tall Other feeds from the ravaged, lifeless body that had been the babe's mother.

The three do not hesitate; they move forward and draw thin silver swords.

They never stand a chance. The Blood-King raises his

head from his feeding, and spears them with his stare. They stand still, as if frozen to the spot, while the new Boy-King's guards start to cut them to ribbons. Mortally wounded, the last yet living manages to raise his head.

"The Pharaoh will have your head, I have seen it," he says to the tall Other.

"Aye," the Other replies grimly, "But my son will be King of Kings." The three like Sean die, cut to death by the guard's swords.

"So, you see," the voice said in Sean's head, "You have not the power to defy me."

"You forget," Sean replied. "I am an Officer of the Watch."

He leaned forward and lifted the bloody eye from the chalice.

Rollo stood thirty yards from the defender's circle, a broad smile across his features, his fangs showing brilliant white over his lower lip.

"First I will drink from you," he said. "Then I will have the wolf tamed. What do you think? Will I make a good guard for my King?"

Martin did not speak at first. His officer training had come to the fore, and he realized he was looking for a quick kill. He purposefully made himself slow down. He stopped moving forwards, coming to a halt five yards from the officer.

"You'd make a good arse-licker for your Maid. Tell me…is his shit sweet?"

"Sweeter than my good Mother's. Tell me," the Other said. "Has she opened her legs for you yet? Or has she forsaken you for the new boys? She always did like them young and succulent."

Martin nearly moved forward then, but Rollo seemed to enjoy listening to himself talk, and he was gaining valuable time for young Hillman. He was amazed that the Other was not pressing his army into attack; but if there was one thing he'd learned about the Blood-King and his "children" it was that vanity was by far the strongest of their vices.

"So are we going to have at it?" Rollo asked, "or are you going to just stand there and admire me?"

"I was merely wondering if you fight as well as you talk," Martin said. "It took a lot more of you and yours to subdue me in Newcastleton."

Rollo laughed, and behind him the Others in earshot laughed along, a dry, throaty thing with no humor in it.

"I think I have the besting of a whelp like you," he said, and finally moved forward.

Martin let him come. The Other had no weapons on him, sure of his own ability. Martin believed that he could take the Other down in a matter of seconds, but now was not the time to be showing off his skills. He feinted to the right and thrust the stake forward. When the Other moved to avoid it Martin punched him in the head, hard, sending Rollo staggering to the ground.

He ignored an opportunity to follow up with the stake. Instead he planted his hands on his hips, and let out a bellow of laughter. Behind him his troopers joined in, sending jeers and catcalls echoing around the moor.

"I fear Fitz was right about you all along," Martin said. "Once a mother's boy always a mother's boy."

Rollo smiled thinly.

"I will taste you soon, little boy," he said. "Then I will feed you to my dogs."

"Oh I know all about you and dogs," Martin said. "Although Fitz said you were more partial to planting your member in sheep."

The Other roared, and launched himself directly at Martin. Martin stepped aside, but Rollo had some fighting moves of his own and grabbed Martin's arm on the way past, throwing him off balance.

Martin tumbled into a roll, just managing to avoid the Other's outstretched arms. He slid in a patch of greasy, decomposing flesh, and fell sideways, coating the lower half of his body in noxious slime. He threw himself sideways, expecting an attack, but he turned to find the Other with its head tilted back, letting out a loud bellow of laughter.

Martin smiled grimly and stood upright. He let the Other come to him...every second gained was precious. "Is that the best you have?" Rollo asked, but this time Martin kept quiet, watching the Other's eyes. Thus time when Rollo moved in Martin stepped inside his reach and grabbed him tight with his left hand, punching the stake deep under the Other's ribs. He was careful to miss the heart, but not by much, and when Rollo stepped back Martin's stake was dripping red for the last three inches.

Rollo winced as he felt around the wound.

"Close," he whispered. "I will not let that happen again."

The Other threw itself at Martin, so fast that it seemed to fly. Martin barely had time to get his hand up in front of him before the weight of the Other slammed into him and they were both sent rolling and tumbling in the muck, biting and gouging.

Martin got a finger into the corner of the Other's eye, and something tore, but the Other's fangs were perilously close to his neck. He stuck his knee up, hard, between Rollo's legs, and was rewarded with a gasp of pain and the relaxing of the Other's grip on him. He rolled away, and was pleased to note that Rollo was slower getting to his feet.

Now the Other did not look white...he looked ashen and gray.

"Are you pained?" Martin asked grimly. "We can take a few minutes respite if you need time to recover?"

Rollo snorted. There was little human left in his eyes, and his fingers were curved into talons as he rose and come for Martin once more.

The end was near now...the dance was over and it was kill or be killed. Martin only hoped he had gained enough time. Then he didn't have any more time to think as the Other threw itself on him.

Sean felt the thing scream in his mind, and he felt it try to work its will on him, but his mind was like a slippery rock face and the Other could gain no hold. Sean sensed the fat Other by the fireplace begin to move, but time had slowed and folded. The drips of blood were only now beginning to fall from the gory mess in his hand.

The Blood-King can never truly die, the voice in his head screamed, for we are many who are one.

"Then I will give you the final death many times over," Sean said. "And that I promise, for I am the doom of your kind."

Sean concentrated his mind on the eye. At first he wondered if he was strong enough, then the blood in his palm began to thicken and dry. The white eye clouded, becoming opaque, then gray, then blackening from the edge.

No! the voice screamed, but it was as if it came from a great distance.

The eye blinked one last time, but the tendrils of command it sent out failed to grab hold of Sean.

Slowly Sean closed his fist, crushing the dry, blackened mess that lay there, until the ashes fell through his fist to sift gently in a slight breeze.

Sean felt a slight tingling in his palms, but no more than that as he blew the last of the crumbled ash away.

"It seems dead enough this time," he said, turning towards the fat Other. "What do you think, Lord Falkirk?"

The Other took one look at Sean's eyes and fled the room, his wailing screech trailing after him.

Rollo went straight for Martin's neck, and was only stopped because Martin was able to get a hand under the Other's chin and force it backwards. The Other's fangs were mere inches from his throat.

"The turning did not improve your breath any," Martin said, hoping for a reply, but the Other was past speech.

Martin leaned backwards, taking the Other's weight and turning it at the same time, rolling the Other over his left shoulder and turning himself in the same movement. For a split second the Other's chest lay open to attack. Martin drew back the stake to strike just as Rollo's eyes snapped wide open, and every Other on the battlefield screamed in unison. Martin punched the stake home, and spat in Rollo's face as the life went out of his eyes.

Without looking around Martin walked slowly back to the circle where his troopers were clapping and cheering. He couldn't hear them, for the Others were still screaming. The only thing Martin could equate it to was a wolf pack in full cry. But this was a wolf pack a thousand strong, and the noise was deafening.

Fitz had tears in his eyes as he helped Martin back onto the cart, but Martin didn't have time to react before Megan jumped up and caught him in an all-enfolding embrace.

"I lost one son at the siege of Derby," Megan said, her eyes full of tears. "But I am blessed, for look, the Lord has given me three in his stead." Martin's own eyes began to mist over, but not before he had looked over to where Edward Hillman stood, a big smile on his face and his thumb pointing skywards.

Martin turned back to Fitz.

"Are we ready?" he shouted.

"Aye!" the innkeeper shouted back. "As soon as this infernal caterwauling ceases."

Martin looked over the battlefield. The Others stood, rank after rank of them, their faces raised to the sky, their mouths hung slackly open, the sound pouring out of them like smoke from a wet-wood fire. It had a dirge-like tone, and, even as Martin thought it, the noise abruptly ceased. Out over the moor a lone piper played, the sound drifting in the wind, as lonely as a night owl's cry.

"Someone has died," Fitz said.

"Aye, and the Thane killed him," Harold Hillman said as he clambered onto the cart.

"Nay, young Hillman," Martin said. "Don't go making songs about this one...the pipes only play like that for the death of royalty. We can only hope that the Boy-King has gone to his final death."

Not before you, the well-recognized voice said in Martin's head.

And the horde of Others leapt forward.

Sean let the fat Other go and turned back towards the bed. The four guards had still not moved, not even blinked, but Sean was not stupid enough to believe they would stay like that. He kept his distance from the bed and considered his options. He didn't have many…he had to get Mary Campbell out, and he didn't believe it would be possible without a fight.

Indeed not, the Boy-King said in his head, and once I deal with the Wolf Cub, I will come for you.

Martin, Sean thought, and in doing so gave the Boy-King a chance to withdraw before Sean could go on the mental attack.

Movement from the corner of his eye alerted Sean to the fact that the guards were on the move, and he just had time to get his sword in a defensive position as the first Highlander pressed an attack.

Sean was caught off balance for a second, and that was enough for the Other to force him across the room so that his back was to the fireplace. Even as he fought to defend himself he could see the three remaining guards move to lift Mary Campbell from the bed. He parried a stroke from the Other that was heading for his heart, and stepped forward into the attack.

He realized immediately that he was faster, and stronger than the Other. The Other realized it as well, and it went on the defensive. Sean understood its plan…to hold him up while Mary Campbell was spirited away. He had no time for niceties. The Other drew back its arm, and Sean stepped inside the stroke, giving the Other no room to swing. As the Highlander struggled to free itself Sean leaned forward and, letting the fangs slide from his gums, he tore a bloody hole in the Other's neck.

It stepped back in confusion and Sean took his chance. He turned sharply and brought his sword arm round in a flashing arc. There was still confusion in the Other's eyes as its head bounced on the floor.

Sean was out of the door and after the departing guards before the head stopped rolling.

Master Hillman. Start it up!" Martin shouted. He saw Hillman turn a lever and the water wheel started to move, slowly at first, then with more vigor, until it was only a blur. The lad pulled a second lever, and the arc of water, silver and garlic spanned above them once more.

The Others ran straight into it, as if oblivious to their peril, and they went to the final death in their hundreds once more. The stench was almost overpowering, and a thick pall of greasy smoke hung over the moor for a hundred yards around.

And still they came, marching, almost running, through the corrosive rain, burning and melting even as their lower limbs dissolved into the muck and gore beneath them.

"'Tis folly, I tell you," Fitz said. "He will soon have no army left."

"Either that, or we will run out of garlic and silver," Martin said grimly. "Harold…see if that smart brother of yours has an answer."

The boy left at a run across the defensive circle, but even as Martin turned back to look at the advancing army he could see that there were fewer blue flames rising from the Others. The garlic was still doing its work, but it seemed they were almost out of silver.

"Look sharp, troopers!" Martin called. "It looks like this might turn into a fight fit for men of the Watch after all."

More Others were making it through the wall of water, their flesh sloughing off them. Several even made it to within five yards of their defenses before Martin ordered a volley of fire to send them to the ground.

"I never thought I'd pity an Other," Fitz said, "but if we have to fight them like this, we are little better than they are."

Martin was watching the press of Others keenly.

"Better man our own bellows, Fitz," he said. "It seems Master Hillman's cannon is running short of ammunition."

And still the Others came on.

They pressed forward over the melted and molten bodies of their fallen, those that made it through the curtain of water already leaving sloughed patched of flesh behind them. But closer to the defenders, where the ground was less sodden, they were beginning to make faster progress…so much so that Martin and Fitz were forced to man the bellows.

Once more the stench became overpowering, and soon both Fitz and Martin began to tire at the strain, both physical and mental. Martin called for troopers to take their place as they stepped down.

Megan was at their side immediately, thrusting a flagon of ale at each of them.

"Well, darling," Fitz said. "I'll never let you say again that I never take you anywhere."

She planted a wet kiss on Fitz's head.

"Just let us get out of this alive," she said. "And I'll never leave the inn again."

"I'll hold you to that," both Fitz and Martin said in unison, and they both laughed, but soon stifled the sound as Harold Hillman arrived at a run.

"Edward had less than two minutes left of the garlic," he said. "And the silver is all gone."

"Then we had better get back to our posts," Fitz said, draining the beer in one smooth motion.

"Aye," Martin said grimly. "And start praying that Cumberland does not tarry on his way."

The three highland guardsmen had just reached the top of the stairs when Sean caught the last trailing Other by the neck and twisted, hard. The noise the neck made as it broke was loud in the sudden quiet.

The twice-dead body fell at Sean's feet, but killing it had given the remaining two a chance to prepare. The pair of them stood at the top of the stairs, their swords raised. Behind them Sean saw Mary Campbell. She stood perfectly still, her eyes still seeing somewhere else, somewhere long ago and far away.

The Others were perfectly silent as they pressed their attack. Sean was better prepared this time. He swung himself to the left, leaving one opponent's slash to cleave nothing more than thin air.

The Other swung high, and, instinctively, against all his Watch training, Sean caught the sword in his hand, grabbing it tight as he punched his own weapon into the Other's exposed heart.

The Other fell aside, and Sean dropped its weapon, just in time to parry a blow that would have taken his head off had it connected.

His opponent pressed him, hard, in a flurry of steel clashes that kept Sean on the back foot. Over his opponent's shoulder he saw the bloated Other Falkirk come up the steps and take Mary Campbell's hand, leading her away.

"No. Not again!" Sean shouted, and stepped into the attack. Their swords flashed, sending white sparks flying. Sean left himself open to an attack, and took the Other's sword deep into his side. He leaned over and pulled the Other's weight with him, heaving it off balance. A backhand chop from his own weapon nearly severed the Other's head from its shoulders, and a second finished the job.

Barely pausing, Sean pulled the sword from his side and leapt down the staircase. He caught the bloated Other full in the back, punching his sword completely through the body. The Other fell away, turning, and Sean saw that he had hit the heart. Blood poured from the Other in furious gouts, flowing down the staircase in a river of steaming gore.

"An unfair blow," Falkirk said in a whisper, "I had thought better of you."

Sean was about to reply, then found it was too late…the Other was full dead.

Sean was alone on the staircase with Mary Campbell, and he realized he did not know what he should do next.

The Boy-King spoke in his head once more.

Guard her well, the voice said. I will come for her soon.

Harold Hillman had been right. The garlic for Edward's water cannon ran out little more than two minutes later, and Martin saw with dismay that he and Fitz only had two barrels left for their own weapon.

"Pick your targets carefully!" Martin shouted, "And keep your discipline. Cumberland is coming, and this night cannot last forever."

"No," Fitz muttered so that only Martin would hear. "It will just feel like it."

"Just remember, old man," Martin said, "there is an inn waiting for you in Milecastle."

"Aye," Fitz said with a grim smile. "And 'tis a price worth fighting for." He turned towards Harold Hillman. "Come, young sir. Your brother played his part. Now it is your turn…the men need a fighting song. Have you one at hand?"

The lad started up "The Men of the Watch", quietly at first, but his voice soon rising until it echoed across the battlefield. All around the circle the troopers joined in, bashing weapons, palms and feet against the carts in time to the music.

Martin raised his voice and joined the chorus as the Others began to pour through the curtain of water. Smoke rose from the feet of some, but none were slowed as they came on at a rush. For several minutes Martin and Fitz managed to keep them at bay with their bellows, but all too soon there was a dry sucking sound as the final barrel ran dry.

Fitz dropped his end of the bellows and took up the blunderbuss once more.

"We will share a beer or three when this is over, my Thane," he said.

Martin nodded as he started to load a pistol.

"Aye. I believe I've got a thirst that would give old Menzies a run for his money."

"Then I'd better work up one of my own," Fitz said as he raised the huge gun to his shoulder. "For surely I cannot bear to see a man drinking alone."

Then there was no more time for talk as the air filled with gunshot and smoke once more. The acrid stench of powder stung in Martin's nostril and throat, and his wrist ached as the recoil from his pistol jarred, again and again.

On their arc of the circle the defenders were keeping the Others at bay, but on the far side the defense was less successful. Hand to hand fighting was already breaking out. Harold Hillman was standing behind the line with one of Edward's water sacs over his shoulders, darting forward occasionally to squirt garlic water at any attackers in range. Martin saw that the troopers would not be able to hold on much longer.

"Every third man from me, fall back," he called, and jumped down from the cart. He led six men to the defense of the weak spot and immediately found himself face to face with a drooling Other. Martin fired a pistol full of silver shot into its face and dropped the pistol as the creature fell away…it would be no use in a close fight. He pulled a stake from the bandoleer of the man next to him and let the next Other throw itself forward. Martin used its own weight against it, and needed little force to push the stake all the way to its heart.

Two more Others replaced it immediately, and the men on either side of Martin fell at the same time, both badly bitten.

"Fall back!" Martin called. "Leave the carts, fall back to a square!" The men fell back quickly, but even then they lost another two troopers before the square was formed…six men on a side in three ranks each, one row kneeling and two standing staggered slightly beside each other.

The advancing Others had fallen on the horses the troopers had been forced to leave behind, and the squeals from the doomed animals were terrible to listen to.

Some of the troopers started shooting the horses to save them further misery, before Martin ordered them to stop.

"Save your shot," he called. "We will have our revenge soon enough."

Martin waited until the Others started to pour over the carts before he gave the order.

"Rapid fire in time," he called.

The kneeling troopers fired first, followed at four-second intervals by the half of the rear row, then a further four seconds later by the other half. Then the kneeling men were ready again. In the small area in the center of the square Megan and the Hillman boys doled out shot and powder.

Martin saw with grim satisfaction that the shot was having the desired effect and the bodies of the Other's were beginning to form a wall that the rest of the attackers were having to clamber over.

The noise was deafening, and the afterimage of the barrel-flashes left imprints that were visible for long seconds afterwards. Among the clambering Others the recently bitten horses were starting to rise, red-eyed, from the ground. Fitz blew the head off one with the blunderbuss and Martin put a patchwork of shot between the eyes of another. The defenders poured volley after volley into the ranks of the Others, and one after another they went to the final death.

It wasn't long before Martin began to hear the words he'd been dreading.

"I'm out of shot," a trooper to his right said.

Sean led a docile Mary Campbell down the stairs past the deflated body of the bloated Other, being careful not to tread in the pool of gore.

I have finally gotten her back, Sean thought. Now I don't know how to save her.

He led her out of the tower. Far away to the east he heard a muffled rumbling. It might have been thunder, but Sean knew better.

He realized he was not even breathing heavily. He had bested four Others, five if you counted the bloated one, and he was not even sweating. What's more, his wounds did not bleed. In fact, they were already healing.

Mary Campbell moaned, and something in her jerked, as if she was a marionette being made to dance. Her face contorted in pain, and she fell to the ground, her feet drumming on the soil. Sean had never felt so helpless. He leaned forward, unsure of what he meant to do, just as the woodsman's song filled his head once more and a vision hit with such force that he staggered and almost fell.

He is on the rock altar back in the woodsman's town, and his friend Lennan gives blood that Sean might live

…he is on the shores of the black loch and the serpent gives water that Sean might change

…he is in Alexander Seton's cottage as the old man tells him about the Grand Arcanum …he sees the blood of Baphomet turned to ash in his hands

…he feels once again the sharp bite in the shoulder he sustained in the initial attack on Milecastle

…and finally he hears the water serpent's words once more

…All is one and we are one and we are all together.

He knew what he had to do. He bent and took Mary Campbell in his arms.

Out on the moor Martin realized that the situation was getting desperate. Nearly half of the men were now out of ammunition, and the Others were no longer confined beyond the ring of carts. The advancing horde was less than ten yards away when Martin himself ran out of shot. He turned for more, but Harold Hillman showed him only open palms. Slowly the noise of musket fire lessened until all was quiet. The Others' army surrounded the small square of defenders, and they had lost all the main weapons in their armory.

"Let us see how many we can take with us!" Martin shouted. "And let us die as men of the Watch!"

"Oh, that won't be necessary," a voice said. The army of Others stopped moving forward and they moved aside as the Boy-King came forward, surrounded by a guard of twelve Highlanders in full battle dress.

"You fight well, my cub," the Boy-King said, stepping forward. He looked no more than a pale youth, gaudily dressed more for dancing than for fighting, the tartan of his kilt too colorful, the frills of his shirt too feminine. Martin grinned as he saw the crusted blood at the Other's eyes and ears.

"I am no longer a cub," Martin said, stepping forward. Fitz put a hand on his shoulder, but Martin pulled it away.

"We will end this here, one way or another," Martin said to the innkeeper. "If needs must, you will see that the boys at least stay full-dead?"

Fitz nodded and patted the barrel of the blunderbuss.

"I kept one load of shot, just for that purpose," he said. "But it will not come to that. I feel it in my water. A change has come."

"Not yet," Martin said, taking a stake in his right hand. "But soon."

He stepped forward to meet the Boy-King.

Sean Grant held Mary Campbell up, and offered her his neck. He didn't feel any pain as her fangs pierced his skin and she began to feed.

The Boy-King laughed out loud.

"Ah, my bride is finally taking pleasure in her lover. When she is sated, she will be ready." He turned to Martin. "You will have a new Prince, my cub."

"I have told you before. I am no cub," Martin said, and with the full force of his arm threw the stake straight at the Boy-King's heart, then was dismayed to see one of the guards step in front of the missile.

The guard fell, full dead, and the Boy-King smiled broadly.

"One day you will do the same for me," he said.

"A pet may turn on its master," Martin replied.

"Not if it loves him," the Boy-King said with a smile. "Come to me."

The Other stretched out a hand, and Martin stepped

forward to take it.

"No!" he heard Harold Hillman shout.

Sean Grant was getting weaker. His skin had taken on a gray pallor, and was beginning to flake and crumble, just like the eye of Baphomet had earlier.

I am the balance, he said, and, with the last of his strength sunk bloodless fangs into Mary Campbell's neck and let their blood mingle.

Martin took the Boy-King's hand, just as he saw a deep fear take hold in the Other's eyes.

"No!" the Other shouted and started to pull away.

"Yes," Martin replied.

I am the balance, he said, and tore his newly sprouted talons through the flesh of the Boy- King's arm.

The Other pulled away, leaving a chunk of pale flesh behind, and turned, first walking, then running, his guard following several steps behind.

Martin was too shocked to speak, let alone move. He felt a cold breeze hit his face, then Harold Hillman shouted.

"Cumberland! Cumberland! The Duke has come."

And on the breeze, the bugles and drums of the Protector's advancing army marched onto the field of Culloden.

"Quartermaster," Martin said as he strode back to where his cheering troopers waited. "I need a horse if I am to catch the Maid before he flees."

"I'll find us two," Fitz said, and left at a run. All around them Others were fleeing the field, leaderless and in abject terror.

"You defeated him," George Hillman said, and Martin had no doubt that a song was even now being born in the boy's head.

"No. Not me. Something else," Martin replied. "But the night is not over yet. I intend to catch him, and send him down to his final death.

"I want you to stay with Megan," he said to the boy. "I will find you when it is over."

Just at that Fitz returned, riding a huge gray charger and leading four more horses behind.

"All I could find at such short notice, my Thane."

Martin leapt up onto the nearest mount.

"I go after the Maid!" he shouted, and his troopers cheered. "The rest of you should find an officer in the protector's army and report to him. Fitz. You have the command."

"Not I, sir," the innkeeper said. "I go with you."

Martin noticed that Megan and the Hillman Boys had taken the other mounts.

"It seems the family rides together," Megan said.

Martin signed, but his heart was glad as he urged his horse forward and set off in pursuit of the Boy-King, with Fitz leading the other three behind him.

Sean Grant dreamed, of a man and woman, sleeping contented in each other's arms, a child sleeping between them. The child begins to rage and scream, a temper tantrum like no other, but together, the man and woman sing a lullaby. Slowly, gently, the child calms, until it too sleeps, and all three are rocked in velvet warmth.

The ride was like a journey through hell. Others were trying to flee the field, but Cumberland's forces had then hemmed in on all sides. Martin could see huge carts carrying massive sets of bellows, the spray from them soaking the ground all over the moor, leaving the Others no escape as ranks of red-coated soldiers followed beneath the spray, each with his own sack of deadly fluid to send any survivors to their doom.

Light was just beginning to leech into the eastern sky. Dawn was coming.

"We have won the day!" Fitz shouted.

"Aye!" Martin called back, urging his mount faster, "But look, we are behind Cumberland's main force."

Fitz saw his meaning immediately and nodded as Martin continued.

"And if we made it through, then the Maid must have done likewise."

"Then let us ride faster!" Fitz called. "He will be searching for a place to hole up in the day."

"No," Martin said. "He heads West. There is something there that hurts him."

Martin didn't say it, but somehow he knew what waited in the West. Sean Grant needed him…an officer of the Watch needed him…his friend needed him.

Sean Grant dreamed, of a family, of children, of a gray-haired Duncan Campbell with a grandchild on his knee and a story in his heart. Mary Campbell wept hot tears, and he comforted her as they slept.

Five minutes later Martin caught his first sight of their quarry. They had come down off the moorland and were heading for the coast, and, about half a mile distant, the small band of Others could be clearly seen.

Martin spurred his horse on faster still.

Sean Grant dreamed, of a world without Others, of a world where he could walk the land of Campbell's birth, of a world where night held no terrors but those of man's own making, of a world in balance with itself. In his dream Sean smiled and Mary Campbell smiled along with him.

Martin could see where his quarry was heading. The squat tower showed up almost black against the silver estuary behind it.

Martin's mount was tiring, and suddenly Martin felt urgency, a sense of doom and foreboding. His limbs felt like they were on fire as he threw himself from his horse and began to leap across the stony ground. He ran on two legs like a man, but inside his head he howled, and his joy in the chase echoed around him.

He was closer now, and could see the Others clearly. The Boy-King still ran ahead, and was less than a mile from the black tower, but the guards had fallen back and were a hundred yards or so behind. Martin howled his joy to the moon, and to the West his gray brothers answered in unison. The hunt was on.

He felt more alive than he ever had in his life. It was as if the wind spoke to him, of joy, of freedom, of wild places. He howled again, just for the pleasure it gave him.

He was closing in on the Highlanders fast. He carried no weapons, but he remembered how he had torn through the Boy-King's flesh.

I am the balance, he said, and once more he felt the rough hair run the length of his arm. This time he didn't fight it…he let it take its course. His chest thickened and his teeth suddenly felt too big for his mouth. Everything became sharper…he could see the face of each Highlander clearly, he could smell the stench that came from the Boy-King…and he knew Sean Grant was in the tower…a changed Sean Grant, but one that needed help.

But first, he had to finish the hunt. He sped across a patch of firm grass and launched himself at the nearest Highlander…just as the Boy-King entered the black tower.

Sean Grant dreamed. He was in bed, with Mary Campbell, his wife. She had been having a nightmare, but she was calm now, and the child she cradled suckled at her bosom. She was very pale, and so was the child, but Sean promised to do something about that…he would take them somewhere…somewhere that would bring color to their cheeks and joy to their hearts. What husband would do less for his family?

He was dreaming of warm climes and sunny skies when the intruder burst into their bedchamber, a wild-eyed Other with blood-red runnels of gore running across its face.

The highland Other raised a sword, but Martin feinted to one side and stepped inside it. It fell, full dead, its neck broken, before Martin had time to step aside and engage the next one. His mind was racing…Kill, break, eat.

There were few other thoughts in his head.

I am the balance, he told himself, but there were too many Others. The Highlanders surrounded him, their swords jabbing at him in hot flame. He felt a sudden white flare in his shoulder, then the pain was gone as he tore at the Other's neck with his teeth. Cold blood flowed, but it did not satisfy him and a sword thrust took him in the side, and he howled once more, in pain this time.

And the pack answered.

Sean Grant dreamed. The wild-eyed Other stepped forward towards them.

"No!" it screamed.

It bent forward, and tried to lift the child from between them.

He is mine, a voice said.

Sean thought that he should recognize it, but it didn't sound like anyone he knew from Milecastle.

It was a dream, and Sean knew it to be so, but still, even in dreams, actions were sometimes required. He forced himself away from his bride, and stood between her and the intruder.

Martin turned and pulled a sword from the hand of one of his attackers. The Other hissed at him, like a snake defending its eggs. Without a conscious thought Martin threw the sword in the air, spinning it through one hundred and eighty degrees. He caught the hilt as if he was a practiced juggler and stepped forward into the thrust. The Other fell, full dead, even as Martin threw the sword aside and leapt forward, under the arms of the encircled guards.

The intruder was still trying to reach the child.

He is mine, the voice said again.

"Who are you to decide," Sean heard himself say. "The child is of the balance. Surely he should have an opinion on the way of the swing?"

The intruder laid a hand on the child.

He is chosen. He is the one.

"And what if he decides to be a child, and only a child?" Sean said.

That is not for him to say, the intruder replied.

"No," a new voice said. "But his mother might make that choice for him."

A blade thrust downwards and hit Martin high on the shoulder beneath his collar. He squirmed to one side, and saw the flash of silver as the blade came up again.

I am the balance, he said, but still the blade went up, and the blade came down.

The intruder stepped back as Mary Campbell stood between it and the child. You are mine, the intruder said. Mary Campbell smiled. "I never was," she said, and stepped forward. "But there is a place in my heart for you." She grabbed the intruder in an embrace.

A gray shape came from Martin's left and took the blade meant for Martin. Then another gray, a large wolf, almost tore the Other's head from his shoulders. Suddenly the air was filled with snarling, snapping, and the sharp coppery odor of blood as the wolf pack finally caught its quarry.

Martin was faced with a tall Highlander. The Other smiled grimly as it raised a sword, but it didn't stand a chance. Martin tore out its throat and felt warm blood course in his mouth.

He howled in joy at a successful hunt as he sped towards the black tower.

Sean Grant no longer knew if he was asleep or awake. He was in the black tower, of that much he was certain, but there seemed to be a newborn child at his feet, a child so white it must be dead. Mary Campbell held an Other, the Boy-King, in a tight embrace that at first Sean took to be sexual…then he noticed that the Other's skin was gray, and was beginning to flake. He was just about to move towards the pair when a bloodied, wild-eyed figure burst through the open doorway, and made a lunge straight for the Boy-King. Sean stepped forward and grabbed this new intruder, only to find himself staring into the distorted, blood-crazed face of his Thane. Unlike in Stirling, he knew what he must do…he could see the wrongness, see where the heart of it lay.

He took Martin by the shoulders and dug his hands deep into the flesh of his Thane's arm. His fingers moved through tissue like a fish through water, and it wasn't long before he found what he was searching for. He pulled, and twisted, and the source of the wrongness was in his hand.

Martin blinked and found himself staring into a pair of deep blue eyes set in a face he almost recognized. Then Sean Grant smiled.

"Well met again, my Thane," he said.

"Sean? What has become of you?"

"I might ask the same of you," Sean said. Martin looked at Sean, at the white perfection of his features, then looked at himself, at the clothes covered in grime, gore and the bleeding wounds that still flowed from him.

He burst out in a loud laugh.

"God, I must stink," he said, and Sean joined in.

"As Captain of the Watch, I was too polite to mention it."

Sean stepped forward and took Martin's hand.

"The Woodsman's gift served its purpose," Sean said. "It brought you here, to this place, at this time. But you will not need these again."

He handed Martin three long hairs.

"It is time," Mary Campbell said.

The thing that she released from her grasp, the thing that was once the Boy-King, staggered and nearly fell. It was little more than a dry husk…its skin flaked in a black crust, its eyes mere black pinpricks in a ravaged face.

It staggered towards them.

"You are mine," it whispered. It came forward, arms outstretched. Sean handed Martin a stake.

"The honor is yours, my Thane," he said. "Send him to

his final death."

Martin took the stake as the Other staggered closer.

"You are mine," it whispered dryly.

"No," Martin said. "And we never were."

He plunged the stake deep into the Other's heart, and it fell apart in a cloud of black dust that was immediately dispersed in the draft from the doorway.

Martin dropped the stake and stood for long seconds before turning to Sean, who was standing in the doorway, an arm around Mary Campbell who cradled a child in her arms. The three of them looked like a posed tableaux, a collection of statues by a master sculptor.

"It is over, then?" he said.

"For you, aye," Sean Grant said. "For us, I believe it is just beginning."

"Come with me," Martin said. "Back to Milecastle. There are doctors of the blood, and..."

Sean stopped him.

"No. Can you imagine what the Duke would do to the likes of us?" he held out a pale hand and showed Martin how smooth, how perfect it was. Then he smiled, and pearl-white fangs slid out of pale gums.

"No," Sean continued. "We are not fit company in the Protector's brave new world. And nobody can cure what afflicts us."

"Then where will you go, when will I see you, what..."

"Questions, questions...suddenly my life is full of them," Sean said, and a thin smile played on his lips.

The sound of hoof-beats came to them from a distance.

"There is an old man in a cottage I must find," Sean said. "And after that? I know not. But we must leave now, before we are seen...for we would raise too many questions."

The friends embraced, and both had tears in their eyes as they parted.

When Fitz, Megan and the Hillman boys arrived five minutes later they found Martin standing on the dock, a hand raised in farewell at the black boat that was already well out in the estuary.

Fitz dismounted and turned Martin towards him, looking deeply into his eyes.

"You were too late, then?" Fitz said. "The Maid escaped." "No. He is full dead. Sean Grant sent him to his doom."

Fitz's eyes went wide.

"And Grant? Where is he? And where is yon maiden he was pursuing. And…"

"To quote my greatest friend," Martin said laughing, "'Life is suddenly full of questions.'"

"And will they get answered?" Megan asked.

"In Milecastle," Martin replied. "In front of a roaring fire, with hot pies and porter to sustain us. What say you, Fitz? Shall we become old men in our cups together?"

"I can think of nothing better," Fitz replied.

"To horse then," Martin said. "We ride for home."

The Hillman boys whooped in joy. But before Martin mounted he turned and had one last look at the departing boat, now no more than a speck in the distance.

"Safe journey, my friend," Martin whispered and, opening his hand, he let the wolf's hairs fall from his grasp.

They flew with the wind.

End of the Watchers Trilogy

About the Author

William Meikle is a Scottish writer, now living in Canada, with twenty novels published in the genre press and over 300 short story credits in thirteen countries. His works span a variety of genres, including Horror, Fantasy, Mystery, and Science Fiction.

Printed in Great Britain
by Amazon